Castaways in Time

Books in the *After Cilmeri* Series:
Daughter of Time (prequel)
Footsteps in Time (Book One)
Winds of Time
Prince of Time (Book Two)
Crossroads in Time (Book Three)
Children of Time (Book Four)
Exiles in Time
Castaways in Time
Ashes of Time
Warden of Time
Guardians of Time
Masters of Time
Outpost in Time
Shades of Time
Champions of Time
Refuge in Time
Outcasts in Time

This Small Corner of Time:
The After Cilmeri Series Companion

A Novel from the *After Cilmeri* Series

CASTAWAYS IN TIME

by

SARAH WOODBURY

Castaways in Time
Copyright © 2013 by Sarah Woodbury

This is a work of fiction.

Cover image by Christine DeMaio-Rice at Flip City Books

Comes the sun to the hill ...

To Jolie

Cast of Characters

The Welsh
David (Dafydd)—Prince of Wales
Lili—David's wife; Ieuan's sister
Llywelyn—King of Wales, David's father
Meg (Marged)—Queen of Wales, mother to David and Anna
Anna—David's half-sister
Math—Anna's husband; nephew to Llywelyn
Cadell–son of Anna and Math
Ieuan—Welsh knight, one of David's men
Bronwen—American, married to Ieuan
Bevyn—Welsh knight
Nicholas de Carew—Norman/Welsh lord

The English
Edward I (deceased)—King of England
Humphrey de Bohun—Regent of England
William de Bohun—Humphrey's son
Edmund Mortimer—Lord of the March
Gilbert de Clare—Lord of the March
William de Valence – Norman baron

The twenty-first century English
Jane Cooke—Deputy Director of MI-5
Natasha Clarke—MI-5 agent
John Driscoll—MI-5 agent
Mark Jones—MI-5 agent
Thomas Smythe—Director Cooke's deputy

1

Windsor Castle, England
September, 1289

Bronwen

"**I** know you're busy, but we needed to see you before you left." Bronwen stepped through the doorway into David's office.

David glanced up from the last-minute papers he was signing, looking past her to Lili, who'd entered the room too. He stood to take the sleeping Arthur from Lili's arms and kissed both his baby and his wife. Bronwen smiled, hardly able to believe that this was the same sixteen-year-old boy who'd dropped into her life four years ago when he'd time-traveled back to the modern world, and whose man-at-arms had plucked her from her former life as a graduate student in archaeology and brought her to the Middle Ages with him.

Already dressed in her breeches in preparation for their upcoming journey, Cassie was the last to enter the room. She closed the door behind her and found a chair next to Bronwen, who set the wooden box she'd been carrying onto David's desk.

"Well, isn't this a rogues' gallery? To what do I owe the pleasure?" David leaned back in his chair, rocking his son and smiling at the three women arrayed in front of him. "I've known for a while that you guys were up to something. Are you finally going to tell me what it is?" He spoke in modern American English because Lili's grasp of that language was better than Cassie's Welsh. While they'd started out trying to speak medieval 'English' when talking among themselves, Lili had complained that American crept in at every third word, and she'd had to learn it out of desperation.

Almost breathless with anticipation at what David's response was going to be, Bronwen reached into the box and lifted out a tray.

David recoiled as she'd hoped he would. "What the—!" He cut himself off with a glance at his son in his arms.

Bronwen smiled all the more. Arthur was only three months old, and David was already watching his language.

"It's moldy," he said.

"It sure is," Bronwen said.

David stared at her creation as she placed it on his desk, and then he looked into her face. "Is that a cantaloupe? Or should I say, *was* that a cantaloupe?"

"It was," Bronwen said.

"Where'd you get a cantaloupe?"

"There are some benefits to being the Queen of England," Lili said.

David shot his wife a bemused look. "I'm pretty sure cantaloupe aren't grown in England."

"A Genoese trader brought them to me a few weeks ago," Lili said.

"This one was grown in Italy. She requisitioned ten of them," Cassie said.

Bronwen poked at the fruit with a quill pen from David's desk. "Our friend here is the one that produced what looked like the best mold."

"Why on earth would you want to create moldy cantaloupe?" David said. "And why are you all grinning at me?"

"What we have here, my lord, is penicillin." Bronwen used the honorific because it amused her to do so. "I hope."

"Do we really?" David leaned in to study the mold.

Bronwen recognized the look on his face. It was one he wore when he was giving something his full attention.

"Now that is good news indeed," David said. "How did you know to use cantaloupe?"

"Anna found a discussion of penicillin in those papers you printed out when we were at your aunt's house four years ago," Bronwen said. "Don't you remember including it?"

"I remember printing off the information. I used up a whole ream of paper," David said. "I couldn't tell you half of what I printed out, though, especially the pages that had to do with medicine. I had half a day to sift through the entire internet to collect everything I could think of that could be remotely important to us."

"Okay," Bronwen said. "To summarize: most penicillin molds have no antibiotic properties, and most cantaloupe molds don't either, but in 1941, a woman found a moldy cantaloupe in a market in

Ohio or Iowa or somewhere like that—blue-green and secreting a yellow goo—which the government turned into enough penicillin before D-Day to treat two million injured soldiers."

"Sounds great," David said. "How do we get from here to there?"

"We can't," Bronwen said, "but we can get further along than we are now, and that's what we need Anna for."

"Wait a minute." David looked up from poking at the mold. "Anna's here?"

"No, of course not," Bronwen said. "A rider came in this morning, however, to say that she, Math, and the boys are on their way."

"They're a day or two out, no more," Lili said.

David gave a tsk of disgust. "I'm going to miss them."

"You'll just have to finish up this business with Valence as quickly as you can," Lili said.

Bronwen eyed her sister-in-law. Lili had remained relentlessly cheerful all this week about David's upcoming journey, but the inherent danger in it had them all on edge. Over the last year, William de Valence had been the driving force behind a series of plots against Wales, against Scotland, and against David personally. Everyone knew that Valence couldn't be allowed to continue his shenanigans, but the fact that he was currently residing in Ireland made him difficult to pin down. David had deprived him of his lands in England and Wales already; Valence was supposed to have removed himself from his castle at Wexford in Ireland too, but he continued to range freely throughout his Irish estates, snubbing David's authority.

Thus, that very day, David was leaving with Callum and Cassie for Ireland. The pair had returned from Orkney without having uncovered any conclusive evidence that Margaret of Scotland had been murdered. That failure had made David realize that he had to deal with Valence before anyone else died from unspecified causes. To that end, he'd put together a coalition of barons, both Norman and native Irish. It would be David's first visit since he became Lord of Ireland (and King of England), and he could not postpone it for even one day to see his sister. Gilbert de Clare had already departed to pave the way for David's arrival and to begin preparations for the assault on Valence's stronghold.

"I'm glad she's coming," David said. "I like knowing that all of you will be together for once."

"Quite aside from wanting to see her, making penicillin is something I don't have the knowledge to do on my own," Bronwen said. "Not only does she have all the pages you printed out, but she's been working with Aaron and the other physicians far more than I have. She told me I needed some cantaloupes but not what I should do with them once they started growing mold."

A knock came at the door, and Callum poked in his head. "We're ready."

David held up one finger. "I need a minute, Callum. Probably more than one."

Callum surveyed the three women sitting in front of David and bestowed a grin on them before saying, "I'll tell the men." He held out his hand to Cassie, who rose to her feet and took it.

"I wanted to be here to see your face when you saw the mold, David, but I have a few last-minute things to see to," Cassie said. "This is Bronwen's and Lili's party."

David nodded and lifted a hand without actually looking at her, distracted again by the swath of blue-green mold on the cantaloupe. "Was it hard to grow?"

"It was easy," Bronwen said. "I cut open the cantaloupe and *voilá!*"

"Can penicillin help us with the recent measles epidemic in London?" David adjusted Arthur in his arms. The baby yawned, and David jiggled him a few times to settle him back down to sleep.

Bronwen shook her head regretfully. "Measles is caused by a virus. Some of the policies you instituted have helped control its spread, but only a vaccine is going to seriously curb it. Scarlet fever, on the other hand, is caused by bacteria. This should work on it."

"Thank God," David said. "Tangible results are what we need."

When David had taken the throne of England, it was as if a bomb had gone off in the English court. He was from the outside and hadn't grown up at court with its traditions and expectations, and thus, he didn't take anything anyone said at face value. He was completely willing to shake up the status quo if it meant getting done what he wanted done. Ironically, that made him similar to his predecessor, King Edward, and they had more in common than David might want to admit. Like Edward, he had no patience for blowhards or sycophants and wasn't afraid of making unpopular decisions. But unlike Edward, he was careful to wear a velvet glove over his iron fist, which was perhaps why Valence consistently underestimated him and believed he could defy David with impunity.

Still, in the nine months since his coronation, David had ruffled more than a few feathers. If he could provide real treatment for a disease like scarlet fever, it could go a long way towards getting some of the less enthusiastic barons on board with his less popular policies—among them, issues of education, land reform, taxation, and health care.

Take disease, for example. David and his medical consultants (Aaron, his fellow Jewish physicians, Anna, and Bronwen) had come up with a strategy for impeding the spread of disease, with an eye to the Black Plague, which they could expect to arrive in another sixty years. But *change* was hard for anyone to accept, much less a medieval sailor who'd been taught to view disease as caused by the wrath of God. Or a churchman who believed the same. More than one priest had condemned David from the pulpit for what he was trying to do. Though David had been reluctant to call upon outside help to deal with issues of discipline, he'd asked the Archbishop of Canterbury twice to talk sense into one of his underlings or, if he couldn't, to banish him to a remote monastery.

David had hired cadres of customs officers to manage the quarantining of ships. Before any ship docked on England's shores, the officers identified sick travelers, isolated them, and arranged for treatment. He'd instituted refuse collection throughout London, much to the groans of the populace at first, though he wasn't hearing anything like the complaints he used to get. People were even beginning to admit that it was nice being able to walk down the street without fear of a bed pan being dumped on their heads.

"When Anna gets here, I'll have a better idea of what the timeline might be for getting this stuff to work. We'll have to test it," Bronwen said, already thinking about test subjects and control groups.

"Do you know how hard it is to get scholars to switch their focus from alchemy to the scientific method? To grasp the concepts behind germ theory?" David gestured towards the door, but Bronwen knew he meant the world at large. "I can barely get those yahoos to believe CPR could possibly work, much less that women should be educated equally with men."

"Aaron understands. It's been the basis of the academy he and Anna have begun in Llangollen," Lili said.

"And not a moment too soon." David tapped on the desk with his fingers. "That said, when Anna gets here and you start experimenting with this, we need to put those twenty scholars from Oxford and Cambridge to work. I'm not going to dance around either their egos or their sensibilities any longer. Tell them the invitation is from me." He gave a wolfish grin. "Play off the two universities against each other if you have to."

Lili gestured to the cantaloupe. "At least this is a natural result of exposing fruit to the air. Many of them may have seen mold like this before on apples, which is a source of penicillin too, just not as good."

"It would be best to avoid all accusations of witchcraft," Bronwen said.

"I agree." But then David's brow furrowed. "You know as well as I do that these things go better when you guys work behind the scenes. The midwifery classes are one thing, but when those twenty men sit in that room and are expected to listen to any of you talk, their ears will close. It's inevitable. I'm not saying you shouldn't be there; I'm just saying that we have to think strategically about how to make them listen to women."

"Good thing Cassie already left, or she'd box your ears just for suggesting that any of us step behind a curtain," Bronwen said. "We can't do that, if only because nobody else understands what we're doing as well as Anna, Lili, or I."

"You know I don't like to suggest it," David said.

"We're not going to take a back seat in the experimenting either, if that's what you were going to say next," Bronwen said.

"I wasn't," David said, "but you will make waves if you don't."

"You mean we'll ruffle some feathers when they find out that not only do they have to listen to a woman—three women, in fact—but we're in charge," Bronwen said.

"You said it, not me," David said.

"My only response to that is, *it's about time*," Bronwen said.

"I know it is," David said, "but—"

Bronwen cut him off. "I'm not implying that it's your fault that things haven't improved faster for women."

"It is his fault, just a little bit," Lili said.

"He didn't make the rules," Bronwen said.

David bowed his head. "Thank you for defending me, but I know that I have failed you to a certain extent in this. I haven't pushed like I could have."

"I know why you haven't," Bronwen said.

"It isn't that I don't think women's rights are important—"

Arthur gave a little cry, and Lili reached across David's desk to take the baby from him. "Husband, as long as girls aren't educated equally with boys, as long as they can't represent their towns in Parliament, change won't happen the way we want it to."

Bronwen didn't smirk at Lili's 'we'. One of their first conversations had been about the difference between her upbringing and Lili's, and how Lili admired Bronwen's surety as a human being. Bronwen believed herself worthy of respect and expected men to listen to her. Lili had wanted that for herself, and David had encouraged her, but she was still a medieval woman living in the Middle Ages. For all that they were pressing David now, Bronwen remained realistic about what they could change. *This* was one of those instances, however, when Bronwen was going to hold firm. "This is our project."

"As a compromise, who do we have who could stand up with Bronwen and Anna and lend credibility to their words?" Lili said. "He doesn't have to say anything."

"I wish I could do it," David said, "but I'm leaving today."

Since Bronwen felt she had won the battle, she was willing to give in slightly on the negotiations. "Roger Bacon should do very nicely. The man has pride. He's already entranced at being on the cutting edge of our little scientific revolution. And he listens to me when I talk instead of pretending I'm not in the room."

David dropped the front feet of his chair to the floor with a thud. "Let's talk to him together before I go."

"Can you make him understand what we're trying to do here, do you think?" Lili gestured to the cantaloupe. "We don't want him to undermine what little progress we've made."

"I am the King of England, and Bronwen is a woman unlike any he has ever encountered." David winked at Bronwen. "I'm pretty sure the two of us can convince him."

2

September, 1289

David

"We sail with the evening tide, my lord." Callum halted in front of David and gave him a quick bow. They'd arrived at Cardiff at midday and were departing at sunset, facing an eighteen-hour journey across the Irish Sea.

"How long until then?"

"An hour, no more," Callum said.

"Then I suppose we ought to get everyone on board," David said. "The longer it takes for us to get to Ireland, the more ready Valence will be for us."

The ship on which they were sailing might be called a 'cog' or a 'hulk' by historians. It was an oak-timbered, single-masted ship with a square-rigged sail. Each cog had been fitted to carry between twenty and thirty horses and a comparable number of men. David's ship presented the one exception. He would sail with only five horses and fewer men because, like Air Force One, it had been designed with substantial accommodation for him.

When William the Bastard had conquered England in 1066, he'd brought two thousand horses across the English Channel. David wasn't trying to duplicate that feat. He was taking ten ships carrying two hundred men and horses. In Ireland, they would meet Gilbert de Clare, to whom David had given oversight of the royal estates, and join the army he'd gathered. Dublin was the most common port in Ireland for disembarking, but David had chosen to land at the smaller port at Waterford, far to the south.

"Well, my king." Humphrey de Bohun sauntered up to David. "The time of reckoning has come."

"Don't get ahead of yourself," David said. "We have a long way to go before we can rein in Valence."

Humphrey rubbed his hands together with undisguised glee. "I hear he has dug in at Wexford, and if we're to get to him, we're going to have to dig him out."

David knew that Humphrey wanted Wexford for himself. That wasn't necessarily part of David's plan, though he might have to reward Humphrey somehow if he made a major contribution to the upcoming fight. It made David uncomfortable to know that to the Irish, he was of the conquering nation. The Welsh had always been the underdog, and David liked knowing that his was the side of justice.

Thus, David's sympathies remained with the native Irish people, and one of the more pressing tasks that faced him was how to control all of his Norman barons who viewed Ireland—like the March of Wales—as their own private playground. He couldn't afford to lose their support, especially now. But in the long run, he wanted the Irish to govern Ireland. While the situation with Valence appeared clear cut to David, leaving the issue of Irish independence unresolved was one of the many compromises he'd made since becoming king. Sorting all this out was a delicate task if there ever was one, and how he was going to square his conscience with what he might have to do— or not do—he didn't yet know.

"Son." A hand dropped onto his shoulder, and David turned to see his father standing to his left. "It was good to see you."

"Good to see you too." David went to embrace his father but then stopped himself.

"What's wrong?" Llywelyn said.

David grimaced. "I'm not feeling great." That was, in fact, an understatement. He had a sore throat and ached all over. It wasn't a good way to start a trip across the Irish Sea, but he felt that he had no choice but to continue what he'd started.

His father didn't hide his concern, and they settled for grasping forearms.

"It's why I stayed away from the twins last night," David said.

Yesterday, David's company had spent the night with David's family at Caerphilly. He and his mother had managed a short evening of conversation before she'd disappeared to nurse his twin siblings, and then he'd stayed up talking with his father until well past midnight. Even if David was paying for the late night now, he wasn't sorry. He'd listened to all the advice his father could give him, and he found it terrifying to think that the rest was up to him. David had taken on the absurd mantle of the King of England, but in his father's presence, he realized how little he knew about governing and how much he was still feeling his way in the dark.

Thank goodness he had Callum with him. Callum wasn't David's father, but he knew more about more things than anyone David had ever met outside his own family.

"I'd tell you to be careful, but I know it won't do any good," his father said.

"I'm always careful," David said.

His father laughed. "Except when you're not." Then he sobered and gripped David's shoulder, shaking him a little. "Come back to us."

David nodded. "I will. You can count on it."

"My lord, it's time." Callum reappeared, holding out a hand to David, having overseen the disposition of David's men on the other ships.

"Of course." David patted his father's arm, nodded to Humphrey, who would be sailing on a different ship, and walked up the gangplank in front of Callum.

"Do you get seasick, my lord?" Cassie greeted him from the top of the gangway. She stood with legs spread, as tall as the average man, beautiful and uncommon in her male clothing. She had pulled her cloak close around her against the wind that blew from the east. It meant they would get to Ireland all the faster.

"No, I don't," David said. "My mother does. How about you?"

"I haven't before," Cassie said. "When Callum and I sailed to Orkney, the ride was smooth enough, but there's a chop to the water today that I didn't expect."

David studied the waves that lapped at the side of the ship. All the waters around Britain, the Bristol Channel included, were known for their unpredictability. "We'll hope for the best."

"All aboard who's coming aboard!" The ship's captain ordered the ropes untied. The shallow bottom of the ship meant that, unlike larger sailing vessels in later centuries, it could be moored at a dock. Soon, the wind filled the sail, and the ship sailed out of Cardiff harbor into the Bristol Channel. They'd be sailing west and then northwest, since Waterford was on the south coast of Ireland.

Once David saw that they were properly underway, he turned to Callum. "Let me know if something happens. I'm going to sleep."

"Yes, my lord." Callum smirked.

"You may laugh, but your time will come."

"Of course, my lord," Callum said.

Despite the stress of being King of England, David had managed a good night's sleep most nights but not since the birth of Arthur. Even though Lili or a nanny took on the bulk of the baby's needs at night, David had changed one or two middle-of-the-night diapers. Cassie had given no sign that a child was in the offing for her and Callum, but unless something was very wrong with one of them, children were inevitable. David crawled into his narrow bunk and grinned evilly at the ceiling, thinking of Callum as a father. He'd make a great one.

The old wooden cog was salted and splintered, though it seemed sturdy enough. David recalled the first night he'd been given a room of his own after his father had told him he was his son. David had reveled in the feeling of the down mattress and marveled at what it was like to be alone. Tonight, he missed Lili and Arthur but didn't regret that he'd arranged for every counselor other than Callum to ride in a different ship. On one hand, David might regret avoiding the mountain of paperwork he could have worked through during these eighteen hours. On the other hand, he could sleep instead.

He closed his eyes but found his mind still churning over his last conversation with Bronwen at Windsor. In the nine months since he'd become King of England, he'd upended every aspect of the social order. Bronwen complained about the slow pace of his policies regarding the role of women in society, but the idea of establishing village schools to educate all *boys* in England was terrifying to many noblemen, most of whom couldn't read or write themselves.

David's insistence on educating girls as well as boys, and including their mothers and grandmothers on village councils—not to mention Parliament, which was the next step—had them apoplectic with shock and horror. It was astonishing to David that medieval men wouldn't want their wives and daughters educated, but thousands of years of history couldn't be undone in a year. It probably couldn't be undone in a hundred.

The status of women was just one of a dozen issues at hand. David's lecture on the scientific method at the newly established college of Peterhouse at Cambridge had been given to a packed house. Much of what had gone into that talk he'd plotted out with Callum in a marathon study session. Callum had said openly that he'd survived his first months in the Middle Ages only because of the help David had given him, but from David's perspective, the benefit had gone almost entirely the other way. Callum had himself gone to university at Cambridge, and while David felt himself capable of understanding anything once taught, every day he was reminded of his own lack of education.

When he'd come to the Middle Ages, he'd been a freshman in high school, taking Algebra II and advanced biology. It was only through concentrated study with his mother, Aaron, Bronwen, and now Callum, not to mention the endless pages he'd printed out that frantic afternoon at his aunt's house in Radnor, that he was able to feel like he could hold his own with his elders. He just plain didn't know enough.

All the while, he'd had to deal with numerous sticky political situations. The nobles of England were growing in their acceptance of him—he hoped—but they would lose their faith in him and his ability to lead if he allowed Valence continued freedom to wreak havoc throughout his domains. The man had to be stopped somehow. David didn't yet know how he was going to do it.

He might even have to order the man killed. Humphrey de Bohun was only the most recent baron to suggest rather loudly that a beheading was in order. The delegation from the throne of Scotland he'd spoken in front of had happily concurred. David had reached a point where he needed to act. When he found Valence, he would first try to speak to him, but he assumed that by now, whatever words he used needed to be backed up by an army.

He didn't want more war. But he'd come to realize in the six years he'd lived in the Middle Ages that he had to find it within himself to use force. The key was to understand the difference between using it as a shortcut to get what he wanted and using it for justice.

3

September, 1289

Callum

Callum sat upright with a jerk. Something had woken him, and it wasn't only that Cassie wasn't beside him on the narrow bunk they shared. He threw off the blanket and got to his feet. Because he could see well enough without a lantern to find his clothing and weapons, dawn wasn't far off. Callum pulled on his boots, wrapped his cloak around his shoulders, buckled on his sword, and went to find his wife.

He ducked under the lintel but had to catch the frame of the door in order to keep himself upright. While the weather had been fair when they'd gone to bed, clouds had blown in overnight, and the waves had grown larger. In the murk of the morning, the only real light came from lanterns that lit up the deck bow and stern and swung with the motion of the ship.

Callum found his wife standing at the bow, her hands tucked into her cloak and her hood up against the wind and the chill of the morning. "Why aren't you in bed?" he said.

"As it turns out, I don't get seasick, but the rocking of the ship was bothering me. I lay awake for hours before I decided to get up so I wouldn't disturb you with my tossing and turning." Cassie turned her head to look at him. "That so-called bed was hard, even by medieval standards."

Callum had slept in far worse circumstances, as had Cassie, but instead of mentioning this, he put his arm around her shoulders and looked with her towards Ireland. The fierce wind whipped the waves ever higher, and other than the faraway lights from several of the ships that sailed with them, all he could see were gray clouds and sea.

David had arranged it so that only Callum, in his station as Earl of Shrewsbury, sailed with him in this particular ship. Ever since the White Ship had gone down in the English Channel a hundred and fifty years ago, losing England its prince and the flower of its nobility who'd sailed all in the same ship, no English king had sailed with more than a handful of his retainers in a single craft. To continue that tradition made sense and, in this case, served David's purposes.

Back at home, Callum would have been surprised not to find David up and about by dawn, but here, alone for once, he could sleep without interruption. Most of the time, Callum forgot that David was only twenty years old. For all that he took up more space than the average man, he looked his age—maybe younger. When Callum was twenty, he'd still been growing and had been known to sleep for fifteen hours at a stretch.

Callum moved behind Cassie, placing his arms around her waist and his chin on her shoulder. "The wind is picking up."

She leaned against him. "It's changed direction again."

Callum licked his index finger and stuck it in the air. He'd seen other people do that to gauge the direction of the wind, but all it did for him was make his finger cold. Better to look at the sail above their heads. "It's coming down from the north." His brow furrowed. "That's not usual."

"It isn't," Cassie said. "A north wind is an ill wind; isn't that what the old wives in Scotland say?"

Callum laughed. "You would know better than I. All I know is that we're in the middle of the Irish Sea with no radio or GPS."

"If this turns into a real storm, is it too late to make for safe harbor at Pembroke?" Cassie said.

Callum looked behind them, in the direction from which they'd come. "I can't see land anywhere."

"If I had a thermometer, I wouldn't be surprised to learn that the temperature had dropped twenty degrees in the last ten minutes," Cassie said.

Callum held out his hand as the first drops of rain began to patter onto the deck. "We should get under cover."

Cassie moved with him back towards their tiny cabin, but before they reached it, the captain planted himself in front of Callum. "I swear to you, I inspected the ship myself this morning," he said. "The rudder was whole then."

Callum's stomach sank into his boots. "But it isn't now?" The rudder was a very important part of the ship.

"The tiller has jammed. I can't steer her."

Cassie edged closer to the captain. "Can you rig something up? The way you swing the sail steers us too, doesn't it?"

"Normally, yes, but if this squall becomes a storm, I'll have to shorten sail, maybe even drop it. We'll be dead in the water with no way to control the ship."

Callum lifted a hand to protect his eyes from the rain, which fell harder, sweeping across the deck with each gust of wind. He tugged up his hood, but the wind immediately blew it off his head again. The ship began to rock uncomfortably with each swelling wave. "I'll wake the king. Maybe he'll have an idea."

"He doesn't and knows far too little about sailing." David stood in the doorway of his cabin, clutching the frame and rocking back and forth as the ship dove into another trough and came up the other side. "Captain Evan, do you suspect sabotage?"

The captain bowed low before David. "I couldn't say. I can vouch for every one of my sailors."

"I don't doubt that, since without a rudder, they're in the same predicament as we are," David said. "Presumably none of them have a death wish."

The captain's eyes crossed as if he wasn't entirely sure what David was saying. Callum could have told him that he wasn't the only one who didn't always catch David's meaning.

"Can you fix it?" David said, overriding the captain's confusion.

"Not without getting into the water, which would be deadly in this weather," the captain said.

David took in a deep breath and let it out, and then he stepped out of the doorway to look beyond the rail of the ship. Looking with him, Callum could make out the lights of only two of their ships, both at least two hundred yards to the south.

"What are the odds their captains learned that SOS code like I instructed and will respond?" David said.

"I spoke with them all before we departed. They know SOS, if no other Morse code, but—" Callum peered into the distance. "I do believe one of them is signaling to us!"

David turned back to the captain. "Send out our own signal. We can't help them and can only hope that they have contact with another ship farther to the south. Perhaps they can pass on our distress call."

"Yes, my lord," said the captain.

"Is there anything else we can do?" Callum said.

"No, my lord," the captain said.

"I suggest *pray*," Cassie said.

The captain genuinely laughed before returning to the stern of the ship, passing among the horses that were tied to the deck, heads down. He began shouting orders at his men.

Callum watched for a moment and then staggered towards David's cabin. David and Cassie had already gone inside. They'd pulled the curtain that acted as a door across the opening, but right in front of Callum, the wind half tore it off and whipped it up so it lay in a sodden mass on the roof, the ends flapping every now and then in a stronger gust. Inside the cabin, Callum found Cassie sitting on the end of David's bunk and David gripping the beam that ran a few inches above his head for the length of the cabin. His jaw was set.

Callum lunged for an iron ring on the wall to hold onto as the ship rocked, creaked, and suddenly tipped sideways such that they all slid along the deck.

"The captain said she was sturdy!" Cassie said.

"Like he would have told us otherwise," David said.

"Man overboard! Man overboard!" Through the open doorway, Callum could see the first mate slide down the deck towards the tiller—or what remained of it. "It's the captain!" Shouts and calls intermingled with the horses' whinnies as everyone on board strove to stay upright and alive. The cog fell down into a trough that Callum feared they'd never come out of, but then it struggled upwards once again.

"I suppose we're a little early in time for rubberized lifeboats," Cassie said.

Callum thought she was being remarkably calm. On the next plunge downward, he released the ring he'd been holding and slid across the floor to her. He caught a post with one arm and put the other around her.

David was braced in the doorway, observing the activity outside the cabin without speaking.

"My lord!" The first mate wove back and forth like he was drunk, fighting the wind and trying not to knock into the horses. At the last second, the deck heaved, and he stumbled into David, who caught him by the arms.

"See to your crew, Captain," David said. "Their safety is paramount."

"That's what I came to tell you, my lord," the first mate-turned-captain said. "The rope that attached the dinghy to the ship broke in the last wave. It's already too far away to haul back."

David gave a brief shake of his head. "I'm sorry."

"My lord!" The man was practically in tears, wringing his hands. "I wish there was more I could do. I trusted the captain with my life, but I've already lost him and two more over the side!"

"Tie everyone and everything down," David said. "We can ride her out."

The first mate gave David a wide-eyed look and turned away, responding to a shout from a crewman near the tiller. David continued to gaze stoically, though Callum didn't see how he could see much of anything through the driving rain. Then David released his hold on the frame of the door and strode away, following the first mate.

"My lord, don't!" Callum shouted as loud as he could, but the storm whipped away the sound of his voice, and David didn't turn back.

"We should go after him!" Cassie said. "We could lose him overboard as easily as the captain."

Callum and Cassie let go of their post at the same time and in two steps were able to clutch the doorframe as David had been doing. The crew had pulled down the sail, since it would only capsize the boat in a storm like this. The horses whinnied and tried to rear, though they were tied down so tightly they couldn't. Callum was glad only five had been staked to the deck. If even one worked free, it could maim everyone on the ship in its panic before escaping into the sea. At the other end of the cog, the first mate was trying to hold the ship together by sheer willpower. Callum could see him gesticulating and urging his men on. Through the rain and the wind, Callum couldn't hear what he was saying, but it looked as if they were trying to fix the tiller.

Callum peered through the rain and was about to set off towards the stern of the ship after David, when he reappeared, bringing with him a thick rope. Like everything else on the ship, it was waterlogged, but he managed to tie it around Cassie's waist anyway.

"Get your men out of the hold if they will come," David said.

Callum went to the trap door and lifted it up. At the start of the journey, his men had insisted on staying in the hold, but now a tall Saxon named John scrambled up the ladder. "The hull is breached! We'll drown if we stay down there."

"Unfortunately, we're already drowning up here," Callum said.

Several more soldiers came out of the hold, though not all of them. Callum stuck his head through the trap door. "Come on, men!"

"We're going to die!"

"I can't swim!"

Callum reached a hand down and hauled two more men out before another huge wave swamped the cog and poured water into the hold. Those he'd rescued scuttled to the stern and huddled there with the crew.

David, meanwhile, had pulled out his belt knife and begun working at the ropes that bound the horses.

"What are you doing?" Callum said.

"I'm turning the horses loose. They should have a better chance of surviving out there than on the ship."

Callum would have helped him, but at that moment Cassie screamed and clung to the rail as the plummeting ship swept her off her feet. Callum leapt towards her, catching her around the waist with one arm and gripping the rail with the other. As the ship climbed back up out of the trough, he tied the other end of Cassie's rope around his own waist to link himself to her. If a wave sent them overboard, they could more easily find each other—and save each other—if they were attached together. Callum continued to keep her between him and the rail, both of them hanging on for dear life.

The first mate joined David with the horses, cursing as one of them reared and flailed his hooves. Callum glanced down the deck to his men and was horrified to see fewer of them than before. With the horses finally gone, David returned to where Cassie and Callum cowered by the rail. He grabbed the end of their rope, wound it around his own waist, and then urged them towards the mast.

"David, what exactly are you doing?" Cassie said.

"Saving us, I hope!"

"How is tying us to the mast saving us? The ship is sinking!" Cassie was soaked from head to foot. Rain streamed down her face, and she swept a sodden lock out of her eyes.

"What about everybody else?" Callum said.

"I don't think they want to go where we're going," David said, "and I couldn't ask it of them, even if I could control what happens next."

"What happens next—" Cassie stopped speaking at the look David gave her.

David remained focused on tying the rope to the mast, and then he cinched it tight one last time. "If this turns out like I fear it might, it would be better if we took the ship with us."

"With us?" The words caught in Callum's throat. For months, up until the day he and Cassie met, in fact, he'd longed for this moment. Now that it might finally be here, however, he was terrified. He pulled Cassie close, wrapped his arms tightly around her, and managed a few words. "Hang on to me."

The three of them huddled together on the deck. With each wave, the ship dove and came up like it was climbing a mountain. Cassie peered past Callum to shout at David one more time. "Do you really think that we'll return—"

That was all she got out, because David suddenly stood and faced north, taking the full weight of the storm in his face. To Callum, he had the look of Odysseus, tied to the mast lest he follow the siren song to his death.

"Is this really happening?" Cassie's voice caught on the last word.

"Yes," David said.

The ocean seemed to open up in front of them; they fell into yet another giant trough, and as they came up the other side, the water rose with them. Callum curled himself around Cassie's head and shoulders. But even as he tried to protect her, he was in the water—and then he was water. He couldn't breathe; the world went black all around him for a long count of three, and then—

With a *thud*, he landed flat on his back on the deck, with Cassie on top of him and all of the air gone from his lungs. Callum gasped for breath and then ran his hands up and down Cassie's back, willing her to be unhurt. He breathed easier when she opened her eyes. Her wet hair had come loose from her braid and formed a veil over his face. He swept a length of it aside. The sun was a bright circle overhead in a nearly cloudless sky.

Had they really—?

Someone sputtered beside him and Callum turned his head to see David sprawled beneath the mast, shaking with laughter.

4

September, 2017

David

David pushed up onto his elbows and looked over at Callum and Cassie. They were both conscious, thank God, though Callum was staring at him as if by laughing he proved he'd lost his mind. Given that they'd just time-traveled from the Middle Ages to the twenty-first century, he didn't think anyone should blame him for being a little punchy. Nonetheless, he quit laughing. His stomach clenched at the magnitude of the distance that now lay between him and Lili and Arthur, but as soon as the thought of them came into his head, he brutally crushed it. The only thing that would return him to them was to face full on the reality of his present circumstance.

His immediate concern, beyond the fact of their location, was the precarious condition of the ship. Looking down the deck, it appeared that they no longer *had* a stern at all, which would explain why none of his men or the ship's crew had time-traveled with them. The cog must have split in two on its way to sinking.

The loss of half the cog was daunting, and David hoped they weren't going to sink to the bottom just yet. The cog was riding relatively flat, though with a definite (and disconcerting) tilt downward from where they lay to the water, which lapped ominously at the ragged boards twenty feet away. He was pleased to see that the storm had never happened in this world—or if it had happened in 1289, it didn't matter in the slightest to the sunny morning in 2017 they were currently experiencing.

"I'd ask what happened, but—" Cassie rolled off Callum and sat up, allowing him to pop up between her and David. Neither man said anything, and Cassie finished her thought, "—I guess at this point it's pretty clear." She looked over at David. "You could have been a little less opaque."

"*Time travel* is still hard for me to say out loud, even after all the times it's happened," David said. "And I could have been wrong. We could have just drowned."

Even as he spoke, the cog tipped a bit more towards the stern. Instinctively, the three of them scurried backwards like crabs, trying to bring the damaged ship back into balance.

"I can't believe you brought us back," Cassie said.

"Not on purpose, I assure you," David said. "If prior experience is anything to go by, this is September 2017, but I don't recognize our location. What do you think?" He studied the stretch of land half a mile away and wondered if they could swim the distance if the cog decided within the next minute or two to sink to the bottom. "At least it's green."

"I know where we are. That's the Pennarth head, near Cardiff." Callum made this comment without any inflection in his voice.

The shape of the bluff, now that David had a chance to study it, was definitely familiar. They'd sailed out of Cardiff harbor not twelve hours ago, so David had seen it then. But the adjacent pier and the six-to-ten story buildings lining the esplanade were not familiar. There was no mistaking that they weren't in the Middle Ages any more.

Now that his initial laughter had faded, a heavy weight came to rest on David's heart. He glanced at his friends, sensing that they weren't feeling exhilaration either. For all that both Cassie and Callum had confessed more than once the desire to return to the modern world, actually returning was something else entirely. Now that they were here, they seemed more stunned than anything, and neither smiled. For David's part, he was disgusted. He really didn't have time for this.

"I know that we've been here for two minutes, and it's probably too early to make any decisions or even think about the logistics of getting back, but you have to know that I'm already thinking about it. I'm giving myself two days here, and then we're gone—or I'm gone, if you don't want to come. I don't think I have to tell you that my preference would be for you to stay with me—to return with me—but you'll have to make your own decision when the time comes."

When neither Cassie nor Callum responded immediately, David added, "Not to be overly formal, Callum, but as of this moment, I release you from my service."

"That's not—" Callum cut himself off with a glance at Cassie, who swung her gaze away from the shoreline to look at David.

"Don't be ridiculous. Of course we're coming back with you." Cassie brushed her hands together and stood up.

David pushed to his feet too, clutching at the mast as he found himself swaying—not from the motion of the cog but from the lack of motion. His body had grown used to the rise and fall of the ship, and the current calmness of the Bristol Channel was confusing his inner ear. "I'm really sorry about this, guys."

Cassie looked up at him. The sun was shining above his head, so she put up a hand to block the light. "What are you sorry for?"

"Not giving you fair warning," David said. "I tied that rope around you and didn't say, *I think we're about to be transported to the modern world. Let me know if you don't want to come.* It was selfish of me, but I didn't want to end up here alone. So I made it so you'd come with me if I did."

"If the choice was between drowning and—" Cassie broke off again, swallowing hard.

"I can't say I'm sorry either, given that alternative." Callum took the hand Cassie offered him and got laboriously to his feet, rubbing at his right hip as if it hurt.

David gazed beyond the ship, which seemed to be making its slow way into shore on its own, since the pier looked a little bit closer than before. Perhaps the tide was going in. The three of them stood side-by-side on the slowly sinking cog and thought about what to do next.

"We'll be all right, Callum," Cassie said.

"I know we will." Callum wrapped his arms around her, and they held on for a few seconds before parting with a kiss that David tried not to see. They continued to hold hands, and David felt awkward standing beside them during their marital moment. He cleared his throat, but Callum spoke before David could think of something to say. "Why do we have only two days?"

"Gilbert de Clare will know about the storm. Ships get blown off-course often in the Irish Sea, so he won't think too hard about it if we're late by a few hours or even a day," David said. "But once the storm ends, he'll want to see our ships sailing into port sooner rather than later. He won't know if the reason for the wait is because we delayed our departure from Wales or because we drowned."

Callum nodded. "Clare has the authority to hold the men together for a little while. But the longer you're missing, the more the uncertainty. He and Humphrey de Bohun will consider the consequences of your death for two days. After that ..."

"After that, the race back to London begins. Before you know it, England will have a new king," David said.

"You've thought a lot about this," Cassie said. "Do you have a plan for getting back?"

"Not yet."

"Do you think you *can* get us back?" Cassie said.

"I brought you here, didn't I? I'm willing to bet my own life on the assumption that I can," David said. "It's up to you to decide if you are willing to risk your life at the chance."

"I don't know what to tell you." Callum didn't look at him. "If you had to come here, through no fault of your own, I'm not sorry you brought us along, but I can't think about going back just yet."

"That's okay," David said. "I'm not going back right this second, and a lot depends on what Her Majesty's Coast Guard is planning to do with us." David pointed towards a ship that had just rounded Pennarth Head, coming from Cardiff, and was cutting its way through the Bristol Channel towards them. Above it, a helicopter flew low, also headed in their direction.

"Already?" Cassie said.

"We are listing rather badly," David said.

"I'll handle this," Callum said.

"How?" Cassie said. The cutter was coming on fast. The closer it got, the tinier the cog seemed in comparison.

"I'm still a member of the Security Service, aren't I?" Callum said. The Security Service (known to Americans as MI-5) was the government agency for which Callum had been working ten months ago when he'd thrown his arms around Llywelyn's knees and fallen from the balcony at Chepstow Castle, inadvertently hitching a ride to the Middle Ages.

Cassie blinked at Callum's words, but David laughed and said, "I knew I brought you along for a reason."

"We'd better get our stories straight," Callum said.

"We should tell the truth," David said.

"The truth? What do you mean *the truth?*" Cassie shook her head vehemently. "You've got to be kidding me."

"I'm not." David gestured to Callum. "Isn't it the truth that you were following orders when you tried to apprehend my mother and father at Chepstow?"

"I was." Callum's brow furrowed.

"Then it's also the truth that you continued to serve your country the best way you could, which meant staying close to me. At the first opportunity, you returned to the twenty-first century with the time-traveling King of England in tow."

Callum blew out his cheeks and then laughed. "No less than the truth, as you say."

"If MI-5 was paying attention, they'll know we're here because of the flash," David said.

"That would explain how the Coast Guard was scrambled so quickly. It may be that they're paying more attention than they were last November." Callum turned on his heel and disappeared into the cabin behind them. The roof had been ripped off in the storm, but the walls were still intact. David could hear his boots scraping on the deck as he moved things around inside.

David rubbed his forehead. Every muscle in his body hurt. "Would it make you uncomfortable if I admitted that I'm a little afraid?"

Cassie gave a half-laugh. "Not at all! I am too, and I don't think the truth is a great idea. The people on that cutter aren't going to know who we are. We can let them rescue us, tell them we lost all of our identification and luggage, and then they can drop us on the shore with no more questions asked."

"That's not going to work," David said. "We're Americans. They'll hold us until they can sort out who we are and how we got here. Besides, I don't lie well. Even if they don't understand what is really going on, they'll know something's off."

"For a politician, you are disconcertingly honest." For a few more seconds, Cassie's eyes followed the approaching cutter, but then she faced David. "I know it's too late now, but the instant we woke up, we should have run and not stopped running until we got back home again."

"How could we have done that in the ten minutes between waking up and when that ship appeared?" David said. "Could you have swum to shore?"

Cassie licked her lips. "How do you imagine this playing out? Less than a year ago, they chased your parents halfway across Wales, trying to prevent them from returning to the Middle Ages. Callum came with your mother because he wanted to arrest them. Are these MI-5 agents going to view us any differently than Callum did? They'll lock us up until they can figure out if we're safe to be loosed on the world, and if they do believe us, it's going to be even worse. Time travel, David! You're going to be like every holiday of the year wrapped up in one neat bundle and delivered to their doorstep."

"Cassie—" David began.

"No, David." Cassie glowered at him. "Even after more than six years in medieval Britain, with all the poisonous politics, backbiting, and outright murder, you still think the best of people? They're going to lock you up and never let you out!"

David didn't know what to say. He'd brought his friends here with a certain kind of confidence that never left him. He was the King of England, and that meant he *had* to show confidence at all times. Only his closest friends and family knew how often he struggled with uncertainty. Bile rose in his throat, which was hurting badly enough as it was. He didn't answer Cassie.

She nodded slowly as she watched him. "You know I'm right, don't you?"

"Yes. You're probably right." David could smell the diesel fumes from the Coast Guard cutter, even from this distance. He felt lightheaded and took in a deep breath to steady himself. "I may have miscalculated."

Cassie didn't rub it in, though she could have.

"I'm glad you said something, but now it's too late to do anything but what we can," David said. "It was too late the instant the Coast Guard found us. I'm sorry. We're cornered now."

Cassie didn't answer, just turned away from him to observe the approaching ship.

"I have to tell the truth, Cassie."

"Okay."

"What does that mean?" David inspected the cutter too, acknowledging that its only relationship to the ship they were on was that they were both technically 'ships'. The Coast Guard cutter was metal and sleek, needing a mere handful of men to crew it.

"It means *okay,*" Cassie said. "What's done is done, and we'll deal with what is before us and try to get out of this in one piece."

Then she shot him an actual grin. "It can't be more dangerous than facing down King Edward without a sword."

David managed a laugh, and then Callum stepped between them, holding a billfold in his hand.

"What do you have there?" Cassie took it from Callum and opened it. It contained not money but Callum's MI-5 badge. Cassie stared at it and then at Callum. "I don't know which is more incredible—that you kept it or that you brought it!"

Callum looked sheepish. "I didn't bring it to Scotland, as you well know, but I threw it in my bag this time because—"

"—because you were traveling with me," David said.

Cassie's mouth was open. "I knew you thought a lot about returning to this world when you first got to the Middle Ages, but I didn't know you still did."

"Every day." Callum took in a breath. "We can do this."

"Under the circumstances, I don't think we have much choice," Cassie said, "and I agree that if we stick together, we might get out of this in one piece. I won't lie, David, if you don't want me to."

The cutter pulled up to within fifty feet of their wreck and stopped. A man came out of the wheelhouse and put a megaphone to his lips. "Do you need assistance?" The helicopter hovered overhead.

David laughed at the absurdity of the question. They were standing in a husk of a ship, slowly sinking into the Bristol Channel. What did they need if not assistance?

"Just follow my lead, my lord," Callum said.

"Will do," David said.

If they weren't planning on telling the truth, he might have suggested that Callum cease with the 'my lords', but David was who he was: a twenty-year-old American boy turned King of England. What he hadn't said to Cassie was that he'd wanted to tell the truth because that mantle of responsibility was so solidly his now that he was completely uninterested in pretending otherwise. He'd been arrogant, though, and probably delusional to think that anyone here would accord him comparable respect.

For years, he'd played over and over in his mind what he would do if he ever returned to the twenty-first century. He'd known about MI-5; he'd known that they'd chased his parents across Wales. But he honestly hadn't spent any time thinking about what they might do to him if they apprehended him. He was about to find out.

Callum moved to the ship's rail and held up his badge. "Security Service! I must get these people to Cardiff immediately."

Callum had left his badge in David's care when he'd gone to Scotland, before he met Cassie. David was grateful for whatever impulse had told Callum not to leave it behind this time. That Callum had brought it didn't necessarily mean that he wanted to forsake his life in the Middle Ages, only that he'd been thinking about it. A lot.

Cassie filled Callum's place beside David. "I have a bad feeling about this."

David smirked. He couldn't help it; Cassie had said the phrase so perfectly.

The man with the megaphone peered at Callum's badge, and then someone in the wheel house, whose face David couldn't see because of the glare off the windshield, signaled his approval. The first man gave a quick salute to Callum. "Sir!"

Callum glanced back at David, who shrugged. It was too late to change course now; they were committed. Twenty seconds later, a lifeboat appeared in the water off the back of the cutter and surfed towards the wrecked cog. It pulled up to the side. David and Callum reached over the rail to grasp the hands of the first man out of the lifeboat, the same one who'd spoken to them through the megaphone; they helped him to hop over the rail and onto the deck, and then he handed each of them a life jacket.

"I'm Coast Guard rescue officer Dan Timmons."

"David Llywelyn." David shrugged into the life jacket.

Callum held up his badge. "I'm Agent Alexander Callum."

David did a double-take at Callum's use of his first name. It was completely normal to give it under these circumstances, but this was only the second time David had heard 'Alexander' come out of Callum's mouth. In the first instance, Callum had been drinking mead for the first time and had consumed a few too many cups.

"I'll need to speak to my superiors immediately," Callum said.

"You can radio them from the ship." Timmons words came out clipped. His first priority, as it should have been, was not to chat but to get them off the cog and to safety.

"Thank you," Callum said.

Cassie went first, clambering over the rail with Callum steadying her by holding onto her upper arm. The officer who'd remained in the lifeboat reached for her hand, but as she stepped into the lifeboat, the buoyant surface caused her to lose her footing, and she went down on her knees between the seats. At least she was safe.

David followed, losing his footing as she had, and swallowed down a curse. He felt awkward, completely out of his element, and helpless. The last time he'd come to the modern world, he'd done it accidently-on-purpose to save Ieuan, who at the time had been his man-at-arms and had been wounded by an English arrow. The wound would have been mortal if David hadn't jumped off a cliff with him on the wild theory that putting his own life in danger would transport them both back to the twenty-first century. It had done exactly that. They'd returned to the Middle Ages with Bronwen in the same way he and Anna had come the first time: by almost causing a car accident.

More recently, his mother had jumped with his father and Goronwy off the balcony at Chepstow Castle, also on purpose, to save his father's life. Llywelyn had been suffering from an infection around his heart, which was killing him. They'd returned to the Middle Ages the same way, though with Callum as a stowaway. Today, with the storm raging around them, David had calculated that the odds of ending up in the twenty-first century, rather than ending up dead, were relatively high. In a strange way, it was almost as if he were immortal, except that he was pretty sure that one swing of a sword to his neck would put an end to him in short order.

Still, the risky part was that time travel didn't always happen. Before he was born, his mother had fallen out of the window at Brecon Castle with his father to escape an assassin, and a few years ago she'd been caught up in a storm in the Irish Sea and almost drowned.

Anna had seemed to waver in time at the birth of her first son, Cadell. None of those events had resulted in time travel. The unpredictability of the whole process made him more than nervous about getting back. It made him want to puke.

"What's wrong?" Cassie's voice was a low whisper in David's ear as he struggled to right himself and find a seat in the boat beside her.

"I'm royally ticked off to be here," David said.

Cassie snorted a laugh, a hand to her mouth.

"How about you?" David said.

"Ask me in a few hours," she said. "I think I'm still too stunned to think straight."

"You need to know that I'm serious about the timeline," David said. "To me, this is a raid: we get in, we gather whatever information we can or need, and we get out. Or at least I do," he amended.

"Callum and I are with you," Cassie said, "whatever happens."

David nodded, accepting that she meant it in this moment, though they really would have to see how both she and Callum felt in a day or two, after a shower and the chance to truly consider what they would leave behind to return home with him. Callum, at least, was none too certain that a return to the Middle Ages was what he wanted to do, even if Cassie didn't want to admit it.

Callum and the Coast Guard officer got into the life raft last, and the Coast Guard officer waved at the helicopter, which began to circle around them but at a higher altitude. David touched the artificial fabric of his life vest. He wanted to take everything here home with him, but he would have to make do with filling his brain instead.

"Why not the Bahamas?" Again Cassie leaned in close to whisper to David, though between the noise of the helicopter and the lifeboat engine, she could have shouted in his ear and nobody else in the raft could have heard her.

"Excuse me?" David said.

"Why don't you ever end up some place warm? We could have a hut by the beach, a hammock, and a fruity drink by now."

"Because that's not where I'm needed," David said, taking her question as a serious one instead of a joke.

Cassie made a rueful face. "Leave it to you to be so practical, even when doing something that ought to be impossible."

The lifeboat sped back to the cutter, and David allowed himself to be lifted onto the deck. He followed the others as Timmons led them up to the wheelhouse and indicated a bench seat where they should sit.

"We need the cog towed to the pier," David said. "It's a wreck, but it's medieval. You don't want it sinking into the channel."

Officer Timmons swung his head to look at David. "Did you say the ship is medieval?"

"It is," Callum answered for David.

Officer Timmons seemed to notice their full medieval garb for the first time. Although he said, "Yes, sir," his eyes flicked from the sword at David's waist to Callum's.

Callum pulled his sword three inches out of its sheath. "Believe me, it's real."

"And so is the ship," David said, "though it's hardly seaworthy any more."

Timmons opened his mouth to say something, stopped to think again, and simply said, "The tug is already on its way. My first priority is to get you to shore safely."

David grumbled to himself and sat, cataloguing the contents of the trunk left behind in his cabin. Besides clothes, it held his armor and what passed for toiletries in the Middle Ages. His primary secretary had ridden in a different ship and retained the endless paperwork that went along with being King of England. David was kind of sorry about that now, since such documents could have provided proof that he was who he said he was.

David was feeling more and more anxious, and he glanced at Cassie, who sat beside him. He'd thought telling the truth was a smart move and that if he didn't tell the truth, he had nothing to say. He was a kid named David who'd disappeared with his sister from Pennsylvania almost seven years ago. Was his reappearance on a medieval cog in the Bristol Channel more incredible than the fact that he'd time-traveled to the Middle Ages in the first place?

If his mom and dad hadn't just come here and left again, and he wasn't with Callum and Cassie, maybe he really could have passed himself off as a hapless kid, thrown about by the winds of time. But Callum was in the forward section of the wheelhouse, even now radioing the Cardiff MI-5 office for instructions. At least none of them looked too out of place, except for their cloaks and swords. The design of their breeches was virtually indistinguishable from what modern people might wear, except that they were made from natural fibers and sewn by hand. David liked pockets and belt loops in his breeches, and what the King of England liked, he tended to get.

Self-doubt might be eating David up, but he didn't have time for it any more than he had time to be here. He was just going to have to commit himself to whatever came next and deal with it when it went all wrong.

Which it surely would. He had a bad feeling about this too.

The cutter chugged towards Cardiff's inner harbor and had passed through the locks that protected it when Callum finally came to sit beside Cassie. "My people are going to meet us at the pier."

"What do you mean by *your people*?" David said in Welsh, guessing that for all that they were in Wales, nobody on this ship but they could speak the language, especially the medieval version.

"In my absence, my second-in-command, Natasha Clark, was promoted to the head of Cardiff station," Callum said. "Jones and Driscoll, two men from my team, are also still there."

"Are you ready for this?" David said.

That got him a laugh from Callum. "No. Are you?"

5

September, 1289

Bronwen

It had been five days since David had ridden from Windsor, heading west to Caerphilly and then Cardiff to take his ship bound for Ireland. In that time, Bronwen and Anna had spent hours with the scholars, first explaining the science behind disease and antibiotics, which many had heard before from David, and then putting them to work in the lab Bronwen had converted out of one of the lesser receiving rooms in the lower bailey of Windsor Castle. It might have been a minor room of uncertain use, but it was still forty feet long and thirty wide. Plenty of room for everyone to work.

Many of the men had experience with alchemy: the 'science' of turning base metals into gold and/or finding the *elixir of life,* a serum of youth and longevity. Bronwen had to bite her tongue more than once to keep from making references to *Harry Potter.* Because of this work, and despite its questionable efficacy, the men did know a great deal about trial and error, which was a first principle of the scientific method. Many, Roger Bacon among them, knew how to work systematically and took copious notes about their work.

Over and over during the last few days, Bronwen was reminded that to a less advanced people, science was indistinguishable from magic, and what was basic thinking to a ten-year-old in the twenty-first century was new, radical, and potentially sacrilegious to men living here. Thus the careful explanations, again and again and again, to head off that kind of thinking. As David had reminded her before he left, transparency had to be the order of the day.

The women they'd included among the scientists, mostly midwives and village healers with extensive experience in herbal remedies, had far less overt education in philosophy and religion than the men but far more practical experience in working with and treating ill people. It had been Bronwen's task (only borderline thankless) to take on the scholars today, so Anna had a chance to work with the women. While only a handful had the desire to study with the men in the lab, many more were involved in the actual treatment of patients.

"Anything?" Bronwen said to Anna, who was bent over a pot they'd left in the warm September sun, following a recipe David had found on the internet for 'penicillin tea'. Anna lifted the heavy cast-iron lid, and together they sniffed the brew.

"Vile," Anna said.

"Let me see!" Abandoning the leather ball he'd been kicking with a friend, four-year-old Cadell came racing over. He peered inside the pot. "Ew!"

"It does smell nasty, doesn't it?" Anna said to her son.

"It would be worth drinking if it would save your life," Bronwen said.

Anna settled the lid back on the pot and shooed Cadell back to his game. "That's why I gave a test sample to one of the girls in the infirmary."

Bronwen raised her eyebrows. They'd set up a hospital and quarantine zone in a long low building within the city walls, adjacent to the Windsor parish church. The church was dedicated to John the Baptist and tended by a small community of nuns. Only adults who'd already had the many diseases from which the patients in their hospital suffered were allowed in. Scarlet fever was their primary concern at present. Bronwen remembered vividly a doctor laying her across his lap and firing a shot of penicillin into her rear when she was five years old. She'd screamed bloody murder and had hated visiting the doctor ever since. But if the antibiotics they were developing were going to help these people, they were going to do it without needles.

"Is the girl very ill?" Bronwen said.

Anna's mouth turned down. "It's Jenet."

Bronwen nodded, knowing the girl Anna was talking about. "Hers is one of the worst cases. Nothing we do brings down her fever, and she's very dehydrated." Up until now—as with nearly every illness people suffered in the Middle Ages—she and Anna could do little for Jenet but manage her pain and keep her comfortable.

"Her parents agreed I could give it to her," Anna said. "I explained that the drink was made of moldy bread and water. It isn't really that scary, even for people in this time."

"She kept it down?" Bronwen said.

"For once," Anna said. "Like Cadell, she throws up from the fever, not because she has the stomach flu. She hasn't been able to drink anything for two days, so it was this or she was simply going to die."

"Then I'm glad you did it." Bronwen turned away but then hesitated and looked back at Anna, who had lifted the lid again to look at the liquid in the pot, even though there was nothing to see that was different from before.

"Cadell and Bran are staying far away from anyone who is ill," Bronwen said. "They are as safe as we can keep them."

"Which isn't very safe at all. Fear for them is like a cold fist in my chest," Anna said.

"For my Catrin too."

It was the horror of losing a child to a disease that the twenty-first century had conquered that drove both women on. Bronwen's ten-month-old daughter hadn't suffered through any illness more serious than a cold so far, and because Catrin was her first, Bronwen couldn't understand it the way Anna could. Anna and Math's second son had died of measles at six months old. Even without that practical knowledge, the fear Bronwen felt was enough to bring her to her knees if she allowed herself to dwell on it.

"Math tells me time and again that I have to let the worry go," Anna said. "I know I do, and yet it keeps me awake at night."

"I know." Bronwen touched Anna's arm. "Speaking of sleep, Lili sent word that Bran is awake."

Anna sighed and abandoned her vigil. "You should come too, for Catrin."

"I'll be along in a minute," Bronwen said.

Anna gave one of the young Oxfordians guardianship over the pot and departed, calling Cadell to her. They left the lower ward for the upper one where their family was staying. Meanwhile, Bronwen made her way towards her husband, Ieuan, whom she'd just spied coming through the village gate into the lower ward of the castle. Accompanied by Sir Nicholas de Carew, he'd been heading for the barracks but changed course at the sight of Bronwen.

"We've got trouble," he said as she took the hand he offered. That was all the public display of affection that was acceptable between a noble couple at an English court.

"What kind of trouble?" she said.

"Valence kind of trouble."

Bronwen gasped. "No! How is that possible? He's in Ireland!"

"Apparently, he isn't. One of our riders has reached Windsor with the news that Valence landed a flotilla of ships at Southampton yesterday. They started marching north immediately."

Bronwen put the back of her hand to her mouth, appalled and uncertain as to anything she could say that would properly convey the enormity of this disaster. Valence's plots had marred the whole of this last year, and in several instances it was only through blind luck that David's forces had defeated him. They couldn't count on luck yet another time, especially since Valence appeared to have decided that a straight-forward fight was in order, rather than mucking about with schemes and subterfuge.

"You're awfully calm about this," Bronwen said.

"Panicking won't help." Ieuan touched her cheek with one finger. "We're marshaling our forces, but they're scattered in and around London to keep the peace and ensure the safety of the roads. Dafydd always plans ahead, you know that, though I admit Valence has caught us by surprise."

"England is at peace with Scotland and Wales," Bronwen said. "Who's left to fight—France?"

Ieuan jeered at the idea too. The King of France, Phillipe IV, had grand plans for his country, possibly on a par with David's, but he was exactly the same age as David and was still finding his feet in his domains.

"You say that Valence is marching north. Is he coming here?" Bronwen said.

"My scouts should be tracking him, but only the one rider has arrived at Windsor. He brought the news I told you, nothing more."

Bronwen pictured the map of southern England that David had stuck on the wall in his office. It wasn't a modern map—more a best guess as to places and distances. Many hands, including her own, had gone into making it as accurate as possible. Thus, she knew that it was fifty miles as the crow flies from Southampton to the outskirts of London, where Windsor lay.

"To get here, Valence has to pass through Winchester," Bronwen said.

"We can't deploy an army quickly enough to stop him from taking the city if he wants it," Ieuan said. "I've sent a message to the bishop, John of Pontoise, expressing my regrets, but of course it may be days before I hear back." The cathedral city was the seat of the Bishop of Winchester, a powerful man in the English church.

Bronwen nodded. One of the most dramatic differences between medieval and modern warfare was the lack of information about the movements of enemy forces, or even one's own. "Worse would be to act before you're ready. Valence is crafty. He may be hoping that we'll act rashly, and if we don't do so on our own, he'll try to force us into it."

Ieuan's jaw showed nothing but determination. "I'm glad Math is here. He can help me think like Dafydd might."

Bronwen scanned the bailey, accepting without thinking it strange that everyone looked to David for leadership. He was all of twenty years old, but everyone in Britain knew by now what an unusual person he was. Everyone but Valence, that is. She supposed Valence kept himself going by telling himself that David's victories over him, and the failures of his various plots and plans, had been due *only* to luck. While David admitted that he'd been extremely lucky, the rest of the world believed he was blessed by God.

In the few minutes Bronwen and Ieuan had been talking, word of the invasion had spread, as news did within a castle, in the blink of an eye. Small groups began to congregate in the noon sun. Bronwen looked back to the pot of penicillin tea, noting the half-dozen people who'd gathered around the scholar tending it. Their penicillin was going to get a far greater test than whether or not it would heal one girl—and far sooner than either Anna or Bronwen had anticipated or wanted. They weren't ready for a full-scale war.

"How many men does Valence have?" Bronwen said.

"According to the rider's best guess, some two thousand," Ieuan said. "He brought fifty ships and packed his men into them. What he didn't bring—and thank God for that—was more than a handful of horses."

"He must have been planning this for a while." Bronwen gave a laugh, though what she was thinking wasn't funny. "In order for him to reach Southampton today, he must have left Ireland shortly after David left Windsor. Do you think Valence knows that David isn't here?"

"I couldn't say," Ieuan said. "This is a direct challenge to Dafydd's authority, however, and we'll have to answer, regardless of whether or not Dafydd is here to lead us."

"We can take care of this ourselves. Valence will never get to London." Edmund Mortimer came to a halt beside Ieuan, having entered the castle with two dozen soldiers. Bronwen hadn't noticed his presence earlier since her eyes had been on her husband.

"I know we can." Ieuan gave Edmund a quick bow in greeting.

Edmund turned to Bronwen. "Valence believes himself to be a hero and that the people of England and its barons—" He put a hand on his own chest, "—me among them, will rise up in support of him to overthrow King David's oppressive rule. All he has to do is make the first move."

"Do you really think so?" Had the last months gone so awry and unrest swelled among the populace to such an extent that Valence was right? How had they not noticed?

"Of course not," Edmund said. "I didn't say this was true, only that Valence believes it."

Bronwen shook herself, casting off doubt as reason reasserted itself. "How could he possibly think that the people would rise up and support him? He's not even English. And when he served King Edward, most of your fellow Normans didn't like him."

"'Hatred' might not be too strong a word for what some of us felt about him," Edmund said.

"He's been listening to the wrong people," Ieuan said, "people who tell him what he wants to hear instead of the truth."

"I hope you're right," Bronwen said.

"King David was hailed as king by the people of London and by his barons," Edmund said. "He was crowned by the Archbishop of Canterbury himself. While some lords may have gotten more than they'd bargained for when they agreed he should be king, he has done nothing to arouse the wrath of his people. They love him."

"He *has* cleaned things up a bit," Bronwen said, doubt still in her voice. "Some haven't liked that."

"Corrupt officials never like to be removed from office," Edmund said. "He has the sheriffs in his purse, along with the merchants, and, if I may say so without offending, the heart of every woman from Dover to Chester to York. As long as that is true, he has England."

Bronwen nodded, somewhat reassured. That women loved David was hardly surprising. Not only was he tall, well-built, and good-looking, but he'd established policies about subjects women cared about, from education to medicine to domestic violence, an issue about which no English king had ever had a policy. A Welsh woman had a right to divorce her husband if he beat her. Now, with

David's rule, an English woman did too. The church might not like it, but church and state were not the same thing in David's reign.

In addition, David had summoned his sheriffs and castellans to him at midsummer, after Arthur's birth. The meeting had gotten off to a rocky start because many of the sheriffs had believed David's intent was to either fire them or coerce them. They feared that anyone who failed to toe the line would find himself in prison or missing his head.

With the help of John de Falkes, the castellan of Carlisle Castle, David had eventually convinced them that what he really wanted was to know what everyone thought—about any topic they cared to discuss. The fact that Falkes walked free, despite having imprisoned David and Ieuan once upon a time, went a long way towards persuading them of the king's sincerity.

"Perhaps Valence will garrison Winchester and come no further," Bronwen said.

"That would be best for us but less so for the people there," Edmund said. "Bishop John has not been what I might call a friend, but neither has he been an enemy. He truly seems to care about the welfare of his flock and has no further aspirations beyond the office he currently holds."

That was so rare it actually seemed likely. "And Winchester's sheriff?" Bronwen said.

"Ingeramus de Waleys." Ieuan laughed. "I can't make head or tail of his name, but he seemed to be a solid enough fellow when I met him in July."

"We'll see what kind of mettle he has when he sees Valence's army advancing on the city," Edmund said. One of his men approached, and Edmund acknowledged his presence with a raised hand. The man stopped, waiting for Edmund to complete his conversation with Ieuan and Bronwen.

"I'll let you go," Ieuan said. "We meet in council in one hour."

Edmund put his heels together and gave first Ieuan, and then Bronwen, a quick bow. "I will be there."

Edmund turned away, and Ieuan put an arm around Bronwen's shoulders. "We will need you and your healers and—" He waved his free hand, "—whatever you've come up with."

"Anna and I will do our best, but we're not ready for a war."

"The men will appreciate any aid you can give them," Ieuan said. "Just having so many healers in one place is a blessing. I understand the herbarium is fully stocked."

"It is." Bronwen canted her head, thinking about the exchange between Ieuan and Edmund at the end of their conversation. "Who's in charge of David's forces: Edmund or Math?"

Ieuan's expression was rueful. "You wound me to the core, wife." Then he laughed to show he didn't mean it. "It would surprise you, then, to learn that *I* am?"

6

Cassie

Cassie and Callum had been married only since June, but in the few months they'd been together, she'd prodded him for information about his former life. She knew about his past girlfriends, about his crush on one of his co-workers, Natasha, and the more nefarious workings of his former employer. Or seemingly, *current* employer.

Callum had joined MI-5 after returning from the war in Afghanistan. It had seemed a natural progression for him to move from soldier to agent. Many of his fellow agents had a military background. He knew how to follow orders and to give them, and for the most part, he felt that he fit right in. If nothing else, he viewed it as another way to serve his country. It gave him a focus, too, while he figured out how to cope with the onset of PTSD (Post-traumatic Stress Disorder), a result of his service in Afghanistan.

Callum's arrival in medieval Wales last November had exposed the extent to which he hadn't dealt with it. By the time Cassie had met him, however, he'd begun to conquer his demons. And in the last few months, he'd grown into his role as the Earl of Shrewsbury, a leader of men, and one of David's chief advisors. She would never assume that returning to the twenty-first century would send him into a tailspin, even though she feared this world was going to crush *her*. But she was still surprised at the rapidity with which, in the half hour they were on the Coast Guard cutter, Callum transformed himself from the Earl of Shrewsbury into an MI-5 agent.

The cutter motored up to the long dock at one of the marinas, in deep enough water that it could moor safely; ships far larger than this—a thousand times larger—were moored in the industrial part of the harbor across the bay. Officer Timmons gestured that the three of them should follow him, and he led them to a gangway, which extended from the ship to the dock. A man and a woman waited for them at the other end.

When Callum lifted a hand to them, they responded in kind. Cassie supposed the woman had to be Natasha, and if so, it showed Callum's good taste in women (herself notwithstanding). Natasha wore her dark hair pulled back from her face in a bun but kept the hair around her cheeks loose. She had dark eyes, high cheekbones, and olive skin. If the sun shone a little more in England, her complexion might have been as dark as Cassie's.

Callum went first across the gangway, followed by Cassie and then David. The water lapped twenty feet below their feet, and Cassie averted her eyes, not liking the height and the low railing. When Callum reached the end of the walkway and the concrete pier, he halted so abruptly that Cassie almost ran into him. He put an arm behind his back, reaching for her hand, which he grasped and squeezed once. "Wait a second."

David spoke from behind her. "Callum, what's up—?" But then he broke off before finishing his question. Fifty yards away, on their side of the chain link fence that separated the parking lot—or 'car park' in Callum-speak—from the road beyond, the doors of a black van opened, and five men in full riot gear toting automatic weapons spilled out of it.

"What's going on, Natasha?" Callum said. "I explained when I rang you—"

"Yes, you did, and that's why they're here," Natasha said. "Thames House has some concerns." Located in London, Thames House was the head office for MI-5.

"I'm sure they do." Callum stood at the end of the ramp, watching the men and not letting Cassie or David past him.

"It looks like they have more than *some* concerns," said David under his breath.

"Are we under arrest?" Cassie said.

"We ask that you come with us," said the man standing next to Natasha. "There is no need for alarm."

"We already said we would come, Driscoll." Callum still filled the space at the end of the gangway completely. He held his shoulders stiff, and his hands were clenched into fists. He wasn't giving an inch, and Cassie wondered how long he was going to stand there waiting for Natasha to bend.

"You were right, Cassie," David said. "We should have run."

"I wouldn't have minded if I'd been wrong." Cassie looked down at the water. If push came to shove, it could offer an uncomfortable way out.

"Don't." David caught her hand at the wrist. "We'll get through this." Then he raised his voice to project forward. "It's okay, Callum."

"It isn't," Callum said.

Cassie patted Callum on the back to indicate her support and encouragement.

David reached past her to nudge him too. "We can do as they say for now. Their response isn't totally unexpected, given what happened with my mom and dad last winter."

"But it is unwarranted." Callum finally stepped towards Natasha, looming over her so that he blocked the sun and she stood in his shadow.

Callum meant to intimidate Natasha, and she wilted under his gaze, glancing down at her feet for a moment. Then Driscoll cleared his throat, and Natasha straightened her shoulders. "We mean you no harm, Callum."

"You might not," Callum said, "but forgive me if I have reason to believe, given the army you brought with you, that others do."

Driscoll cleared his throat again. "If you could simply come this way—" He gestured towards a large black SUV parked next to the van the riot team had come in, "—all will be well. You'll see."

Callum let out a sharp breath. "Damn it, Driscoll—"

Driscoll kept a half-smile on his face, not responding to Callum's anger. Callum cursed under his breath again and then reached behind him to take Cassie's hand. He tugged her forward. "This is my wife, Cassie. Cassie, I'd like you to meet Natasha Clark and John Driscoll, my colleagues from the Security Service."

Cassie stuck out her free hand, opting to be polite, though she couldn't say she really meant it. "It's nice to meet you."

To her credit, Natasha didn't hesitate and clasped Cassie's hand in a strong shake. "Lovely to meet you too. I'm sorry about all this."

"I'm sure you're just doing your job," Cassie said.

Callum sent Cassie a sharp look, but she plastered a smile on her face. Then David stuck out his hand to Natasha, who hadn't even looked at him yet. It appeared to Cassie to be a snub, which was odd since David was the reason they were all here in the first place. "I'm David."

"I know." Natasha shook his hand too. She looked like she was going to say something more, but then she bit her lip and kept it back. Too many people weren't saying what they were thinking for Cassie's comfort. That had been a normal state of affairs growing up in her family, but Cassie had become good at reading the nonverbal cues they used. These English people were much harder to gauge.

David, for his part, kept on going. "I understand that you are at least partially acquainted with my mother, Meg?" He said this with an almost-feral smile, which Natasha didn't seem to appreciate since she just jerked her head in a nod.

Callum barked a laugh.

Cassie appreciated David's cynicism, but for her part, she couldn't even marshal a partial smile. A sick pit had formed in her stomach. During the five years she'd lived in Scotland, she'd thought about little else but returning to the modern world, but this wasn't going at all like she'd dreamed it might. When she met Callum, she'd told him that she wasn't resigned to staying in the Middle Ages. The urgency had waned since then, however, and she hadn't wanted to come here today.

Nor had David. Natasha had shaken his hand politely enough, but she seemed oblivious to how important a person he really was. In the course of the last fifteen minutes, Cassie had come to understand better why David had been determined to return to the Middle Ages as soon as he could when he'd come here the last time and why he was more than a little annoyed to have their journey to Ireland interrupted. He'd had a plan, and now that plan was going to be continuing without him. Or more likely, it was going to fail.

David couldn't stay in the twenty-first century. He had a family and a job to do. Unfortunately, these British secret agents had the look of people who might have the ability to stop him from doing it.

Few walks had ever seemed as long as the one from the dock to the SUV. They weren't physically constrained, but agents penned them in and had closed off all the exits. Callum's teeth were clenched together, and he had a grim set to his face that Cassie hadn't seen since they were in Scotland and he'd had to convince a hall full of Scottish noblemen to listen to his plan for their future. She could practically see the gears churning in his mind, trying to figure out a way to turn what was happening to their advantage. Cassie couldn't see it herself.

This was the first time she'd been to modern Wales; she'd never left her half of the planet before she time-traveled to Scotland on Meg's coattails. Other than the fact that both she and Natasha spoke English—or a variant of it—she couldn't see how they could have anything in common or how she was going to be of any help to Callum in navigating the next few hours. This was far worse than when she'd ridden with Callum to Stirling Castle and been overwhelmed by the expectations of the Scottish noblemen. The feeling of helplessness grew stronger with every minute that passed.

When they reached the SUV, Natasha opened the rear door and gestured that they should get in. Cassie glanced at Callum, not willing to do anything Natasha said without his approval, but he jerked his head in a nod. With every fiber of her being screaming at her not to get in the car, Cassie ducked inside and scooted over so Callum could sit next to her. He didn't follow her immediately, though, instead stopping with one foot in the car and the other still on the ground.

"Natasha." He said the agent's name not as a question, but as a command, like a mother might bark at a child she'd caught doing something wrong. "Where are they taking David?"

"It's fine, Callum," Natasha said.

Cassie leaned forward and peered through the window at Natasha, who stood on the other side of the car door. One of the riot troopers stood next to Callum. From their stance and the way they were preventing Callum from backing out of the car door, it obviously wasn't *fine*. Natasha was lying, and from the determined set to her jaw, she wasn't going to back down about it either.

"David!" Callum pushed at the doorframe, and it was only then that Cassie saw what had disconcerted him: the agents had herded David toward a second SUV, one Cassie hadn't noticed before because it was parked on the other side of the bigger van.

"I'm just following protocol," Natasha said, "which I'm surprised you don't remember."

"If this is protocol, why haven't you separated me from Cassie?" Callum said.

"I will if you don't get in the vehicle right now," Natasha said. "We're taking you to be debriefed. That is all."

Callum stared at her for a count of ten. Cassie honestly didn't know if his glare was a precursor to fighting or if he was going to capitulate. He clearly didn't want to give in. His hand twitched towards the small of his back where his gun was holstered underneath his tunic, but then he let it fall. While it was better than a sword, one gun wasn't going to get any of them very far against the hail of bullets Natasha's men could direct at them. Finally, Callum nodded and got in the SUV. At the same moment, the agent in charge of David put a hand on top of his head so he wouldn't bang it as he ducked inside the rear seat of his SUV. Then all the doors slammed closed.

For a moment, Cassie and Callum were alone inside the vehicle. One agent still stood outside Callum's door, while a second held the driver's side door handle. Both were listening to Natasha and didn't get in the vehicle immediately.

"I shouldn't have called them," Callum said. "I miscalculated."

"David said the same, but he was right, too, that by the time the cutter was approaching the cog, it was too late to do anything else," Cassie said. "Since we have no passports, the Coast Guard officer would have held us somewhere. Once they discovered who you were, we would have ended up with MI-5 anyway."

Callum put a hand on Cassie's knee. "Thank you for not being angry."

"Anger is pretty much the last emotion I'm feeling," Cassie said. "Despair, maybe."

"I thought I'd have some measure of control." Callum curled his hands into fists for perhaps the eighth time in the last twenty minutes. "I didn't think Natasha would send the news of our arrival up the chain of command so quickly. I was naïve."

"Possibly she had no choice. She seems very by-the-book," Cassie said.

"She is. I should have taken that into consideration." Then Callum shrugged. "Admittedly, you're right about the lack of choice. The scientists would have recorded the flash of our entry into this world, whether or not we rang anyone afterwards. They could have sent out the news within ten seconds. That Coast Guard cutter got to us quite fast. I neglected to ask why they responded so quickly, and for all that Timmons looked twice when I held up my badge, he was more uncertain than surprised, like he expected more resistance than we gave him."

"Even though I think we should have resisted," Cassie said, "being the object of a manhunt throughout Wales while we tried to get to Chepstow's balcony wouldn't have been fun."

Callum laughed. "I suspect they won't be accommodating if I ask to take you there. Half of them were with me the last time."

Cassie laughed too, which was a nice change from anxiety. Then she sobered. "Just tell me what to do, and I'll do it."

Callum looked over at her, a flash of a smile still on his lips, before he focused again on his surroundings. "We can't fight this many men. There's a reason swords went out of fashion, you know, and so far nobody's patted me down to look for the gun."

"So we play along?" Cassie said.

"That was David's plan, and that's what we'll do," Callum said, "up until the point we decide otherwise." Callum held her hand in his, absently rubbing the back with his thumb until Cassie made him stop.

Callum moved a few inches closer to her. Sometimes when Cassie was struggling with something in her head, she didn't want to be touched, but she was grateful to know he was here. Cassie's heart kept beating hard as the driver and the man who'd met them at the pier—Callum's colleague, Driscoll—got into the SUV. A minute later, they pulled out of the parking lot and started driving through the streets of Cardiff. Callum appeared to settle into a state of semi-alertness to wait for something to happen. Their doors had locked automatically, and she didn't try to unlock one. With David riding in the car ahead of them, out of earshot and out of reach, there wasn't any point.

Driscoll had shot a quick look at Callum when he'd entered the SUV but then faced resolutely forward. He held himself stiff, clearly under pressure, but since Callum didn't say anything, Cassie didn't either. She'd lived alone in the woods for many years and had felt comfortable with silence even before then. Hunting with her grandfather, she'd learned to still herself to listen to the forest. This was a city, however, and was so typically modern that she could have been in any country in the world. There wasn't anything about it, other than an occasional street sign in Welsh, that told her she was in Cardiff.

She studied the streets and buildings with intensity, trying to memorize where they were going. Callum would know all that already, of course, but she needed to face the fact that they might separate her from him, as they had David, and she might have to figure some of this stuff out on her own. She needed a lot more information about who these people were and what they wanted before she could even formulate the right questions to ask. Until then, she would do her best to help Callum, or at the very least, not get in his way.

She half hoped they'd end up in an underground bunker like in *Torchwood*, but after twenty minutes, they pulled up in front of a nondescript office building, gray, with five floors of windows above a lobby and a massive antenna array on the roof. For a minute, they waited in the street at the entrance to the building, double-parked, and then they took a sharp left and rolled down a long ramp into an underground garage.

"Is this where you worked?" Cassie said.

"Yes." Callum sat straighter in the seat. He'd had to adjust his sword to an awkward angle in order to sit next to her, since modern SUVs weren't designed to accommodate medieval weaponry. Like Cassie's, his linen shirt and wool cloak were still damp from the sea.

The humidity was steaming up her window, since the driver had turned on the heat.

"If they keep us separated for long," Callum said, "I'm going to be very unhappy."

Cassie was already unhappy. The van with the riot squad had pulled into a space ahead of them. Beyond it, the SUV into which they'd put David parked across three spaces. Nothing happened for a few seconds, and then the doors opened. One of the agents hauled David out. He was wearing handcuffs and had a bag over his head.

"Callum!" Cassie surged forward in her seat and then sat back, having forgotten that she was still seatbelted in.

"I see him." Callum ground his teeth.

"What could they be charging him with?" she said.

Nobody in their vehicle gave any sign of getting out. Driscoll was completely focused on the computer tablet in his lap and hadn't looked up. All Cassie and Callum could do was sit, watching Natasha march David across the garage, heading towards the elevators.

"They don't necessarily have to be charging him with anything," Callum said. "Since 9/11, there's been some leeway in the timeline for arrests. Especially considering his lack of papers and the way we came here, I'm sure they could easily trump something up having to do with terrorism."

They'd been speaking in medieval Welsh, even though Cassie's spoken use of it was still pretty poor, but Callum had said the last sentence in English. That distracted Driscoll from his tablet enough to turn around in his seat. "You think that little of us, do you, Callum?"

"You tell me, Driscoll," Callum said. "Do you see what they've done to David?"

Driscoll's brow furrowed. "What are you—" But then at the look on Callum's face, he turned to the front in time to see David disappearing into the elevator, his arms locked behind his back and Natasha holding his arm since he couldn't see anything through the bag. Driscoll sat back in his seat. "Huh."

Callum leaned forward. "What's going on, John?"

"I don't know. But I promise you I will find out."

"What's going to happen to us?" Cassie said. "Why don't we have bags on our heads?"

"My orders were to provide you with necessities and space in a conference room to write your report." Driscoll looked back at Cassie. "Together."

Callum pointed at Driscoll's tablet. "What are they saying about me?"

"Nobody's saying much of anything yet," Driscoll said. "You've just arrived."

"They're saying something," Callum said. "I caught a glimpse of what you were writing on your tablet. What are they passing my disappearance off as—some sort of PTSD mental break?"

Driscoll grunted. "It's one option. You were with the Security Service long enough to know how this works."

"I was," Callum said. "That's why I'm asking."

"Some have wondered if you're safe on your own or if you should be moved to a psychiatric facility."

"I can guess who might have asked that," Callum said.

Driscoll tsked through his teeth. "He's not the only one." He held up his tablet so both Cassie and Callum could see it. It showed a message board with comment after comment appearing and then being superseded by another.

"MI-5's very own Facebook," Cassie said.

"And just as useless," Callum said.

Cassie leaned forward to match Callum. "They ask about Callum's mental state while dragging David off for interrogation? How does that make sense? If they believe David came from the Middle Ages, they have to believe it of Callum too."

"Humans are quite capable of holding two contradictory viewpoints simultaneously and believing them both," Driscoll said.

"What about me?" Cassie said.

"I have no information on you, but judging from your accent, you're American, yes?"

Cassie nodded.

"Then I imagine you will be deported to the United States in due course, unless something can be worked out with your embassy," Driscoll said.

"Callum and I are married!" Cassie said.

"Where is that recorded, again?" Driscoll said.

Cassie's mouth dropped open, and she stuttered, "But—"

Callum pulled on the handle to the door beside him; it didn't open. "Driscoll—"

"Right." Driscoll opened his door and got out and then opened Callum's. "I'm not telling you what *I* think but what others are saying, Callum. You need to be prepared for questions."

"I can answer any question," Callum said, his voice a low growl.

Leaving the driver to park the SUV in the back of the garage, the three of them followed the path David and his captors had taken. Driscoll provided their only escort since all of the men in riot gear, plus Natasha, had gone with David.

Cassie caught Callum's hand. "They really *don't* view us as a threat," she said in Welsh.

"It seems not," Callum said.

"What do they think David is, though?" Cassie said. "A nuclear bomb?"

Cassie had to say the last two words in English, since they didn't exist in medieval Welsh, and Driscoll overheard. "You don't want to say that out loud. You two need to keep your heads down and your stories straight."

Callum tightened his grip on Cassie's hand. "If it's all right with you, Cassie, I'll do the talking."

Cassie nodded, thinking how odd it was that in the Middle Ages she'd fought so hard for her right to be treated like a human being. She'd seen the mistreatment of women—and the assumption that they weren't as intelligent or as competent as men—as something to be fought against. And yet, her first hour in the twenty-first century had already reduced her to the status of non-person, to be seen and not heard. And this time, it wasn't men as a class doing the dehumanizing but a faceless bureaucracy that had decided David was a threat to the British state.

She bit her lip, finding amusement in the thought that MI-5 wasn't far off in thinking that. David might be a twenty-year-old kid, but he'd grown from a high school freshman in a little town in Oregon to the King of England in less than seven years. While she and Callum were smart and resourceful, and she had faith that as long as they worked together, they could figure any problem out, David was a different animal entirely. He was smarter than anyone she'd ever met. He was analytical, a creative thinker, and *driven* to a crazy degree. MI-5 really had no idea what they were in for.

7

September, 2017

David

David had seen the way the wind was blowing as soon as that van of military police showed up, so he wouldn't have said that having the agents separate him from Cassie and Callum was unexpected. It was unfortunate. Even worse than the abruptness of his incarceration was the fact that nobody so far had asked him any questions or spoken to him beyond a few direct orders. They'd walked him from the garage to an elevator, descended two floors until he was in the bowels of MI-5 headquarters (or what he had to assume were their headquarters at Cardiff, given that he couldn't ask Callum where they were), and into an interrogation room.

That it was an interrogation room he had no doubt. It was painted vanilla white on the ceiling, floor, and walls, with one wall taken up by a grayed out, ten-by-five foot picture window that mirrored his reflection back at him. David assumed it was one-way glass without bothering to put his nose right up to it to see if he could see anything of the room on the other side of the wall. That would be too humiliating.

After Natasha removed his handcuffs and hood, he unhooked his wool cloak from around his neck and hung it over a chair. The wool had mostly dried in the warmth of the car, but he felt his toes squishing a bit inside his boots. He hadn't slept in his armor, so he hadn't been wearing it when the storm came. It would have been a bear to remove by himself, and he strongly suspected his captors wouldn't have been of any help. It would be nice to get it back once they were done examining it. It fit him perfectly.

The agents had already taken his sword from him, along with his three knives (one from his right boot, one from up his left sleeve, and a third from his waist), and patted him down looking for anything else he could use as a weapon. David wondered if Callum had received the same treatment; David knew about the gun, of course. As far as David knew, Callum had left the cog with it still in its holster at the small of his back. He made a note not to mention Callum's use of it in Scotland to MI-5.

Once Natasha left him alone, a quick twist of the door handle proved that it didn't twist at all, and a single pace around the room showed David that he wasn't going to kick his way out of this cell either. Where was young Thomas Hartley when he needed him? David faced away from the one-way glass. It felt awkward to know that others whom he couldn't see were watching him.

"So. David Lloyd. Or did you want to go by something else?"

He turned around at the sound of Natasha's voice. She had pushed open the door to the room, already speaking before she was halfway through it, with a file open flat in her hands.

"'Lloyd' was my last name before I found out the identity of my true father," he said.

Natasha dropped the manila folder on the table that took up a good portion of the center of the room, pulled out the chair closest to her, and gestured that David should sit in the chair opposite. Unlike the walls, the table was black, finished with a utilitarian lacquer, and the chair was blue plastic with metal legs. It rocked under David's weight as he sat in it. He appreciated the chance to rest without having to show Natasha how much he needed it. The initial adrenaline rush of their arrival in the twenty-first century had passed, leaving him a little shaken. His sore throat and achiness hadn't seemed like something he could pay attention to in the middle of a storm in the Irish Sea, but now he had to admit that his throat was exploding out his ears.

"And what is your name now?" Natasha said.

David smiled. "David Arthur Llywelyn Pendragon, King of England."

Natasha stared at him, open-mouthed. "Really? That's what you're going with?"

David looked back at her, surprised at her surprise. Did she really not believe him? She had to have known his origins, since she'd spoken with his Uncle Ted. But then he remembered that he'd become the King of England after his mom and dad had returned to the Middle Ages from their brief sojourn in the twenty-first century last

November. Before his crowning, David had been 'merely' the Prince of Wales.

"Callum, Cassie, and I decided that we wouldn't lie to you about where we've been and what we've been doing," David said. "By telling you the truth and nothing but, our stories will be the same, and you won't be able to trip me up in lies, which I don't tell well anyway."

Natasha leaned back in her chair, tapping at her lip with one finger and studying David. "Tell me why you think you're the King of England."

"Excuse me?" David said. "Why I *think* I'm the King of England?" He hadn't intended to be combative from the start, but his hackles had risen right out of the gate at being accused, essentially, of being deluded. "That sounds like you're trying to psychoanalyze me."

Natasha pressed her lips together and then said, "Perhaps I should start again. Please tell me what you've been doing since that December day when you disappeared from Pennsylvania in your aunt's minivan and dropped off the official record."

David nodded, placated somewhat by the little victory but telling himself not to be sucked in by her capitulation. She was probably the 'good cop'. She'd try to put him at his ease and get him to reveal pieces of himself he might rather not have discussed. Still, as he'd said, if he didn't lie, they would gain nothing but the truth. It wasn't as if he'd done anything illegal. "I assume you've heard most of my story already from my Uncle Ted."

"I didn't know about the King of England part," Natasha said. "It would help to hear it from you from the beginning."

David canted his head, studying her. "If you're the good cop, could I have a hamburger and fries or maybe fish and chips before we begin? I haven't eaten since 1289, and my story is going to take a while."

David thought he detected a twitch of a smile on Natasha's lips. *Good.* Callum had spoken to David of his life in Cardiff, mentioning Natasha specifically. Callum and she had been friends of a sort. She had implied to Callum on the docks that the show of force wasn't her idea, and perhaps his incarceration wasn't either.

"I might be the bad cop," Natasha said.

David dipped his head as if she were a visiting ruler and he was sitting on his throne. "I have no intention of underestimating you."

"You don't know what I'm capable of," she said. "This could simply be the calm before the storm."

David couldn't tell if she was joking, so he decided to play it straight. "True. But I live in the Middle Ages. How afraid do you think I'm going to be of what you might do to me? I've killed men with a sword." David dropped his voice slightly, not so much feigning regret (which he did feel), as playing it up for her benefit. "Too many men."

Natasha paused for a beat and again, he could tell that he'd surprised her. "I'll see what I can do." She stood and left the room.

David sat in the chair for another minute, waiting for her to return to tell him that the food was on its way. When she didn't come back right away, he got to his feet and began circling the room, trying not to think of himself as a lion in a cage. Almost worse than being penned in was that this interrogation routine was wasting his time. If he had two days in the twenty-first century, he had a lot to do and not much time to do it in. He needed access to a computer and a phone.

The thought of a phone brought him up short, and he stopped his pacing. The first people he needed to call were his Uncle Ted and Aunt Elisa. For all that Uncle Ted had cooperated with MI-5 last November when David's mom and dad had come to the twenty-first century, David assumed he'd done it out of naiveté, not maliciousness. After all, Uncle Ted had aided and abetted Mom by getting her duffel bag from her room and leaving her the key to his rental car. For the rest, if they stuck him in a room like this one, Ted may have felt he had no choice but to cooperate. David had been brought here in a hood and handcuffs like he was a terrorist. Maybe they'd done the same to Uncle Ted.

The image of what Ted (and his parents) had gone through last year suddenly gave David a very different perspective on Callum. MI-5 was his agency. Interrogations were something he ordered and took part in. While the transition from high school freshman to Prince of Wales hadn't exactly been easy for David, he could see why the transition from agent to medieval man would have been even more difficult for Callum. He'd gone from being the head of his MI-5 section to being baggage, with no job, no authority, and unable to communicate with anyone but David's family. It was pretty much the reverse of what was happening to David now.

On the other hand, Callum had proved himself to be a reasonable person. Chances were, Natasha was too. David walked to within a foot of the one-way glass, put his hands on his hips, and said, "I believe I'm entitled to a phone call."

His statement didn't elicit a response—from Natasha or anyone else.

David stood staring at the mirror, contemplating what to do if Natasha didn't come back soon. He'd all but made up his mind to pretend to have a seizure when the door opened again, and Natasha came through it with a white sack. The smell of fried fish rose from it, and David's mouth watered. Sore throat or not, he really was hungry.

She raised the sack high to show him that she'd brought what he'd asked for. Before she could close the door, he took two steps towards it, trying to see past her into the hallway. He caught a glimpse of a white corridor stretching for at least thirty feet with several doors opening off of it. He hadn't tried to disguise what he was doing, and she very pointedly handed him the bag and gestured that he should resume his seat. Then she closed the door behind her. Another half hour and he was going to insist on using their bathroom (or 'loo', as he reminded himself to say). He needed to get himself a better look.

Bevyn had told him a long time ago that soldiers should eat and sleep when they could, so David accepted the bag of food. "This isn't drugged, I hope," he said.

Natasha gave him a withering look. "We wouldn't do that."

"Uh huh. You put a sack on my head." This time, instead of sitting in the chair, he perched on the edge of the table, swinging one leg. "Did that come from you or your boss?"

Natasha pressed her lips together.

"What's his name, by the way?"

"Her name, and it's Director Jane Cooke."

David nodded. "I stand corrected. Ultimately, I'd like to speak with her, but for now, I need to use your phone, and I need access to a computer, a printer, and a backpack to hold what I print out."

As he'd foreseen when he sat on the table, Natasha had to turn in her seat and look up to talk to him; she wasn't the only one who could play power games. "We'll see about getting you what you want after you answer my questions."

"How about, I won't answer your questions until you get me what I want," David said. "Truthfully, I don't need to tell you anything, and you can keep me locked up here for the next two days if you choose. But if I have to stay in the twenty-first century, I'd like to use the time wisely, and that doesn't mean sitting in this room staring at you all the day long."

"The sooner you talk, the sooner we'll let you go."

"Is that a fact?" David said. "Why should I believe you?"

"Because you have no choice," Natasha said.

David took out a chip and popped it into his mouth. He chewed, thinking. "How about an exchange?"

"I'm listening," Natasha said.

"I tell you something, you give me something, I tell you something, you give me something. Since you started with the food, which is good, by the way, so thank you, you can go next. Ask me a question."

Natasha shifted in her seat, and David thought she looked pleased that he'd capitulated so quickly. Of course, she didn't know how easy it was for him to talk; he had nothing to lose, and who didn't like talking about himself? He'd led a pretty incredible life these last six years. David was almost looking forward to telling someone about it and seeing Natasha's face as she listened. He didn't care so much if she believed him. He was pretty sure she wasn't prepared for what he was going to ask for in return either.

"You say you've been living in 1289. How did you arrive back here?"

"Did you note the listing hulk the tug was hauling behind it as we left the marina?" David said. "We came in that."

"So I gathered," Natasha said. "I mean *how*? The mechanics of it. What was happening to you in the Middle Ages such that you ended up here?"

"Since last year, a baron named William de Valence has been causing trouble for me and for England. I was sailing to Ireland with several hundred men and horses, with the express purpose of dealing with him once and for all, when we encountered a storm in the Irish Sea."

Natasha eyed him and then flipped through a series of notes in the file folder she'd brought. "I guess I don't understand what you're saying. What does a storm at sea have to do with you coming to the twenty-first century?"

"Our ship was going down; my life was in danger. Thus, the time travel," David said.

Natasha continued to flip through the papers in the folder. "This—" She looked up at David. "This is new, you mean? No one in your family has ever traveled to or from the Middle Ages as the result of a storm at sea."

"No." David shrugged and then asked a question of his own. "You're telling me the sensors didn't pick up the flash?"

Natasha pursed her lips.

"Yeah. I thought they might have," David said.

"That's why you came quietly, isn't it?" Natasha said. "You knew that we knew you were here."

"Callum told me you would know," David said. "I suspected you would chase us if we ran."

Natasha looked down at her paper, suddenly still, which David thought was odd. Did she really think Callum wouldn't have told him? He wished he knew what Callum had revealed so far, if anything. Had he mentioned that he was the Earl of Shrewsbury? Somehow, David guessed not. David, for his part, resolved to keep Callum and Cassie out of this conversation with Natasha as much as possible. He would tell the truth, but his friends weren't here, and he didn't want to guess what MI-5 thought about them—or had done with them.

"Your mother ran," Natasha said.

"With good reason, as it turned out," David said.

Natasha grimaced. "We knew at the time that we'd fumbled the initial contact."

"And yet, given your treatment of me, you learned nothing from your encounter with her. If you'd picked us up at the pier without your jackbooted thugs, put me in a conference room, and asked your questions with the three of us together, this could have been so much more pleasant for all of us."

"As was the case with your mother, it wasn't my call." Natasha had the fortitude not to eye the one-way glass, though David did. Natasha could still be playing the good cop, or she could be telling the truth, not caring that her superiors were present and aware of the fact that she'd just disowned them.

In the end, it didn't matter to David if his incarceration was Natasha's decision or someone else's, because he was still locked up and distrusted. "Callum assured me that your sensors were sensitive enough to detect my location. You might not know that I had come through, but you would know that one of my family members had. I decided I'd spare you having to chase me around Wales for two days until I could figure out how to get back home." He looked pointedly at the door. "It seems I made a mistake."

"I repeat: we mean you no harm," Natasha said.

David stood. "I guess I'll just leave, then." He went to the door and pressed on the handle, which wasn't a knob but a lever. It didn't move. He looked back at Natasha, who'd turned in her seat to watch him try the door.

She didn't admit wrong-doing but merely pointed at the chair opposite her. "Please, David. Don't make this more difficult than it already is. Sit."

"I'll sit if you stop pretending that you're my friend or on my side or that I'm anything but a prisoner." David folded his arms across his chest.

"Fine. This can be adversarial if you want it to be. Sit," she repeated.

"Oh, so now it's *my* fault," David said, but he returned to the chair opposite Natasha and sat in it, rocking it back on the rear legs. The muscles around Natasha's eyes tightened, telling David that his sullenness annoyed her. *Excellent.*

"Who is William de Valence?" Natasha said.

"Now, now." David wagged a finger at her. "You got your question—more than one, in fact. Now I get what I want. I need a computer connected to the internet, a printer with paper in it, and a backpack. And I need to talk to someone from the CDC."

"You need to talk to whom?"

"Someone from the Centers for Disease Control," David said. "It's in Atlanta."

"I know it's in Atlanta," Natasha said.

"Or if you prefer, I can talk to someone who works for an equivalent institution in the UK. Your choice."

"Why do you want to speak to someone at the CDC?"

David tsked through his teeth at the question. "We're looking at measles, scarlet fever, dysentery, leprosy, not to mention the Black Death coming up in sixty years. I've got some big problems on the horizon, and I need help dealing with them."

Natasha stared at him. "You really think you're going back to the Middle Ages, don't you?"

"Do you really think you can stop me?" David crumpled the now empty lunch sack and lobbed it towards a garbage can in the corner. He raised two fists in the air in victory when it went in, sparking a cough of laughter from Natasha. Then he lowered his arms. "I'm the King of England."

"So you said."

"Then you must realize that I have a job to do, and I can't let anyone stop me from doing it. Now, are you going to get me what I need, or are we going to stare at each other for the rest of the day?"

Natasha rubbed her chin and didn't answer.

David leaned forward, aiming to sweeten the pot. "If you find me a laptop sooner rather than later, you can ask me all the questions you want while I work."

8

September, 2017

Callum

"Have I mentioned that I love you?" Cassie stood beside Callum at a picture window, admiring the view of downtown Cardiff. With five stories above the lobby floor, the MI-5 building (called 'the Office' by everyone who worked in it) certainly wasn't the tallest building in Cardiff, but from their angle, they could see the old castle standing on its motte, overlooking the old city. Callum could hardly believe that he'd been in this very spot the day before in 1289, riding a horse to the harbor where they'd boarded the ships to Ireland.

"You have." He put his arm around his wife's waist and pulled her to him. "As you should."

"Are we being monitored?" Cassie pulled back a little.

"We should assume it," Callum said.

"Good," Cassie said and gave him a long kiss.

Callum broke off the kiss with a laugh. "The transition leaves you breathless, doesn't it?"

Cassie shook her head. "I've been here only a few hours, and it's already as if the last five years never happened." She smiled. "Except that I'm standing here with you."

"Five years ago, I'd just left the army and joined the Security Service. I came to Cardiff a little over a year ago, six months before the events at Chepstow Castle. The city hasn't changed at all."

"Which is what makes this so hard," Cassie said.

Callum nodded. "Because we *have* changed. For the better." As much as the medieval world had knocked him flat when he'd first arrived, it had been transformative. How could it not?

"Anyone who could see Cardiff in 1289 would be appalled at what's been done to it," Cassie said. "Have you noticed the air?"

"It was the first thing I noticed," Callum said. "Well, other than the thousands of buildings, of course. That gray pall hangs over everything, even when everyone here thinks the sky is perfectly clear."

"They don't know what they're missing." Cassie looked up at him.

"This world can't turn back the clock. It's too late."

"But we can," Cassie said.

Callum was silent a moment. "I'm going to have to think about this." He'd experienced culture shock a time or two. If he stayed, he would again, but that didn't mean he couldn't be happy here in the end.

"Can you talk to me about what you're thinking?" she said.

"If the Security Service really accepts me back, I could serve David just as well—or maybe better—from here." He couldn't say to her that the idea of risking her life to return to the Middle Ages had his heart stopping in mid-beat.

"Our obligations are very real in both centuries," Cassie said. "I need to talk to my grandfather."

Callum kissed her again and then said, "I will go wherever you go. For better or for worse."

"I know," she said, "but this needs to be *our* decision. Together."

"It does seem that we have a little time to think about it." Callum rubbed at Cassie's arms, feeling the soft wool of her cloak under his hands. She'd put the cloak on over the top of the dry clothes she'd changed into: trousers and shirt that fit the modern world. He'd had the cloak made for her especially for this trip, an evergreen hue, thinner for early fall weather, with embroidery at the edges: tiny stags from the McCallum crest she'd modified for his own use as the Earl of Shrewsbury.

In turn, she adjusted his tie. The first thing Driscoll had done was find them new clothes. This suit, in fact, had been one that Callum himself had kept in his office as a spare. At his departure, it had gone into the Office's collection. More than one agent had hurriedly found himself a new shirt from the wardrobe before reporting for duty after being up all night on a case—or having spent the night some place other than his own home.

After that, Driscoll had left them in a small office adjacent to this conference room, where they'd spent over an hour concocting

Callum's report on an old-fashioned typewriter. The powers that be had put a moratorium on any kind of written electronic communication until further notice. Callum hadn't known if that extended to shutting off the cameras that monitored them, but he and Cassie had assumed it didn't. Cassie had insisted on talking normally because they had nothing to hide, just as David had said. Callum had gone along. They *had* been living in the Middle Ages. Whether or not anyone believed them didn't change that fact.

Callum had started out typing with his usual two fingers until Cassie had elbowed him out of the way to finish it with all ten. They'd written volumes about specific experiences but remained light on the personal details. Until Callum knew whom he could trust, he was determined to say as little as possible about anything but his mission.

The door to the conference room opened, prompting Callum to release Cassie. Driscoll stood hesitating in the doorway, but then someone behind him urged him forward, and a small crowd entered the room. Driscoll gestured to the conference table, which took up the central portion of the room and had fifteen chairs around it. "Please, sit."

Callum held out a chair at the end for Cassie before sitting himself. The chair was faux black leather, soft and padded, and he took a moment to revel in the way it rocked back gently under his weight, cushioning him in a fashion he hadn't experienced since last November. As a companion to the King of England, he merited goose down bedding, but there was something to be said for memory foam.

Eight of the chairs filled with men Callum knew marginally well, and then the last person entered the room: 'Lady Jane' Cooke.

Of uncertain age with too-stiff over-permed hair, she was the dragon-boss of the Security Service, the Deputy Director General, whom everyone was, quite frankly, terrified to cross. It was her husband who was the physicist at Cambridge and the friend of David's Uncle Ted, who'd started this ball rolling in the first place. Her boss, known as the DG (the Director General), was a political appointee who had little to do with the actual running of the Security Service.

Lady Jane stalked to the seat at the head of the table, which everyone had wisely left vacant. Her secretary hastened to pull it back for her, and she sat. Callum had steered himself and Cassie to the opposite end when Driscoll had suggested they sit, and now the two women—the only women in the room—glared at each other from opposite ends of the table. Callum fought a smile. If she'd been born in another time and place, Cassie would have had the wherewithal to fill Lady Jane's shoes.

The two women continued to look at each other, though both of their expressions had softened slightly by the time the men in the room arranged themselves and removed files and documents from their briefcases. Their electronic tablets remained resolutely dark. Then they all waited, pen to paper, for Lady Jane to say something.

"Put everything away," she said. "I don't want anything we say here to leave this room."

The men hesitated for a second and then obeyed. Callum continued to rock back in his chair, studying everyone else. This was little different from the daily conferences with David in the hall of whatever baron or nobleman he happened to be meeting that day. David would gather minor lords and their underlings together, listen to them bicker about this and that, their rights and responsibilities. Meanwhile, he'd be gauging their strengths and weaknesses for himself—and relying on Callum as a second pair of eyes.

Lady Jane straightened the edges of a stack of papers in front of her, which appeared to be Callum's report, and then looked straight at Callum. "So. You're back."

Callum righted himself in his chair and clasped his hands on the table in front of him. "Yes, ma'am."

"Perhaps you would introduce me to your companion?" She looked down her long nose at Cassie.

Callum held out a hand to Cassie. "Director, this is my wife, Cassandra. Cassie, this is the director of the Security Service, Jane Cooke."

"It's nice to finally meet you," Cassie said, completely without irony.

Lady Jane inclined her head regally. "And you as well." She looked around the table at the men in the room. "We have all read your report, Agent Callum, but of course we have many questions. Smythe, you may go first."

Callum controlled his expression as best he could. Thomas Smythe was now Lady Jane's right hand man, and he made Callum's skin crawl. To everyone else, he was eminently respectable in his suit and tie, with chiseled jaw and firm handshake from hours spent in the Security Service's athletic facility.

"Who is the man downstairs?" Smythe said.

"David. He's the King of England," Callum said.

With a nod from Lady Jane, Smythe reached into his brief-case for a folder and pulled it out. He flipped through the pages, read a few words silently to himself, and then said, "Edward I was King of England in 1289."

"In this world," Cassie said. "He's dead in ours."

Smythe raised his eyebrows, and Callum cursed under his breath that she'd given them away with the *ours*.

Cassie had her arms folded, elbows resting on the conference table. She leaned into them. "This isn't time travel, you realize? It's an alternate universe."

"We understand that, *young lady*," Smythe said, though he couldn't have been more than a few years older than Cassie, a year or two younger than Callum, who was thirty-five.

Cassie narrowed her eyes at him. "I don't think you do." She looked around the table at the men. "All of you sit here with no idea what you're dealing with or *who* you're dealing with. David is *the King of England*." She pounded a fist on the table. "You should not be keeping him here against his will. He has a country to run, and many lives depend on him." She gestured to Callum. "His job is to act as David's ambassador, to advise him, and to keep him safe. David has been surviving death threats since he was fourteen years old. He fought King Edward in single combat at sixteen. How many of you would have run screaming from the room if faced with any of the enemies either of them have encountered in the Middle Ages? You people are petty and insignificant in comparison."

Even Callum was stunned by Cassie's vehemence. But proud, too, of course.

"Really!" Smythe stuttered his objections, and the other men murmured their disapproval.

Lady Jane lifted a hand to end all discussion. "I have changed my mind. Please clear the room."

Lady Jane's words, coming hard on the heels of Cassie's tongue lashing, caused several more mouths to drop open. Nobody moved but Driscoll, who went to the door like he couldn't get out of the room fast enough.

"Now!" Lady Jane clapped her hands. But when Callum and Cassie started to rise, she added, "Not you two."

With some under-the-breath complaining, the men rose to their feet, fumbling with the items they'd brought, and followed Driscoll out the door. Lady Jane moved down the table, pulled out a chair next to Callum, and sat in it.

"The cameras are off; it's just the three of us. I want to hear what you have to say for yourself." Lady Jane held up the report. "This is the bare bones, and I want the details. I trusted you to apprehend David's parents. What happened?"

Callum found Lady Jane's demeanor somewhat dismaying. She was speaking like a mother instead of a boss. "I tried." He just managed not to shrug, which would not have *done* in Lady Jane's presence. "Coming on top of the shambles Smythe made of the Aberystwyth situation, my team had a few mistimings too, along with what I'm guessing was a too-helpful custodian?"

Lady Jane nodded. "We interviewed all the staff at Chepstow after you disappeared. While you and your men were watching the castle's front entrance, the maintenance worker let Meg and Llywelyn into the castle right under your nose."

Callum scowled. "I tried to stop them from jumping, and they ended up pulling me over the balcony wall with them. We went from 2016 Chepstow to 1288 Windsor in a blink of an eye."

Lady Jane's brow furrowed. "Windsor? Why Windsor?"

"Because, as Meg put it," Callum said, "that's where she was needed."

Lady Jane gave a very unladylike grunt, but Callum couldn't tell if she was dismayed or approving of what he'd said. Lady Jane now eyed Cassie. "That was quite a speech you gave. You are from Oregon, are you not?" Lady Jane pronounced the name of the state as 'Are-eh-gone' which Callum knew from Cassie to be incorrect. Neither he nor Cassie chose to mention it.

"Yes," Cassie said.

"And you saved his life?"

"Yes." Callum took Cassie's hand.

"Hmmm." Lady Jane looked from Cassie to Callum. "What was it like for you?"

"I thought about how to return to the twenty-first century every day," Callum said, without hesitation. "Until that could happen, I focused on continuing my mission, as ordered."

"You believe you have done that?" Lady Jane said.

"When I discovered I had traveled with Meg to the Middle Ages, I took it upon myself to do what I could to learn of that time and serve my country as best I could, even from there," Callum said.

"And here you are, back again," Lady Jane said, "almost as if you'd planned it."

"Yes, ma'am." Callum straightened in his chair. "I did."

"Tell me, what do you see as your responsibilities going forward?" Lady Jane said.

"The same as they've been, from the moment I joined the Security Service," Callum said. "And I think it's time you told me your objectives in this. What, exactly, are you doing with David?"

"What needs to be done," Lady Jane said.

"No," Callum said and then overrode Lady Jane's protest. "I spent nearly a year working my way into David's confidence, and within ten minutes you have undermined the relationship I've spent all this time building! Why is he in interrogation? Why is he being treated like a criminal?"

"It was deemed appropriate," Lady Jane said.

"At least let me talk to him," Callum said. "He will be more cooperative if he sees me working with you."

Lady Jane looked over the top of her glasses at Callum. "I will take your suggestion under advisement. I believe it has merit." She almost sounded regretful.

Some of the fire left Callum. "You're not in charge, are you? Who is—the Home Office?"

Lady Jane's eyes narrowed. "I serve my government, as do you."

Callum sat back; he could press her no further. "Of course."

"I'm glad to see you safe and sound. You've brought us a very valuable asset indeed." She straightened her suit jacket with a jerk. "Your government thanks you."

Callum dipped his head. "As I said, I was only doing my duty."

"And we will see that you continue to do so. You will be reinstated, of course. Full back-pay."

"Thank you, ma'am." Callum didn't know what else to say. He didn't know that he could stomach working underneath Smythe, but he needed to stay close to David, and this was the way to do it.

Then Lady Jane took a mobile phone from the side pocket of her suit jacket. Setting it on the table, she pushed it with one finger toward Callum. "That's your new mobile. Passcode 6631, same as before. The standard numbers have been inputted into the directory."

Callum looked at the mobile without picking it up. Unlike Cassie, he had nobody to phone. "Thank you."

Lady Jane pushed back from the table, and Callum hastily stood to match her. "We'll have to sort out your living situation. You'll be staying here for now." She strode towards the door but stopped before opening it, wavering, and then came back a few steps towards Callum. It was strange to see her hesitant, after she'd appeared so confident before. "Callum, I must tell you that this case has attracted attention from outside the Security Service. Other parties—interested parties—might question your allegiance."

Callum swallowed hard. "I see."

"You have been gone ten months, so you don't yet understand, but what faces us today is bigger than David. Bigger than you can imagine. It may be that you are the only one who truly under-stands our mission. Your ability to see the truth of a situation has al-ways been one of your greatest assets."

"Ma'am—"

"In fact, I am counting on it." Lady Jane turned on her heel and departed.

Callum gazed blankly at the closed door and then sat back down in his chair, absently picking up the mobile as he did so.

Cassie leaned forward. "What was that about? What is she counting on?"

"I think Lady Jane just gave me a new mission," Callum said. "Something is going on here, something that has her running scared."

"Director Cooke, you mean?" At Callum's nod, Cassie added, "Did she have to be so cryptic? What did she mean by interested par-ties?"

"I don't know." Callum entered the passcode and flipped through the screens. The mobile was an upgrade from his old one, with many more bells and whistles.

"Maybe I shouldn't have come on so strong," Cassie said. "I keep seeing David with that hood over his head."

Callum rocked forward. "Not at all! What you said was bril-liant. I think it made all the difference, and I truly enjoyed the look on Smythe's face as you set him down."

"Why was he promoted?" Cassie said.

"Rumor has it that he has connections on high," Callum said. "I don't doubt it now. *Interested parties* means politics and money."

"So … what do we do next?" Cassie said, looking around the room.

Before Callum could answer Cassie's question, Driscoll opened the door. As before, he paused, running a hand through his hair and staring past them out the windows set in the opposite wall. Several other men hovered in the corridor behind him, but he closed the door in their faces.

As he did so, Callum's phone vibrated with an incoming text. He clicked on it and saw it was from Lady Jane:

Don't trust Driscoll. Don't trust anyone.

Callum stared at his phone and then up at Driscoll, who slapped the leather tablet he'd been carrying on the table and plopped himself into one of the vacant chairs opposite Cassie and Callum. "David really believes it."

"Believes what?" Callum hastily closed the message and dropped his phone into his suit pocket.

"That he's the King of England."

"He is the King of England," Cassie said, "in 1289."

Driscoll threw up his hands and then dropped them onto the conference table. In yet another gesture of despair or capitulation, he slouched further in his chair.

Callum leaned forward with his elbows on the table. "Lady Jane seems to have no problem believing us. Why do you?"

"Honestly, Callum. It can't be true."

"Then what's your explanation for all this?" Callum said.

"I don't have one!"

Callum and Cassie exchanged a glance, and then Cassie put a hand on Driscoll's arm. "Imagine how I felt when I arrived in that Scottish woods when a second before I'd been in Oregon. It's hard to accept, but everything becomes easier once you do."

"That's what my parents told me about belief in God," Driscoll said. "What do you want me to say? That I believe you have spent the last ten months living in the Middle Ages? It's a fairy tale."

"I have spent the last ten months living in the Middle Ages," Callum said. "Whether or not you believe it doesn't make it less true."

Cassie tapped her fingers on the table, watching Driscoll. "Let's put the truth of what we say aside for the moment. Lady Jane said that we were to stay at MI-5 for now, since we're homeless. That's all very well and good, but it seems to me that nobody is quite sure what to do with us. You left the door unlocked, and you aren't holding us. Yet somehow, I get the feeling that security isn't going to let us walk out the front door either."

"We have nothing to hold you on, and Callum is one of us," Driscoll said. "Lady Jane has made that abundantly clear. You are being reinstated."

"That's what she said to me too," Callum said, not sharing what she'd said afterwards—or her text. "Has she said anything to you about what that entails?"

Driscoll pursed his lips. "That I don't know. Not head of Cardiff station, not right away."

"I gather Natasha has been running things since I left," Callum said.

"She has done a creditable job," Driscoll said. "She hasn't put a foot wrong. I find it likely that Lady Jane will transfer you somewhere else, rather than transfer or demote her."

"Why would Lady Jane do that?" Cassie said. "Callum is a wealth of information about the Middle Ages. If they want to continue this project, they need him."

"They have David," Driscoll said, "and Callum is too close to this. Removing him is standard procedure. It's why he hasn't been asked to join the interrogation."

Cassie mouthed the word *interrogation* and scowled.

"So they do question my loyalty," Callum said.

Driscoll shrugged. "It's going to take time to know where anyone stands."

Cassie pushed up from the table. "I need to call my grandfather."

"That can be arranged," Driscoll said, "but it's just seven in the morning there. Do you want to wake him up?"

"He'll be up," Cassie said. "And if he's not, he would want to be woken."

Driscoll nodded. He went to the door, spoke to someone beyond it, and then waved a hand to Cassie.

Callum stood too. "Do you want me to come with you?"

"I'll be all right." Cassie squeezed his hand and left the room.

Callum let her go. He didn't want to be naïve about all this, but he hoped this wasn't just being used as an opportunity to separate Cassie from him. So much still didn't add up.

Don't trust Driscoll. Don't trust anyone.

Driscoll returned to his chair, wrinkling his nose as he sat. Callum wanted to laugh. He guessed that Driscoll remained three seats away because Callum smelled as he always did—of salt and sweat—but to Driscoll, he would smell a little ripe. Callum had grown accustomed to living without modern perfumes and deodorants, but it wasn't as if he'd showered that morning either.

"What's happening with David, exactly?"

Driscoll coughed. "So far he's asked for fish and chips, a computer, and to speak to someone at the CDC."

"And what has he told you?" Callum said.

"That he's the bloody King of England!" Driscoll said. "You were on a ship bound for Ireland, chasing a lord named Valence, when you were hit by a storm and *boom!* you're here. It's exactly what you wrote in your report."

"Have you hauled the cog out of the water yet?" Callum said.

Driscoll chewed on his lower lip. "We're working on it. Our researchers from the university want to know where we found a medieval cog, and we're not answering."

"That was quick work," Callum said. "In fact, everything has happened too quickly. How is Lady Jane even here?"

"She arrived last night for the annual review of our office," Driscoll said. "That you came today is viewed by her as manna from heaven. Smythe has been walking around with a stupid grin plastered on his face, annoying everyone by telling us how pleased Lady Jane is with his performance."

"*His* performance?" Callum said.

"The show of force at the dock was his doing," Driscoll said, "sanctioned by those higher up."

"Who?" Callum said.

"I don't know."

"Naturally," Callum said sourly. "What's next, then?"

"The wheels of bureaucracy can move fast when they choose to," Driscoll said. "Lady Jane has been in contact with the DG and the Home Office. Likely, David will be transported to London by this evening."

Callum tapped his fingers on the arm of his chair. Driscoll leaned across the table towards him and lowered his voice. "Listen, Callum. The higher-ups—" He broke off and looked furtively around the room.

"Are we being recorded?" Callum said.

The conference room was one that in the past had been a work space for Security Service agents, not a place where they kept suspects or those under interrogation, even peripherally. Come to think on it, this was the room in which they'd last gathered before going after Meg and Llewelyn at Chepstow Castle. The wall screen was black, and the conference table was new. It disturbed Callum slightly that it had taken him this long to notice where he was.

"No," Driscoll said, "not here. But Callum, they are going to want to know some things. They're going to want to use David."

"What do you mean *use* him?" Callum said.

"You need to start thinking like a politician. Certain people— important and powerful people—see this as an enormous opportunity."

"An opportunity for what?" Callum said.

"If we can find a way to use whatever is inside David to send men back and forth to the past at will, think of the knowledge to be gained! Not to mention the access to resources that have grown scarce on our planet. Think about it: precious metals! Untapped oil reserves! This isn't a few quid we're talking about. To the Home Office, it could be a matter of *billions* of pounds."

Callum's mouth fell open. Cassie had been right. They should have run.

9

September, 1289

Anna

Anna couldn't decide which concerned her more—that Valence had landed a fleet of ships at Southampton or that she and Bronwen were suddenly expected to produce a magic potion that would heal all wounds—for that was the gossip her maid was hearing in the corridors. The witchcraft trials hadn't yet overtaken Britain, but superstition and ignorance underlay suspicion of anything different or new, and Anna and her family had rightfully always feared it.

For now, she was faced with saying goodbye to her husband, who had a war on his hands, the parameters of which they didn't yet know. "When do you leave?" Anna said.

"I ride out within the hour," Math said. "William de Bohun volunteered to ride to London with twenty men to gather reinforcements between here and there. He, Ieuan, and Edmund Mortimer have already left. If Valence marches this way, we will have the men to defend Windsor. Don't worry."

Anna took a deep breath and eased Bran, who had fallen asleep, from her breast. She laid him on the bed beside her. He was her third son, but only the second living, since she and Math had lost little Llelo at six months old to a measles epidemic when Cadell was three. Now at nearly four, Cadell had already had measles, an easy bout of scarlet fever at the start of the current epidemic, and chicken pox. Mumps, rubella, whooping cough, and a host of other diseases awaited him in the next few years. If he could survive them, if he could reach the age of ten, he had a good chance of living into his fifties. Provided he didn't die of the other major cause of death for men: war.

Such was the reality of the medieval world, and the older Anna grew, the more she wondered if choosing this life had been the right decision. And then she looked from Bran to Math and knew why she had chosen it and knew that if she could travel back in time again to her earlier self, even knowing what she knew now, she would make the same choices all over again.

"Why have you given Ieuan overall command?" Anna said.

The corners of Math's mouth turned down as he looked at her. "You object that we've elevated him thus?"

"Not at all!" Anna allowed herself a burst of laughter before her fear reasserted itself. "I just can't believe Edmund or Carew gave way. Ieuan is a Welshman, and while his English and French are improving, he is not one of *them*."

"Ieuan has stood at Dafydd's side since he and Bronwen arrived at King's Langley before Arthur's birth," Math said. "He has familiarized himself with the full extent of Dafydd's forces in London and the surrounding area, far more so than any other lord barring Dafydd himself. These barons all have their own men and estates to see to. It is Ieuan who has trained Dafydd's standing army, and we all agreed that it should be he who leads them."

"I didn't even know David had a standing army. Papa doesn't." Given Anna's occasional disbelief that she was really living in the Middle Ages, the fact that her baby brother was the King of England had been known to stymie her completely. She supposed that for him to have a standing army was small potatoes compared to that.

"King Llywelyn doesn't have anyone to war with these days," Math said. "It's not as if England or the barons in the March are going to be raiding his lands any time soon."

"He has defenses—" Anna said, defending her father.

Math came forward to sit on the edge of the bed. "I'm not criticizing Llywelyn. God knows I'm grateful that the wars with England are over, along with the constant skirmishes along the border. All I'm saying is that Dafydd does not have that luxury. He has had to think several moves ahead, if not the whole chess match. Unfortunately, he miscalculated in thinking that Valence would stay in Ireland."

Anna accepted her husband's explanation, no longer offended. "Just be grateful that he had the foresight to insist that Cassie and Callum were the only ones to accompany him. That said, do we have enough men to defeat Valence?"

"The scouts report that two thousand men landed at Southampton. We can only pray that this is Valence's only force. We hope that his goal for now is to carve out a place for himself in the southwest while Clare and Dafydd are away. Then he can begin to woo the other barons to his side," Math said.

"I suppose he'll promise them the usual: land and money under his dispensation," Anna said. "How many takers might he have?"

Math shrugged. "Edmund would know that better than I. A few, certainly. I'd like to defeat him before any of the wavering decide to take Valence up on his offer, believing he can give them more than Dafydd has or can."

"David has tried—"

"Again, I'm not criticizing your brother," Math said. "He has taken the long view, as well he should and as only he can, but he has been none too gentle with some of the barons he views as particularly stubborn or arrogant. They've taken offense. Valence speaks their language better than Dafydd does."

"David's French is fine," Anna said.

Math laughed and gently rubbed Anna's arm. "I'm not speaking of his fluency, *cariad*."

Anna had known that, actually, but she still found herself angry on David's behalf with all those Normans who were backing into the future instead of turning around and running towards it. "What are we going to do about it?"

"At this point, I can do nothing but go to war," Math said. "These barons wouldn't listen to me anyway."

"Their wives might listen to me, though," Anna said. "I know that David would have to approve any promises, but would it hurt to identify those who are wavering and sweeten the pot for them? The crown of England has more resources at its disposal than Valence."

"Bribe them, you mean?" Math said. "Don't you have enough on your hands with the baby, Cadell, and this penicillin problem?"

"We have twenty scholars working hard, and Bronwen knows what she's doing," Anna said.

"What are you suggesting?"

"I could at least find out *who* might be wavering and what might encourage them to stand firm a while longer, long enough for you to take care of Valence's army."

"Will their husbands listen, though?" Math said.

"Do you listen to me?" Anna said.

Math looked affronted. "Of course."

"The longer I've spent with noblewomen, the more I've come to realize that they are no more content, most of them, with doing as they're told than I am," Anna said. "Some have empty heads, it's true, and too many haven't been educated or haven't read enough beyond the Bible to have the proper knowledge to *think* with. But when pressed, or shown evidence, they can think. And none of us like seeing our sons die."

As Anna had grown more animated, Math had moved closer. He put his hands on either side of her face and kissed her gently. "Okay. I'm convinced. But you take care. Far worse would be to push one of these would-be traitors into Valence's arms."

"I'll be careful, though it's you who needs to hear that more." Anna leaned into her husband. He wrapped his arms around her, and they held on until a low knock came at the door.

"That's for me." Math kissed Anna one more time and then went to the door.

"Say goodbye to Cadell before you go," Anna said.

"Where is he?"

"I arranged for him to 'help' in the kitchen while I put Bran to sleep."

Math laughed. "I'll see to him."

"I love you, Math," Anna said.

He kissed his fingers and blew the kiss to her. "And I you."

After Math left, Anna arranged for the nanny to watch over Bran, who would sleep for several hours (she hoped), checked on Cadell, who was elbow deep in bread dough, and then went to find Bronwen. Anna peered through the crack between the frame and the door at Bronwen's sleeping daughter. The late afternoon sun shone through the window, making an elongated rectangle on the floor. Bronwen had pulled the curtains around the four-poster bed so the sun wouldn't shine on Catrin's face.

Bronwen came to stand at Anna's shoulder. "Today is one of those days."

"What do you mean?" Anna said.

Bronwen drew away from the door and leaned her back against the wall in the corridor. "Much of the time since Catrin's birth, I've felt like my head is stuffed with cotton. I can't see or think about anything further than a few feet around me. It's like I'm wrapped in Styrofoam."

"I hadn't noticed anything wrong with you." Anna squeezed her friend's hand. "You're a wonderful mother."

"It's not a lack of love for Catrin I'm feeling." Bronwen rubbed her forehead with the heel of her hand. "My love for her is as fierce as I can imagine love ever being, but I haven't had space in my head for anything but getting through the day."

"I can quote a parenting book at you, if you like," Anna said. "Something about how easy it is to get in the habit of meeting everyone's emotional needs but your own."

"Do I need to ask why you were reading a parenting book at seventeen?" Bronwen laughed, and Anna was glad to see it. "I probably read that somewhere too—or at least, I've heard that from other mothers. A friend of mine who had a baby back in the old world told me that if she had four minutes by herself a day, just enough for a quick shower, she was lucky. And more often than not the baby would start crying while she was still soaking wet."

"We can't take showers." Anna laughed now too, a hand to her mouth.

Bronwen smiled. "And we have nannies and maids and servants around every corner to fulfill any wish. We're rich and privileged. More than one woman in the village at Buellt birthed ten children by the age of thirty-five and works from dawn to dusk with little help. I'm spoiled and I know it, and yet—"

"We are all spoiled, Bronwen," Anna said. "Compared to the Middle Ages, the twenty-first century spoiled us rotten, and it has continued here, though admittedly, the standard for what constitutes 'spoiled' is a lot lower."

"Which, to steal an already overused cliché, is why our responsibilities are even greater," Bronwen said. "I know. I'm honestly grateful to you for putting me to work, even if now I have too much to do."

"Yeah, well, guess what I just did?" Anna said and then continued without waiting for a response. "I told Math that I would take it upon myself to weasel my way into the confidences of various noblewomen, trying to gauge if their husbands will continue to support David despite Valence's pleading."

"Despite Valence's outright bribes, you mean?" Bronwen said, thinking like Math.

"You'd go that far?" Anna said.

"What would you call promises of land, even in Wales, after he defeats David and then your father?" Bronwen said.

"Is that a fact or a guess?" Anna said.

"A fact," Bronwen said. "Everyone thinks they're keeping secrets, but nobody really can. Not at Windsor and certainly not at Westminster."

Anna stared at her friend, a bit stunned at the calm way she had delivered that news. "Does David know?"

"Sure. Why do you think he decided that he had to deal with Valence *now*?"

"Do you know which barons are at risk?"

"Not Edmund, thankfully, not even a rumor of that. Not Bigod, even with the war in the Severn Estuary and the bad blood it created between his family and ours. Not the Bohuns, despite all expectations to the contrary. David was most worried about the Burnells and the remaining Giffards."

"What about the Percys?" Anna said.

"Henry Percy is the only male left in that line and he, like William de Bohun, worships the ground David walks on," Bronwen said. "Percy arrived this morning, by the way. He fancies himself a scholar. Have you seen him yet?"

Anna shook her head.

"I told him to introduce himself to you, but with all that's been happening, I can see why he hasn't yet managed it. I put him in the guest quarters in the lower bailey."

"He may end up regretting that he threw in his lot with us," Anna said with a laugh, though it wasn't really funny, given the war they were facing.

"Bronwen!" Lili's voice carried up the stairwell, and while Bronwen took a quick glance into her bedroom to make sure Lili's call hadn't woken Catrin, Anna hurried towards the stairs.

She leaned into the stairwell, searching for her sister-in-law. "What is it?"

"Valence has come!"

"What?"

"What was that?" Bronwen arrived at Anna's side at the same instant Lili appeared at the top of the stairs. It was first time Anna had seen Lili wear breeches in a long while.

"Ieuan has sent word back," Lili said. "Valence didn't stop at Winchester. He's by-passed it completely and has almost reached Windsor."

"Four hours ago, all he'd done was land at Southampton!" Bronwen said. "How did he get from there to here in so short a time?"

"Either our scouts were bought off or totally misled. Valence landed late yesterday afternoon and has force-marched his men across country with little rest since they disembarked from the boats. They are within striking distance of Windsor town," Lili said.

Bronwen turned to Anna. "Fifty miles in twenty-four hours is just barely possible."

"He hasn't quite come fifty," Lili said. "Not yet. While our muster was to be at Basingstoke, it's too late for that. The few men Ieuan had already gathered are defending the bridge across Bourne Creek for now, but we don't have the men to keep it. Ieuan hopes he can hold it long enough to allow a full retreat into Windsor."

"How many fighting men do we have here?" Anna asked. Math hadn't said.

"Not even a hundred," Lili said, "including the archers."

Bronwen's brow furrowed as she looked at Lili. "Why don't we have more men?"

"Ieuan and Edmund Mortimer left Windsor with their men-at-arms and knights," Lili said. "All that's left to us are the usual fifty who live at Windsor plus the personal guards of the various noble-men who have come."

"And we lost twenty of those to William de Bohun's departure." Anna's throat closed over the horrible odds they were facing.

"We'll need every one of our scholars," Bronwen said, "Henry Percy included."

"We'll make them see the need," Anna said. "We can appeal to their romanticism. They're young. They won't have learned to fear war yet, most of them."

"Windsor town has a defense force too, doesn't it?" Bronwen said.

Lili nodded. "Ieuan's been teaching everyone over the age of ten to shoot."

"Will Ieuan be among those who retreat into Windsor?" Bronwen said, and Anna could see her holding her breath in hope.

Lili shook her head. "Both he and Edmund Mortimer are riding with the few who can be spared to reconnoiter Valence's lines and to gather all the men they can from the villages and towns around Windsor, particularly along the Thames River. Valence won't have run through them on the way here."

"That leaves Math to defend Windsor," Anna said.

Lili nodded again. A hollow space opened up inside Anna's belly, which was then filled instantly with fear.

"Why isn't Valence marching on London?" Bronwen said. "I would have thought that Westminster would be his goal if he is to take the kingship from David."

Anna shook her head, pushing down her anxiety so she could think. "Valence knows that the Londoners won't willingly support him. He'll need to show them proof of his power before they let him into the city."

"Besides, last Valence knew, Dafydd was here, and thus his treasury is here," Lili said. "The path to the crown goes through Windsor, not Westminster."

"Or maybe he knows that David has gone to Ireland," Anna said. "Valence may hope to stage a coup. David could return to find his castle held against him, and Valence seated on his throne."

"That cannot happen," Lili said darkly.

"Regardless, Lili, why are you dressed like that?" Anna said.

Lili looked down at her breeches and then back up at Anna. "What do you mean?"

"Do you really intend to fight?" Anna said.

"Of course I intend to fight," Lili said. "Math will need every archer. He will need me."

"But—"

"How can you even ask if I'm going to fight? You of all people?" Lili said.

"What do you mean *me of all people?*" Anna said. "If my brother were here, he would question you too."

"He wouldn't stop me," Lili said. "And that's not what I meant. Am I any less of a queen than Matilda, who led King Stephen's forces after Empress Maud imprisoned him? Am I any less of a woman than Queen Gwenllian of Ceredigion, who led the fight against the Normans while her husband was away?"

"I've heard you tell that last story before, and you always leave off the ending where the Normans win and they hang her from the battlements," Anna said.

"Still, my point stands," Lili said.

"You have a three-month-old son to care for!" Tears pricked at the corners of Anna's eyes, but she fought them back. She couldn't believe how unreasonable Lili was being. "Even after all this time, you still feel as if you need to prove yourself?"

"What are you talking about—prove myself? That's not it at all." Lili was now standing right at the top of the stairs with Anna, their noses only six inches apart. "Math needs every archer on the battlement, and I am an archer. You—you and Bronwen—have spent the last six years fighting for the right to live your life here on your own terms, to use the gifts God has given you even though you were born a woman, and yet you deny the same right to me?"

Anna stared at Lili for a second, swallowed hard, and then brought the volume of her voice down a dozen notches. "You think that I don't want you to fight because you're a woman?"

Lili looked nonplussed. "Isn't that it?"

"No, you little fool! I don't want you to fight because I love you!" Anna's throat closed over the terror that welled up inside her. "You could die!"

Instantly, Lili's expression softened, changing from one of defiance to understanding. She stepped closer, first putting a hand on each of Anna's arms and then pulling her into a tight embrace. "You can't keep everyone wrapped in padding, Anna. You have to let us live. *You* have to live."

Anna buried her face in her hands, realizing she had been feeling the same as Bronwen, like she was wrapped in Styrofoam, and hadn't known it. Either that or it was just the opposite: she felt too much. "Sometimes the fear of losing any of you overwhelms me to such a degree that I can't breathe. I can't handle another loss like Llelo. I don't want to ever feel that kind of pain again."

Lili rubbed her back, and then Bronwen, who'd been standing to one side and not interfering in Anna's argument with Lili, wrapped her arms around them both. "The twenty-first century has all the same problems, Anna. You just didn't know it at the time because you hadn't experienced a loss like Llelo. It hurts, and then it hurts a little less. We pretend that death doesn't walk with us there, but when we do that, we are lying to ourselves."

"You know that you'll see your Llelo again, don't you?" Lili said. "He's in heaven, waiting for you."

Anna sobbed and laughed at the same time. Such surety of faith hadn't been hers since Llelo died and maybe long before that.

Lili swept aside Anna's tears with her thumbs. "Come. We have work to do."

10

September, 2017

Cassie

Seven in the morning was long past her grandfather's usual waking time, since he would have seen to his horses at five, so Cassie dialed his number without a qualm. The fact that her hands were shaking had more to do with the emotions welling up inside her than what she feared might be her grandfather's reaction to her call.

"Hello?"

"Hi, Granddad. It's Cassie."

Cassie had expected the complete silence on the other end of the line, and it didn't bother her. In her mind's eye, she could see her grandfather gathering himself together, processing those few simple words she'd just said, and reconciling himself with the five years they'd been apart.

"Cassie. It's good to hear from you."

A sob rose in Cassie's throat, but she swallowed it back. "I never thought I'd hear your voice again."

"I missed you." He paused, again with a silence that Cassie didn't fill. She waited ten seconds, which was a long space of silence over the phone, and then he said, "What happened to you, Grand-daughter?"

"I don't know if I can even tell you, Granddad," Cassie said.

"Cassiopeia—" It was her grandfather's nickname for her because he had never liked 'Cassandra'. "I saw the plane come in. I saw the hole in the ground it didn't create when it didn't hit that mountain. I mourned for you, but we had no body to bury and no story to tell. You were simply gone from this world."

Her grandfather often spoke this way when he was being formal and serious, and this time his words gave Cassie the opening she needed. "That's exactly it, Granddad. I've been in a different world. The plane took me to the Middle Ages. To Scotland." Cassie held her breath, and this time the silence stretched on so long that she did start to grow concerned.

"Is that so, Cassie?"

"Yes, Granddad." Cassie had been so intent on her grandfather's reaction to her phone call that she'd barely looked up from the desk that held the phone. The door to the room was closed, but a prickling at the back of her neck told her she was being watched. She glanced up to the ceiling and then around the room. She couldn't spot a camera, but now that she was calmer, she acknowledged the high likelihood that her conversation was being monitored.

"Where are you now? How are you speaking to me?" her grandfather said.

"We came back today, Granddad. To Wales," Cassie said.

Her grandfather made a *tsking* sound through his teeth. "The phone cut out for a second. Did you say you're with whales?"

"No, Granddad. I'm in Cardiff, Wales. The country. It's part of Great Britain."

She could feel her grandfather nodding at the end of the line. "I've heard of Wales, Granddaughter. My father was a mechanic at an airstrip during the war."

Her grandfather meant World War Two. She hadn't known her great-grandfather well, since he died when she was six, but she remembered the stories he told. At times, it seemed like he lived more in 1944 than the present. It put a momentary smile on her face to think that she wasn't the only one with a penchant for time travel.

"How did you end up there?"

"Well—" Cassie fought for what to say, how to explain. "It's too long a story, and I know someone is listening on this line. We were sailing to Ireland in a cog—a medieval ship—when we were caught in a storm like the one on the mountain five years ago. I'm with—" she stopped and thought again, "—we're-we're in the custody of MI-5, which is like the FBI for England." She'd stuttered because she didn't know how to begin explaining about David and his family and how they'd changed history, not to mention that she was married to Callum, a white Englishman. Though as a veteran himself, her grandfather might have more in common with Callum than they might think at first.

"I thought you said you were in Wales?"

"England owns Wales—" Cassie shook her head, even though her grandfather couldn't see it. "Listen, Granddad, I will tell you all about how and why, but right now I just wanted to say that I love you, and I missed you, and I would never have left if I could have helped it."

"I know that," her grandfather said. "I've always known that."

"It's because of everything you taught me that I survived the last five years on my own."

"Will I see you, Granddaughter?"

"I-I-I don't know. If I don't call again, please don't worry. I'll come to Oregon when I can." Cassie paused. "How's Mama?"

"She's fine, as far as I know."

Cassie didn't want to delve further into that comment and chastised herself for being such a bad daughter. But *as far as I know* could mean a lot of things, including that her mother wasn't at all fine and had fallen back into her addictive behaviors. "And how are you, Granddad?"

"I had this thing with my heart two years back," he said. "I'm fine now, just slower than before."

"Oh, Granddad." Cassie's heart ached at the thought of all the time they'd been apart, and at all that they no longer knew about each other. "What thing?"

"They called it a *cardiac event*." She could feel the shrug, even six thousand miles away. "It comes with growing old."

"I'm sorry I wasn't there," Cassie said.

"You going to tell me about this Middle Ages thing?"

As his speech grew more casual, Cassie could tell that he was more at ease with her now, as if they were sitting on his porch on a hot August day, drinking lemonade and talking.

"Not right now, if that's okay," Cassie said. "I want to talk to you about it in person."

"I'll wait, then," he said, leaving *but don't wait too long* unsaid. Her grandfather was in his early seventies, and if he'd had one 'cardiac event', he could have another.

"Yes, Granddad." Cassie teared up again. "I have to go."

After they hung up, Cassie leaned both hands on the desk, collecting her thoughts and trying to bring her emotions under control. She'd needed to speak to her grandfather, just to hear his voice again, but now that she had, her old life and all that she'd left behind, and lost, came rushing back. She wished an ocean and a continent didn't separate her from him.

It could be Callum was feeling the same. Cassie wasn't worried that he missed his old girlfriend. He loved Cassie. But David had been right to question how they would each feel about returning to the Middle Ages with him. It wasn't hot showers and coffee that would keep Cassie here. She'd learned to live without those things. But the people ... to return to the Middle Ages would be to turn her back on her family, on her obligations, and to die to them all over again.

She took in a deep breath and let it out, trying to put the uncertainty aside for now, and went to the door. Callum opened it just as she reached it, and they stood looking at each other for a moment without speaking.

"Are you okay?" he said.

"I guess so. That was a difficult conversation."

"Is your grandfather all right?"

Cassie nodded.

"I wish I could make it easier for you." Callum reached for her hand. "Come on."

Cassie strode down the hall with him, hustling to keep up with his longer legs. "What's the hurry?"

"We are meeting Driscoll in ten minutes in the cafeteria but arriving from a different direction," Callum said.

"You want to see how freely we can move about the building without an escort," she said, not as a question.

"Yes." Callum drew out the 's' in a hissing sound. "I'd like to avoid Smythe or Lady Jane, if possible."

Cassie could understand why Callum wouldn't want to run into Smythe, but she had kind of liked Lady Jane. She reminded Cassie of her father's mother, who'd died when she was fifteen. Cassie hadn't been very close to her father's side of the family—the white side—but she'd spent a little time with her grandmother. She'd been a smart, tough woman, who in a cultural opposite to the Indian side of Cassie's family, was always happy to speak her mind and cared not at all that nobody wanted to hear it. Even so, one day after she'd lectured an uncle in no uncertain terms about the error of his current course of action, she'd put her arm around Cassie's shoulder and whispered: *always certain, sometimes right*, mocking herself for her outspoken ways.

Cassie had laughed and gotten along well with her grandmother after that. Lady Jane seemed to be cut from the same cloth, and Cassie hoped that maybe she would have her grandmother's common sense too.

Cassie and Callum took the stairs down to the lobby floor but stopped in the stairwell before exiting through the door. Callum peered through the narrow glass window into the foyer beyond it. A bank of elevators faced them, and several people got on and off.

"No alarm yet," Cassie said.

"Seemingly not. Maybe we need to give it another minute." Callum went through the door. To their left was an expansive lobby that was divided in half by a glass partition and guard boxes. Anyone coming into the Office had to pass through security scanners before entering the building proper.

"Would your ID get us past that if we had arrived like normal people?" Cassie said.

"My badge wouldn't," Callum said. "It has a bar code that in the past was updated once a month. This, on the other hand—" He pulled out his phone, "—this has all the updates programmed into it. Did you know that at the airport check-in you can scan your mobile, and it substitutes for a boarding pass?"

Cassie stared at him. "No."

"MI-5 identification now operates on the same principle."

"What if you lose your phone?" she said.

"It's the same as losing your badge." Callum shrugged. "At the very least, if there was a question as to my identity, my iris won't have changed."

"We don't actually know that, though, do we?" Cassie said as the new idea struck her. "Could the time traveling have altered our DNA? Have we been disassembled and reassembled like on the transporter platform in *Star Trek*?"

Callum glanced at her, his eyes widening, but with a smile on his lips. "I don't think I want to know the answer to that." Leaving his phone on, Callum put it back in his pocket.

Cassie eyed the action. "You want them to stop us."

"I want to know if they feel the need to."

Instead of heading out to the lobby, Callum turned the other way and walked past the elevators and into a maze of branching corridors, all unlabeled. He reached an equally unmarked set of double doors and pushed through it, revealing a fully equipped cafeteria.

Driscoll was already seated at a table on the left-hand wall, near a bank of windows that overlooked a central courtyard. He'd been talking on his cell phone as they entered the cafeteria but waved them over when he saw them. "I chose an assortment: soup, bread, fish and chips." He gestured to the food on the table in front of him. "I didn't know what you liked, and I know it's been a long time since you've eaten anything like this. Can I get you a coffee, Cassie?"

"Yes, please." Cassie accepted the seat Callum pulled out for her. He was being particularly chivalrous today, and she couldn't decide if it was for Driscoll's benefit or if the change of scenery had awakened old habits.

Driscoll seemed to have gotten on board with the time travel thing or was pretending really well for their benefit. He set a cup of coffee in front of Cassie with what looked like Bronwen-proportions of cream and sugar in it. Cassie hadn't witnessed Bronwen's habits in person, of course, since coffee wasn't available in the Middle Ages, but she'd heard about them.

"What nosh did you miss the most?" Driscoll seated himself across from them.

"Nosh?" Cassie said.

"*Nosh.*" Driscoll snapped his fingers. "You know, *food.*"

"Oh," Cassie said. "That would have to be chocolate—"

"Potatoes—"

Cassie laughed and poked Callum in the shoulder. "You are just so *English* to miss potatoes."

"You don't have potatoes in the Middle Ages?" Driscoll's brow furrowed. "How is that possible?"

"They're what David calls a New World food," Cassie said. "They weren't brought to Europe until after 1492. Same with chocolate."

Driscoll was staring at her with his mouth open. "How do you *live?*"

Cassie laughed. It felt good to be having a regular conversation with someone who was truly *listening* to her instead of questioning her sanity.

Callum leaned across the table and lowered his voice. "Have you heard anything?" He didn't have to explain to either Cassie or Driscoll that he was asking about David.

Driscoll shook his head. "I haven't had a recent update."

"How about a less recent one, then?" Cassie said.

"He's in basement two in one of the interrogation rooms," Driscoll said. "Natasha is with him."

"What about the sack over his head?" Cassie said. "That didn't look good."

"I can assure you that he's fine." Driscoll put down the cup from which he'd been drinking.

Callum sat back and tapped his fingers on the table. "I need to know what's happening with David. I need to be part of his interrogation."

Driscoll shook his head.

"I've been reinstated," Callum said. "How can they not let me in?"

"*I* might not be let in," Driscoll said.

"Then we'll have to get through to Natasha," Callum said.

"You're not understanding me," Driscoll said. "Lady Jane herself has taken over Cardiff station. She's the one you have to get past. David is not your responsibility now. Let it go."

"We can't let it go. You are literally asking for something we cannot do," Cassie said.

Callum had moved infinitesimally closer to Cassie while they'd been talking and had started pressing gently on her right foot. He was trying to stop her talking, and it occurred to her only now that Callum might not trust Driscoll, and she was kind of running at the mouth. She put her lips together and sat back. "You're right. We need to be patient."

Callum draped his arm across the back of Cassie's chair. "The mission is paramount. While all I want to do is help, I can accept that my help is not wanted at present. Tomorrow I will speak to Lady Jane about what I *can* do."

Cassie cleared her throat. "Lady Jane said something about housing us here in the Office. Is that what you understood?"

Driscoll nodded. "Yes."

"Personally, I'd like to see a little of Cardiff." Cassie glanced at Callum. "I'm particularly fond of the castle."

"You aren't supposed to leave the building," Driscoll said. "If you try, I believe you will be stopped."

"Both of us?" Cassie said.

"For now." Driscoll's phone beeped at him. He pulled it out and read the screen. "I have somewhere to be."

"Where?" Callum said.

"Nothing important." Driscoll rose from his seat, about to leave, but then he hesitated.

"What is it?" Callum spoke softly. "What's going on?"

Driscoll jerked his head, as if he'd decided something, and then turned back to them, leaning on his hands, which rested flat on the table. "I want to do what's right. If you need help, you can count on me."

The reversal was a bit too sudden for Cassie, and she didn't need Callum's warning touch to know that caution was required. She put her lips together and let Callum do the talking.

"I'm glad to hear it," Callum said.

"If time travel is real, I want to be a part of it," Driscoll said. "But I don't believe in using David, even in the name of national security, and you need help from someone on the inside. In return, I ask that you take me to the Middle Ages with you when you go."

His words left Cassie stunned, but Callum contemplated his former colleague without a change of expression. "It's not an easy life. Why would you want to come with us?"

"Why wouldn't I?" Driscoll looked down at their upturned faces. The slightly ironic expression he'd worn up until now was wiped away in favor of a bright-eyed enthusiasm.

"What about your wife?" Callum said.

"She left me three months ago, we have no kids, and I haven't spoken to my parents in two years," Driscoll said. "I have nothing to keep me here."

"I lived there for five years," Cassie said. "I know what it's like and what it takes, and you really don't want to come with us." The conversation with her grandfather had shaken her a bit, and she didn't know any more if she herself wanted to go back, but now wasn't the time for waffling on that decision in public. She and Callum needed to have a serious talk about all of this. But not now, not in front of Driscoll.

"I do," Driscoll said.

"I don't know what to say. I don't even know where to begin." Callum rubbed at his chin.

Driscoll looked at his phone again. "For now, you should sit tight. I'll touch base with you later."

Callum grinned. "You've been watching too many American police procedurals. I almost hear a southern accent in there."

"Shut it," Driscoll said, though he smirked as he pushed off from the table and departed.

11

September, 1289

Anna

The five minutes it had taken for the three women to travel from the upper bailey to the lower one had been spent in heated argument, and this time Anna found herself on the side of practicality, rather than emotion. The tears in the stairwell had wrung her out, but because of them she'd been forced to admit—to herself only, since neither Bronwen nor Lili had said it out loud—that she'd been thinking entirely about herself. *She* didn't want to hurt more. Well, *who did?*

And they were right about the living part too. She hadn't been living. She'd been going through the motions, even after Bran's birth. Her family had been kind enough, and loving enough, not to slap her out of it. Somehow she was going to have to let this fear go, not simply shove it down deeper inside herself and pretend it wasn't there. The middle of a siege seemed both hardly the time, and the perfect time, to start anew.

"We have to bring them inside the castle, Anna!" Bronwen said.

"We can't," Anna said matter-of-factly. "You know we can't."

"They'll die out there," Bronwen said. "If Valence gets through the walls, his men will show no mercy."

Anna stopped and turned on Bronwen. Lili stayed two paces away, not interfering, for which Anna was grateful. Lili had known instinctively that the patients in the infirmary adjacent to the abbey could not be brought inside the castle itself. The city walls would protect them and the nuns who cared for them. Bronwen, however, wasn't seeing it their way.

"Some of them are very ill, Bronwen," Anna said. "Many will die, no matter what we do for them. What happens when we bring them inside the castle and they start to die in here? Where will that leave us? Are we going to put wounded men alongside sick children and hope both groups survive that contact? You'd be all but writing a death sentence for the injured!"

"But—"

Anna put her hands on Bronwen's shoulders. "You must know that my heart agrees with you, but my head says we have to be practical. I hope Valence doesn't breach the walls of either the town or the castle, but it's as likely as not that he will do both, given time. Not everyone has an equal chance to live, and right here, right now, is where we start to triage."

Bronwen looked like she was going to argue some more. In fact, Anna had rarely seen her so passionate about anything.

"What would Ieuan tell you to do?" Anna said.

Bronwen stuck her finger in Anna's face. "Don't bring that *listen to your husband* crap down on me." She was speaking full American now; Anna wasn't sure Lili could keep up, which was probably a good thing. "I put up with it most of the time, but just because we live in the Middle Ages doesn't mean we have to act like it. Lili is right about that, at least."

"I wasn't suggesting anything of the sort," Anna said. "I was merely pointing out that in this we *do* need to think like medieval people. The sick are in quarantine. We didn't house them inside the castle in the first place for that reason—and it was a good reason. Do you want to expose Catrin to scarlet fever? Or Arthur?"

Bronwen stabbed the toe of her boot into in the dirt of the bailey. "But they'll die." She sounded sad now, and tired. They all were tired and the battle hadn't even started.

"We don't know that," Anna said.

Lili stepped between them and put her arm around Bronwen's waist. "Dafydd has done everything in his power to protect this castle and Windsor town. He spent the last two months strengthening the town walls. Perhaps he had a vision of the future and knew that it might be the only thing standing between us and death. Regardless, given the suddenness of the threat, we are as prepared as we can be." Between the twenty-foot-high town wall, begun under Edward and finished very recently, and the moat created by water diverted from the Thames, Valence wasn't going to break through their defenses quickly.

Bronwen closed her eyes and rubbed at her temples with her fingers, finally calming down.

Though Anna wasn't going to admit that David had the *sight*, Welsh blood or not, Lili was right that David had planned ahead. It was bad enough that people routinely referred to him as the return of King Arthur. David wasn't King Arthur, and she wasn't Morgane, even if she grew more and more into the role with every year that passed. David had named his son 'Arthur' because of that legacy, though few people beyond Anna and her mother truly understood the cynicism behind that act—and the extent to which it had been a blatant political ploy.

It had been unlike David, and thus exactly like him too.

"Even if we are forced to retreat to the castle as a last resort," Anna said, "and Valence's men overrun the town, they won't want to get anywhere near our patients. They know what scarlet fever looks like and how contagious it is."

"They could set fire to the abbey and burn everyone inside it," Bronwen said.

Lili stepped in. "They will do the same to the castle if they can. In fact, with the abbey in the center of Windsor and the castle forming part of the defenses of the town, it is the castle that is in the more vulnerable position." She looked at Anna. "We should think about moving the children to the northwest tower of the lower bailey, where they can be protected by the river and the walls. It's the most defensible tower in the whole castle."

Their conversation had carried them into the lower bailey Lili had mentioned. The gatehouse lay just in front of them, and the stairs up to the southern battlements formed a line to their left. Anna wasn't sure if Bronwen had even heard Lili, since she turned away and mounted the stairs without responding. Lili and Anna followed. Many of the scholars had heard the news of Valence's approach; they'd had the same idea. Anna found herself standing on the wall-walk with Lili on one side of her and Roger Bacon on the other.

"War is the last recourse of the wise and the first of fools," he said by way of a greeting.

Anna glanced at him. "Who said that?" If it wasn't Shakespeare or the Bible, she wasn't going to guess.

Bacon mumbled something under his breath that Anna didn't catch and then said, "I did."

Anna gave a low laugh. She was sure the internet in the twenty-first century was full of pithy quotes by Roger Bacon. She wouldn't be the one to ask if this quote got passed down through the ages, though it sounded familiar to her, like maybe Plato had been the one to say it first. From where they stood, she could see the dust churned up by Valence's approaching army. It hung in the air, the particles glinting in the light of the setting sun. The soldiers marched up the King's Road, which led to the main gate of the town of Windsor.

The gate itself faced southeast, overlooking the lands that fed the town. Anna was no farmer, but she recognized the different grains by now—barley mostly, but also wheat—interspersed with pasture where sheep and cattle grazed and patches of woods. The castle was located in the northeastern corner of the town, accessible only from the town itself. Thus, its walls formed a protective curtain around that quarter of Windsor, which had only two entrances: the southeastern gate on the King's road and a northern gate that guarded the bridge across the Thames River and the road to London. The original castle, built at the time of the Norman Conquest, occupied a natural chalk mound overlooking the Thames River. The castle had been much expanded since then with the addition of two more baileys and a dozen towers.

"They've already raised the sluice gates," Bacon said.

Anna stood on her tiptoes and peered between the crenels, looking straight down into the frothy water below. Since its completion, the moat had been filled only once, as a test case.

Here at Windsor, the Thames flowed west to east, heading towards London. The town had been built on the south side of the river. After consulting a host of engineers, David had built a dike and installed a sluice gate at the northwestern end of the town. The gate could be opened at need to divert a portion of the Thames into the moat that now surrounded the town and castle on the west, south, and east sides. The water then flowed back into the Thames at the northeastern side of the castle.

Though impressive, and even to Anna's modern eyes, sophisticated, this kind of project had been done before at other castles. David had simply taken the best of what had been tried to its logical conclusion.

"You could have run, my Queen," Roger Bacon said, leaning back to look past Anna to Lili. "You should not feel that by fleeing Windsor, you would have abandoned us. Your duty to your country and husband would be, first and foremost, to protect your son."

Anna didn't tell him how strange it was to think that the country to which Bacon was referring was England, not Wales.

For her part, Lili calmly shook her head. "Quite aside from the fact that I am one of the few people in this castle who can shoot a bow, Math felt the risk of leaving outweighed the risk of staying. Valence force-marched his men night and day to get here. Our own riders were barely ahead of them."

"Which is why, up until an hour ago, we thought they hadn't yet passed Winchester?" Bacon said.

"Exactly," Lili said. "Math's concern is Valence's penchant for constructing plans within plans. Who's to say that he didn't send a contingent of men to block the road to London in the hope that he could capture me as I fled the city with Dafydd's heir? If Valence does, in fact, believe Dafydd is here, he might even be hoping that Dafydd himself would retreat to Westminster."

"Even Valence can't imagine that King David would abandon his people," Bacon said.

"I didn't say so, sir," Lili said. "I merely suggested that Dafydd might have left his men to defend the town until he could marshal an army to come to their relief."

"Ah, that is a good thought," Bacon said. "Did you know that I have made a particular study of battle tactics employed by the Greeks and Romans and am writing a definitive work on the strategy of war? Depending upon how this ends, Valence's maneuvers might be worthy of a mention."

"Is that admiration I hear in your voice?" Lili said, bemusement in hers.

"I would prefer that the only mention of Valence is in defeat," Anna said. "We all might be more interested today in what the ancients said about defending a besieged position."

"They spoke of it often, of course." Bacon bent his head to look at Anna over the top of his glasses (a gift from David). "It would have been better if we hadn't found ourselves on the defensive in the first place."

"Obviously," Bronwen said under her breath from the far side of Lili.

Bacon didn't seem to have heard her. "I may have a few suggestions for our commander." He tapped a finger musingly to his lips, unaware that Bronwen was about to throttle him.

"It may be that my husband would be happy to hear them," Anna said, with a grin at Bronwen, who rolled her eyes. "I will take you to him."

Anna gestured Bacon down the stairs to the lower bailey, but while Lili followed, Bronwen caught Anna's sleeve. "You can't be serious?"

"Maybe he can be of help," Anna said. "Math is overseeing the destruction of the bridge across the moat. Perhaps he'll find Bacon as amusing as I do."

Below them, Bacon stood talking to Lili, her quiver on her back and her bow in her hand. A half dozen other archers clustered around them. Bacon appeared to be pontificating yet again on military strategy.

Anna bit her lip, fighting back a smile, but when she caught sight of Bronwen's face, she sobered. Bronwen said, "I'm sorry that I argued with you about moving the patients in the infirmary. It was wrong of me."

Anna put a hand to Bronwen's cheek. "I understand why you did. I know you are worried about them. And about all of us. I am too."

"It's times like these I hate the Middle Ages."

"Ieuan will gather the necessary men and return at the front of an army," Anna said. "Valence will find that he cannot maintain a siege when he faces opposition from the castle and his flank."

Bronwen took in a deep breath and let it out. "I asked earlier why Valence had chosen to march on Windsor instead of going directly to London. Now that I've had time to think about it, either scenario—that he thinks David is here or that he knows he isn't—presents us with a problem. If Valence knows David left for Ireland, then someone informed him of that fact and made quite an effort to do so, given the distance between Windsor and Ireland. As Lili pointed out, Valence would believe that we're less well-protected with the king gone, and since David wouldn't have taken the treasury with him, it is now exposed. Capture that and he goes a long way to putting the crown of England on his own head."

"And if he doesn't know that David has left for Ireland?" Anna said.

"Then he seeks to challenge David outright," Bronwen said. "I can't decide which is worse."

"How can he think to challenge David with only two thousand men?" Anna said.

"Either he has more allies than we thought, and thus more men, or he has something he believes will call into question David's right to the throne."

Anna shook her head. "That, at least, is unlikely. David rules because the people chose him and the barons called for it, not because of his bloodline, whatever people think that may be."

One of the stranger twists of fate had been the falsification of David's family tree. Bishop Kirby had forged a paper that 'proved' Anna's mother was the illegitimate daughter of the old King Henry (and thus King Edward's half-sister). He'd done this in the hope that David would take the throne under false pretenses, at which point Kirby could show proof that the document had been forged. David, for his part, had strenuously denied any such claim, burned the paper in front of half the nobility of England, and been crowned king anyway. By now, most of England believed him to be Henry's grandson, and this, along with the Arthurian mythologizing, had been ultimately impossible for David to refute.

"Then it's something else," Bronwen said, "and the traitors are among those barons who we believe to be unswervingly loyal. Math needs to watch his back."

"I will tell him," Anna said.

"I will see to moving the children to the northwest tower."

Anna let Bronwen go, collected Lili and Roger Bacon, and then made her way through the unusually empty streets to the city gate. Normally at the close of the day, people would be coming home from a day of work in craft hall or field. Church bells tolled for vespers, but a glance down a side street showed her that the only parishioners hurrying to evening devotions were elderly. Tonight, the obligations of Windsor's people would be of a different sort entirely.

Anna found Math conferring with his captains in a house adjacent to the city gate. The house belonged to one of the aldermen and like most structures in Windsor had a thatched roof. It would burn if Valence shot fire arrows over the walls.

At the same time, the house was more substantial than the typical dwelling, with a complete second floor and an interior stairway running up a side wall of the house. Opposite the main door to the street was another doorway, which opened onto a courtyard behind the house, revealing the house's kitchen and washing areas. A woman in a faded dress, with two children under five playing at her heels, unpinned laundry from a clothesline near a well.

The men stood in the main room of the house, gathered around a table upon which a map of the city of Windsor had been laid flat with weights at the corners. Anna recognized most of the men surrounding Math. Many were of noble birth but some had been given a place because Math, or more likely, Ieuan, believed them to be worthy of it, regardless of their birth.

Anna looked from one face to the next, wondering who among them she needed to fear or whom David, in the end, would need to call out as a traitor. Her brother had drawn the best of the English nobility to him, many of them as young as he or younger, with the cast of hero-worship in their eyes and without a shred of cynicism. In David, they'd found the intersection of life and legend. The adulation was annoying at times, and Anna made a point to tease her brother about it whenever she could. Fortunately, he (mostly) hadn't allowed it to go to his head and found it more of a burden than a benefit of being King of England.

Math looked up at their approach. His eyes narrowed at the bow in Lili's hand, and she raised it in salute. With a nod at his men, who continued to talk around the table, Math came to where Anna, Lili, and Roger Bacon stood to one side of the main doorway. "What are you doing here?" Math put his arm around Anna's shoulders and kissed her temple.

"I have some words of wisdom for you, young man," Bacon said, without waiting for Anna to answer.

Bacon sounded so much like a pompous professor that Anna couldn't help smiling.

Math gestured towards the table and the map of Windsor that took up three-quarters of it. "I would be pleased to hear you out if you will give me a moment with my wife and sister-in-law."

Bacon put his heels together, bowed, and was soon absorbed in conversation with Sir George, the steward of Windsor Castle, who was among the men looking at the map. Anna's first impression of George had been that his personality consisted of bluster and little else, but he seemed to know how to talk to Bacon, which was more than she did.

"So." Math looked from Anna to Lili. "Tell me what you're doing here."

"I brought you Roger Bacon," Anna said.

A smile twitched in the corner of Math's mouth. "Am I supposed to thank you?"

"You can thank me," Lili said. "I brought you archers. Where do you want us?"

"Us?" Math ran a hand through his hair. He had the look of a man about to argue.

"Yes," Lili said.

"I'd tell you 'no,' but the truth is, I need you. It's tragic how few Englishmen know how to shoot, even after working with Ieuan for three months."

"Ieuan has shot a bow nearly every day since he was nine years old," Lili said. "It's going to take time to train the English." And then she laughed. "I can't believe I just said that. Who would ever have thought we would have *wanted* them trained?"

"The Welshmen we brought should help," Anna said.

"That's certain. Ieuan left me the best archers among them," Math said. "But fifty archers can hardly cover the entire circumference of the city and the castle. We're going to be spread thin."

"Our chances improve if Valence didn't bring many archers with him," Lili said.

"Right now, I can think of few things that would please me more," Math said. "But you know as well as I do that if Valence pays them enough, he can find Welshmen to fight for him."

Anna made a face. "I hate that."

"It's the way of the world." Math still hadn't let go of Anna, and now he moved his arm to her waist. "Why is Roger Bacon here, really?"

"For exactly the reasons he said. He wants to bring you the wisdom of the Romans and Greeks," Anna said.

"What is the phrase you all use?" Math said. "*You've got to be kidding me?*"

Anna couldn't help smiling. "Give him two minutes of your time, that's all. David thinks he needs him, and I don't want to be responsible for driving him away. How soon will Valence reach us?"

"It won't be long now," Math said. "By nightfall, he'll surround us. We don't have enough men to stop him from doing whatever he wants outside the walls."

"Send the wounded to the middle bailey," Anna said. "Bronwen and I will see to their care."

"Any chance the penicillin will be ready by midnight?" Math said.

Anna raised a shoulder in a half-shrug. "I guess it will have to be."

12

September, 2017

Callum

Without asking any questions, Cassie took the hand Callum offered and departed with him, not out the door they'd come in or in the direction Driscoll had gone but through the French doors that opened into a courtyard adjacent to the cafeteria. Enclosed on all four sides, it had been intended to provide a moment of greenery and peace to the often-harried Security Service personnel, though Callum had never seen anyone sitting on the benches set there for that purpose. Senior staff ate lunch elsewhere, and any underling with a desire for promotion ate at his desk. The rest of the time, as this was Wales, it rained.

Callum and Cassie walked casually in the late-afternoon sunshine along the grass-lined concrete pathway, heading for a door that would take them back into the building, except on the opposite side of the courtyard. They reached it just as someone came through it.

"Ta," the man said as he held the door for them.

Callum knew him. He was one of the technicians in the research library, but for the life of him, Callum couldn't remember his name now, so he just said, "Thanks," and gave the man a quick smile.

There was an awkward moment as Callum urged Cassie past him and into the building, and then as Callum turned away, the man said, "How are you?"

"Good. Very good," Callum said.

"What are you—?"

But Callum didn't want to take the time to field questions he couldn't answer and strode away down the corridor, Cassie at his side. As he led her up flights of stairs through the levels of the building, picturing the floor plan in his head and seeking privacy, he was strongly aware of the badge in his pocket, next to his mobile phone. He forced his brain to work like an agent instead of the Earl of Shrewsbury. David's future might depend on it.

Walking through the Office, he felt almost like a ghost of his former self. He'd been the commander here, and whether or not that might be his job again, for now others had taken over. That ass, Thomas Smythe, who'd bungled the initial pick-up of Meg and Llywelyn, had somehow been promoted to Lady Jane's second-in-command. The promotion stank of corruption, and Lady Jane's words implied that other things had changed as well for the agency in his absence and not for the better. He knew he had changed, as Lady Jane had noted, and he hoped that distance would allow him to see clearly. It was what she wanted. Callum just hadn't yet figured out what he was supposed to be looking at.

"That was a very strange conversation we just had with Driscoll," Cassie said. "Are you wondering what's really going on?"

"It was almost as if he was trying to trap me in a lie or get me to admit that I'm considering breaking David out of here." Callum went over their conversation word for word in his mind. As far as he could tell, he hadn't admitted to anything Driscoll didn't already know. On impulse, he felt in his pocket for his mobile phone and powered it off.

Don't trust Driscoll. Don't trust anyone.

"Up until three minutes ago, I thought Lady Jane meant for me to work within the parameters of the Security Service," Callum said, "which is why I remained so open and civil with Driscoll. But if David is being moved to London tonight, we're going to lose him. He'll be out of Cardiff and possibly out of the Security Service's jurisdiction. The Home Office is a black hole that not even David, with all his gifts, can climb out of."

"Maybe Lady Jane has already fallen in," Cassie said.

"There are enough cameras in this building to ensure that we've been watched everywhere we've gone," Callum said. "Plus, technology has improved in the five years since you were here last. Some of what you may have seen in movies has become real. All anyone would have had to do to tag us was to pat my shoulder. The tracking device is the size of a tick. It doesn't give out as strong a signal as for a mobile phone, but if we stay in range, we're an open book. Did anyone touch your skin? Did someone pat you on the back or on the hand?"

"I definitely shook hands with several people, including Natasha and Driscoll, who also clapped you on the shoulder."

Callum pulled up, cursing. "We're wearing clothing acquired for us here. I'm an idiot." He'd halted in the middle of the corridor and now stepped to one side to allow several people to pass them, briefcases in hand and jackets slung over their arms or shoulders. The end of the working day had come. Callum let several more people who'd come out of nearby offices disappear around a corner, and then he tugged Cassie into the loo. He locked the door behind them.

"I suppose it was too much to ask that you'd choose the women's bathroom for this?" Cassie said.

Callum was glad to see the amusement in her eyes. "I was convinced at one time that IT had put cameras in here, but I'm taking it on faith today that they haven't." Callum slipped his arms out of his suit jacket and shook it out.

Cassie unhooked her cloak at the throat, and they took turns inspecting each other's clothing. Neither found anything that raised their suspicions, not even a slight discoloration indicating they'd been sprayed with an ultraviolet tag.

Cassie set her folded cloak on the counter and studied Callum. "You look very dashing. I've always loved a man in a suit."

Callum looked down at himself. He'd grown used to medieval clothing, but this suit fit him like no clothing had in a long while. The coat was a little tighter in the shoulders and arms than he remembered, and the trousers were looser in the waist. He had to admit, too, that it felt odd not to have his sword resting on his left hip.

"Let's wash our hands," he said.

"Why?" Cassie said, going to the sink and turning on the water.

"I haven't worked here for ten months," Callum said. "But I know what my colleagues are capable of. I'm being paranoid on purpose."

"Just because you're paranoid doesn't mean someone isn't out to get you," Cassie said, laughing.

Callum laughed too and dried off, marveling to himself at how far he'd come from the man who'd returned from Afghanistan with an obsessive need to wash his hands. Then he went to the door, unlocked it, and peered into the corridor. It was empty. He'd chosen a loo on the top floor on purpose, assuming that as the offices emptied, this corridor would have the least amount of traffic. It might be all hands on deck for a certain percentage of agents involved in the time travel project, but most of the secretarial staff would still have been given leave to go home on time.

He looked back at Cassie. She hadn't put her cloak back on, and with regret in her face, she shoved it into a corner underneath the sink counter. She then joined him in the corridor. "I really love that cloak, but I'm too noticeable when I wear it here."

"We'll come back for it," he said, knowing even as he spoke that they might not get the chance, and that Cassie was noticeable here no matter what she did or did not wear. She was stunningly beautiful, and not for the first time he found himself marveling that she'd agreed to become his wife.

Cassie shrugged. "All I have is what I stand up in. I've been in that position before and may be again. Tell me what's next."

"I have yet to see one member of my former team," he said.
"Who's that?"

"Mark Jones. He didn't work for me for very long, but I thought he had the most potential of any of my staff." He shot her a grin. "He had the typical computer bloke's disrespect for authority that was sometimes a pain in the arse when I was his boss but makes me think now that he might be of use to us."

"*Might*," Cassie said.

Callum shrugged. "It seems worthwhile to feel him out before I come up with a plan for getting to David." He set off down the corridor towards the last door on the left.

"Or he could turn us in before we even start," Cassie said, hustling after him.

"At this point, we have so many problems, it would hardly be worse." He stopped and looked at her. "Let's pretend I didn't just say that."

When they reached the door and its scanner, Callum hesitated. He would have preferred a more anonymous entrance, but there was no way through the door without leaving a trail. He put his eye to the box and let it scan his iris.

"Most everyone has gone home. Do you think he will have left too?" Cassie said.

"In the seven months I knew him, Jones never went home before eight in the evening." Callum squared his shoulders and went through the door into the strange inner sanctum that was the Security Service's secretive technology department. Faced with an all-white corridor, with no windows or adornment other than a red fire extinguisher in a glass case in the corner, he took the passage to the left. He and Cassie walked quickly but steadily, trying to imply deliberation but not haste. They reached Jones's lab, and with a wink at Cassie, more for luck than because he was feeling that optimistic, Callum opened the door.

Jones sat on an ergonomic ball instead of an office chair, facing a bank of computers and monitors that took up a ten-foot table on the far wall and an equally long table on the adjacent one. The room had no windows, and the air conditioning was set to arctic temperatures. Jones had at least twelve computers running simultaneously in various places in the room. He had been focused on one screen when they entered but looked up from what he was doing at the sight of Cassie and Callum.

"I've been tracking your progress." Jones came to greet them, grabbing Callum's arm and tugging him inside. Before he shut the door behind them, he took a quick look down the corridor. "I might not be the only one." Returning to his desk, Jones gestured that Cassie and Callum should sit opposite. "Every corridor, every office, up to and including the janitorial closets, is monitored. You know that, right?"

"Even the loo?" Callum said.

Jones snorted. "Especially the loo. Where have you been living—under a rock?"

Cassie laughed. "I think the Middle Ages are the definition of *rock*."

Jones barely blinked. "I assume you have a plan for getting David away, Callum?" Jones didn't ask this accusingly but as if he really wanted to know.

Callum studied Jones. Coming on the heels of Lady Jane's text about Driscoll, Callum thought about leaving the room without another word but decided he would treat Jones as he had treated Driscoll: with a friendly face and with the idea of getting what information he could. He hadn't come here with a plan, just a hunch, and was a little stunned to find that Jones was already three steps ahead of him. "I see there's no keeping secrets from you."

Jones lifted his chin to point at the computer monitor beside him. "They'll know I talked to you but not what about. I can head them off for a while, just by saying you came by to introduce me to your wife."

"Who's *they*?" Callum said.

"Smythe for starters," Jones said. "The layers of paranoia go all the way to the top."

"Are you offering to help us with David?" Cassie said.

Jones cleared his throat. "I—" He stopped and shook his head.

"I understand. Don't worry about it." As he spoke, Callum put a hand on Jones's shoulder. It was a gesture he used often in the Middle Ages to settle a man in his charge. It had been automatic for Callum to do the same with Jones, but Jones looked down at his shoulder out of the corner of his eye, as if he couldn't believe Callum was touching him. Callum dropped his hand. "I appreciate you talking to us at all."

Jones nodded. "I can do that."

"You are alone in this lab now?" Callum said.

"Yes, and—" Jones swept his eyes furtively around the room before continuing, "—its sole purpose is to work on your problem."

Callum's eyes narrowed. "My problem? What are you talking about?"

Jones waved a hand up and down the length of Callum's body. "The time travel issue."

"Oh," Callum said.

"Coming back here with *him* was probably the worst thing you could have done."

"Believe me, we didn't mean to," Cassie said.

Jones shook his head. "I read your report, but if you could have done anything else—"

"Tell me what you know." It came out as an order, but Callum was well aware that it was he who was the supplicant and at Jones's mercy. If Jones showed anyone the images of Callum and Cassie in the loo, it would be enough to condemn him.

"To begin with, the Security Service have been working with Meg's DNA and blood work for the past ten months, and now they'll have David's," said Jones.

"Wait a minute," Cassie said. "Meg's blood work? How would they have come by that?"

Jones rubbed at the bridge of his nose with his thumb and forefinger. "If you give me a minute, I'll explain." He took in a deep breath. "When Meg was here last, the research labs had come as far as cataloging the instances where she, Anna, or David *traveled*."

"Right," Callum said. "We understand that."

"What you may not know is the rest of what has happened. Meg was seen by a midwife at that clinic outside of Aberystwyth. As part of a routine examination for a pregnant woman, the midwife ordered a blood draw and various tests," said Jones. "The Security Service acquired that blood and took over a lab north of Cardiff for the sole purpose of analyzing Meg's DNA, trying to isolate what is in her makeup—in the whole family's makeup—that allows her to shift between worlds. Meanwhile, here in Cardiff, we're working day and night on the physics of what they can do, as well as our surveillance systems."

"What kind of surveillance systems?" Callum said. "I get the feeling you don't mean cameras at every round-about."

"I do not," said Jones, "though Britain now has five million cameras in use, and I have access to all of them except those on closed systems."

"Five million?" Cassie said. "How is that possible?"

Callum's jaw would have been on the floor too, but he already knew this from when he worked here before. He hadn't been gone as long as Cassie.

"Five years ago, we had two million," said Jones. "But that's not what I'm talking about."

"You'd better tell us," Callum said.

"We are preparing not only for David or Meg's return but trying to identify any other people who might be doing what David's family is doing."

Callum stared at him. It had honestly never occurred to him that there might be other families out there like David's. "We don't know of any other *travelers* to Wales—"

"Wales, England, Germany or Borneo, we don't care," said Jones. "We're looking purely for the ability to shift, whether to the past, to the medieval world you came from, or to a different one entirely."

"Wow," Cassie said. "You're serious about this."

"That's not all," said Jones. "Another section is trying to build a device."

Callum and Cassie absorbed that stunning bit of information in ten seconds of silence.

"You're trying to build a time travel device," Cassie said, "like in *Dr Who*?"

"*Yes!*" said Jones, clearly excited about that in a way that he hadn't been about the DNA.

"I hope you aren't using a blue police call box," Cassie said, deadpan.

Jones gave her a sour look, but Callum said to Cassie, "How do you know *Dr Who*? I've only ever met three Americans who've watched the show, and one was David."

"My roommate in college watched three seasons in one weekend after a bad break-up. I had no choice." Cassie bit her lip. "Did you ever notice how the Doctor always shows up when he's needed, even if he intended to go somewhere else?"

"Kind of like David," Callum said, "except I can't see how he was needed here."

Jones waved a hand to draw their attention. "Regardless, now they have access to his genetic material too."

Callum ran a hand through his hair and got to his feet, pacing back and forth in front of Jones's monitors. He couldn't believe what he was hearing, but then again, it shouldn't be surprising that once the Security Service accepted what was happening, it would try to control the process in every way anyone could think of.

He paced back to Cassie, who was looking down at her feet. "Driscoll indicated that large amounts of money might be involved," he said.

"*Mucho* money," Jones said. "On top of which, the Americans have discovered that there's a puzzle to solve and are screaming at us to share the rest of it with them."

"The family is technically American," Cassie said.

"*Technically.*" Jones scoffed. "We're not going to share. Not something this big, and especially not if the Americans can throw more money at it than we can. They'll want to take over."

Cassie had her arms folded across her chest. "David doesn't know any of this. He's down in the interrogation room, possibly spilling his guts. We have to get to him."

"You can't *get to him*, as you say," Jones said flatly.

"We have to try," she said.

Jones was still shaking his head. "Since you left, Callum, the entire station has been focused on this problem to the exclusion of all else. Smythe has gone somewhat mental on the subject."

"He's trying to atone for screwing everything up the first time," Cassie said, and when Jones stared at her, she added, "Callum told me."

"What did happen when I went off the balcony at Chepstow Castle?" Callum had an almost morbid interest in the answer to this question. It was like attending his own funeral.

"Initially, the focus was on damage control. Several of our men witnessed your fall: Leon from the battlement and others, whom Natasha sent to find you when your mobile cut out, from the balcony itself. Having you disappear like that wasn't something Lady Jane or anyone else could dismiss, even if they wanted to, which they didn't. Natasha was pretty gutted to learn you'd gone." Jones said those last words casually, but then he reddened, glancing at Cassie before looking towards a monitor.

Cassie appeared oblivious, but her poker face was excellent, so Callum might well hear about Jones's comment later.

"So what happened after Callum vanished?" Cassie said.

"Everyone stood there at first like they couldn't believe it," said Jones. "I was communicating with Natasha and had been watching the live feed from the castle's cameras. While none were pointing at the water, three tourists caught the fall on their video phones. I killed the cell towers in the area before any of them could upload to the internet. After that, we shut down the town completely. Between you and me, it was probably a violation of their rights, but before anyone could leave Chepstow, they had to surrender their cameras and mobiles for inspection."

Cassie looked at Callum, a little open-mouthed. He nodded. "You've seen only the tip of the iceberg of what we're capable of."

"After that, Lady Jane sent Smythe to settle things down. He's a ponce, but he really pushed us; I've kipped in the office more times than I can count in the last six months. A team cleaned out your flat, moved your money to an offshore location, and scrubbed the internet clean."

"Hard to do," Callum said.

"That was my job," said Jones. "You'd be amazed how significant your presence was, even with your service here."

"I had a life before the Security Service, believe it or not," Callum said, taking the news of his invisibility in stride.

"You don't now," said Jones. "You have no living family, so disappearing you was easier than some."

"So I don't exist at all?" Callum had expected no less and had ordered the same kind of scrubbing twice before for other agents caught in compromising circumstances. The Security Service deliberately recruited unattached people for that very reason. While those agents hadn't time-traveled to another universe, they'd committed unforgivable breaches of security and had to be virtually killed and reborn as someone else.

"You're dormant but not dead," said Jones. "Now that you're back, it won't be hard to resurrect you. You'll have been on assignment in as remote a place as Lady Jane can dream up."

"You mean like Scotland?" Cassie said with a laugh. Jones looked at her quizzically, and she explained further: "He's MI-5. You guys don't go to Madagascar."

"We do when requested for training or in a goodwill exchange," said Jones. "Lady Jane will come up with something plausible."

"Well, don't start the process yet." Callum looked at Cassie. She raised her eyebrows, and as he continued to look at her, she shrugged. He continued, "We don't necessarily intend to stay." He didn't mention Driscoll's odd request.

"No. You don't mean it!" Jones's mouth fell open.

"I do mean it," Callum said.

"How could you return?" said Jones. "I thought you couldn't time travel without David?"

"We can't." Callum looked harder at his former colleague. "You don't really think you're going to be able to prevent him from leaving if he chooses to, do you?"

"You do!" Cassie poked a finger at Jones. "Haven't you learned anything at all from Meg's disappearance?"

Jones shook his head and didn't seem to have heard Cassie's protest. "You still don't understand. Our superiors are going to do everything in their power to prevent him from returning—and when I say *everything*, I mean it. He's in their clutches now."

"I think I liked it better when you didn't believe us," Cassie said.

"Those days are long gone," said Jones.

"I wonder how David is taking being believed instead of dismissed?" Cassie said.

Jones made an involuntary motion with his hand.

Callum's eyes narrowed. "What is it?"

"The plan was not to tell him," said Jones.

"Not to tell him that you believed him?" Cassie said, and when Jones nodded, she added, "That's twisted and a little sick."

Callum squeezed her hand. "David can take care of himself." He turned back to Jones. "Have you managed to discover anything from Meg's blood?"

"At one point, Smythe assured Lady Jane—based on no evidence—that identifying what allows the world shift would be a doddle. He assumed, as did we all, that her DNA would be different, but so far—nothing," said Jones.

"I can't tell you how happy I am to hear that," Cassie said.

Jones smirked. "That's not to say we aren't trying with everything we've got to break down her genome nucleotide by nucleotide. Meanwhile, we've had better luck with the *when* than the *how*."

Callum nodded. The moment their time-traveling occurred had been the crucial piece of knowledge that had allowed Lady Jane's husband to backtrace the family's world shifting in the first place.

"What's that supposed to mean?" Cassie said, looking from Callum to Jones and back again.

"It has to do with what happens to time and space," Callum said.

"Of course." Cassie wrinkled her nose at him. "That explains everything."

"It does, in fact," said Jones. "I've all but identified the exact wavelength and frequency of the intersection between the two worlds that David's family manages to manipulate."

Callum exchanged a glance with Cassie. She looked as concerned as he felt. Jones seemed pretty pleased with himself, but to have the Security Service so invested in this project was not good news. Callum much preferred it when Meg's file was buried under a dozen others on his desk.

"We have our work cut out for us, I guess," Cassie said.

Callum rose to his feet.

Jones held up one finger. "One moment." He turned back to his desk, checked a few things on his monitor, and scribbled onto a notepad. It seemed Smythe was still driving his staff hard. Jones then walked to where Cassie and Callum waited by the exit and stuck out his hand to Callum. "Good luck."

"Thank you." Callum shook.

Then Jones shook Cassie's hand, but as he turned to open the door to let them out of the room, he slipped a piece of paper into Callum's left hand. Callum covered up the action by hustling Cassie ahead of him and pocketing the paper. Jones clearly didn't want a camera to see what he'd done; Callum would have to look at what he'd given him later.

Cassie didn't argue with the way he urged her on. Instead, as Jones closed the door behind them, she said, "How are we going to get out of here unseen?"

"I don't want just to get out of here," Callum said. "I want to find David and then get out of here with him."

"Yeah, yeah, I know. But how are we going to do that—?"

Cassie's question was interrupted by a distant klaxon coming from the depths of the building.

13

September, 2017

David

They'd brought David the computer and hooked it up to the internet as they'd promised. Once that was accomplished, he answered Natasha's questions while he worked, as he'd promised. The brand of computer was one he'd never heard of, and a quick check of the specs showed him how the world had changed in the four years since he was here last, in ways that he probably couldn't even begin to catalog. His fingers had been itching for a chance to check out Natasha's cell phone since she'd set it on the table between them. He wanted to take the computer home.

As soon as he got on the internet, however, it was clear that MI-5 was censoring it. He should have expected it, given this cave they were keeping him in, but he was disappointed that he didn't have access to his old email account. They hadn't yet given him the phone call that he'd asked for with someone from the CDC either. He wouldn't have minded if they'd listened in, if only because they might begin to believe the truth of what he was saying. They also hadn't let him call his Uncle Ted, which was starting to annoy David a lot. He wasn't a terrorist, and they shouldn't be allowed to treat him like one.

The internet was so much vaster than four years ago, and there was a lot more information to sift through. The papers started piling up in the printer, and every few minutes, David got up to retrieve what he'd printed out and stick it in the duffel bag they'd brought him. Honestly, he couldn't even begin to articulate how excited he was to have so much information at his disposal once again. Admittedly, he wasn't too happy to learn that regular old penicillin wouldn't work to fight the Black Plague when it came around. He needed *streptomycin*, which wasn't the same, wasn't made the same way, and would mean acquiring a bunch of ingredients Anna didn't have access to. It was frustrating.

He did acquire some new recipes for penicillin, though again, the ingredients were going to be a bit hard to come by in the Middle Ages. The best recipe was created in a medium that included *corn steep liquor*. Corn was a New World food and didn't exist in Britain in the Middle Ages. He would have to figure out what else they could use that was close to the same. "When do I get to talk to someone at the CDC?" He looked up at Natasha.

"We'll see how the day goes," Natasha said.

David ground his teeth. The day was almost over. He rose to his feet for the eighth time, glancing at Natasha's downturned head as he dropped onto the table the extra pages that always seemed to print at the end. For a second as he looked at them, he wavered on his feet, and the text on the papers blurred. He couldn't chalk it up to standing too fast, because this was the third time it had happened in the last twenty minutes.

He was losing the battle with his body and could no longer deny the symptoms that had only gotten worse since he'd spoken with his father on the pier at Cardiff: his throat was so sore he could barely swallow around it, he was hotter than normal, and he had a headache. In the past, even before he found himself in the Middle Ages, he could often fight off being sick simply by being determined *not* to be sick, but the power of positive thinking wasn't working for him today.

He sat in his chair and stared at the keyboard, trying to figure out what to do. Natasha still wasn't paying attention to him. She had a notepad in front of her, since apparently (except for his laptop and her powered off cell phone) no electronic devices were allowed in his interrogation room, and she had just asked him to relate how King Edward had died. Her eyes tracked between her writing and the papers on the Black Death, which David had printed out but hadn't yet put into the backpack.

David made a split-second decision and gave in to temptation, following through with a plan he'd been concocting for the last hour but had been nervous about implementing. He lay his head down on the table in mid-explanation. Given that he had been relating the story of the fight with King Edward where David had punched the king in the face, it wasn't too surprising that Natasha noticed he'd stopped talking.

Her pen hovered over the paper for a second, waiting for him to continue, and then she looked up. The sight of David with his head on his arms brought her to her feet in an instant. "What is it?"

"I don't feel so good."

Natasha's hand hovered over David's head, but she didn't touch him. "Is that a rash on your cheek?"

Other than the one-way glass, which was darkened so it didn't show color well, David hadn't had a proper chance to look at himself since he'd arrived in the twenty-first century. If he'd had a rash earlier on the ship, Cassie or Callum would have noticed it, so maybe it had just developed. His throat sure hurt; he wasn't faking that either. And now that his head was on the table, it felt good to close his eyes. "I probably have scarlet fever. London was experiencing an upsurge in cases when I left, and we'd established an infirmary at Windsor to take care of patients."

Natasha backed away from him, taking little steps at first and then faster ones as she closed in on the door.

"It's okay." David put out a hand, which stopped Natasha's retreat, but she didn't move forward to take it. "I looked it up, and scarlet fever is just strep gone bad, which I didn't know before. It's common in this world too, though I'm kind of old to get it." He'd also read that since scarlet fever derived from strep—as in strep throat— you *could* get it twice, though it wasn't a common occurrence. That wasn't good news. Anna and Bronwen were counting on the fact that they'd both had scarlet fever as children to provide them with immunity.

David's stomach clenched at the thought of their babies and the threat untreated scarlet fever could pose for them. He needed to get *home*. Though now that he thought about it, he wouldn't do anyone any good as long as he was sick; it was better all the way around for him and everyone else that he *was* here. Once again, the world shifting had come through for him, more than at the initial moment where it had saved his life. For all the technology that MI-5 was throwing at the problem, they weren't going to be able to rationalize their way out of this one. He didn't have any midichlorians in his bloodstream. A supernatural explanation for his world shifting was the only one that made sense to David, and at this point, he was pretty sure he didn't want to inquire any more deeply into it than that.

Natasha was still staring at him, so he flopped the same hand in her direction. "A good dose of penicillin, and I'll be fine."

But by his last words, he was talking to himself. Natasha had fled. David lifted his head, surveying the room and the door that Natasha had left open behind her. He had a moment where he thought about getting to his feet and following her, maybe even running, since he wasn't as sick as all that, but he abandoned the idea. He didn't think he'd get far. Better to try this first. He rested his head on the table again. The black lacquer felt cool on his cheek. He closed his eyes.

A minute later, though it could have been longer since he thought he might have fallen asleep without meaning to, he opened his eyes to find the room full of people in full hazmat suits: white coveralls and helmets, taped at the wrist and ankles, with rebreathers making them all sound like Darth Vader. Satisfaction coursed through him. MI-5 was taking his illness seriously. The hazmat suits alone told him they were concerned that his brand of scarlet fever was new—or rather, old—or maybe just that he was extremely contagious. Considering the number of people in the Middle Ages who died from what was a very treatable disease in the twenty-first century, David couldn't blame them for being concerned.

Someone shook his shoulder. "Sir. Sir."

"What?" David lifted his head and then decided he'd been better with it on the table. No way was he getting out of this now that he'd started it. As he'd discovered when he'd taken Ieuan to the twenty-first century, once you were on the medical train, it was nearly impossible to get off. And in this case, he didn't want to.

"We need a stretcher," the man said to someone behind him. "When is the ambulance due to arrive?"

"Any minute, sir," a second man said.

"And the quarantine unit at the hospital?"

"Dispatch said that by the time we get him there, they'll be ready."

David observed the next half hour through eyes kept at half-mast. The two men who had spoken first were joined by a third, and the three of them placed him onto a stretcher. A fourth person— David thought she was a woman—stuck an IV in his arm and hung the solution bag above his head on a metal hook. The first man had him stick out his tongue to culture his throat.

"This is a classic presentation of scarlet fever," he said to the person standing at David's head, handing off the culture to him while accepting a syringe. He pushed up on David's side, forcing him to roll onto one hip. Then, without warning, he jabbed the needle into David's rear.

"Ouch!" David said. "What was that?"

"Benzathine penicillin," the man said.

"Whatever happened to pills?" David said.

"For this, they don't work as well," the man said.

Then they wheeled him out of the interrogation room and down the corridor to the elevator.

"We'll take care of you, son," said the third man, who'd arrived last. He spoke in American English.

David turned his head to one side, trying to make out the face behind the man's plastic mask. He couldn't see much beyond a lock of gray hair, which fell across the man's forehead, and owl-round glasses through which he gazed speculatively at David.

"Thank you." David closed his eyes. He really did feel terrible. And for all that he would have been much happier were Lili here, part of him was glad that she wasn't. Even though he longed for her touch on his forehead, he wouldn't want her to worry about him more than she already did.

The elevator doors opened, and the men wheeled David inside. They rose up, and then when the doors opened, Natasha was standing in the entrance to the garage. She, too, wore a hazmat suit, and she walked with him as they wheeled his stretcher to where the ambulance was parked.

The change in scenery had David feeling momentarily alert. Not only was he out of interrogation, but they were taking him out of the MI-5 building! "I'm surprised they're letting you walk around,"

David said to Natasha. "You were exposed to me. Why aren't you quarantined too?"

"Why do you think they've made me wear this suit?" she said. "I'll be given my own bubble at the hospital, just like you."

"A bubble, huh?" David said. "That'll be fun."

"I really appreciate what you've done for me," Natasha said, deadpan, and for the first time, David understood what Callum might have seen in her. Admittedly, she hadn't been at her best and had been uniquely stressed out for the last six hours dealing with him.

"What about Cassie and Callum?" David said. "They could be sick and not know it."

"My God." Natasha came to a full stop. She pulled her phone from the messenger bag she wore diagonally across her chest and dialed awkwardly through the gloves that impeded her fingers.

David missed the beginning of her conversation since he was being loaded into the ambulance, but after a few minutes, Natasha climbed into the back with him. She grinned wickedly. "Driscoll will share my prison if he's not careful."

"Are they sick?" David held his breath. His plan depended on the three of them being in the same place. Since he didn't know where Cassie and Callum were, he had to do the best he could with what he had to work with.

"Not yet." Natasha's phone rang. She looked at who was calling and then answered. "Do you have them?"

David couldn't see her face pale behind the plastic face guard, but he could tell from her tone of voice that she was worried. "Well, find them!" She hung up.

"Where are they?" David said.

"Driscoll ate with them in the cafeteria not long ago. He told them to stay put while he saw to—" Natasha cut off what she'd been about to say, "—some other business, and they disappeared."

"Surely you have cameras everywhere?" he said.

Natasha paused before speaking. "Not enough, apparently, since they aren't on any of the video we do have. Security is backtracking through it now to find where they were last seen."

"Where's Director Cooke in all this?" David said.

"She and Smythe will meet us at the hospital. They weren't on-site when this happened."

David nodded, surprised she was telling him all this. "This could have been handled better, you know."

"I know," Natasha said. "Believe me." She gazed out the rear window of the ambulance.

David reached out a hand and touched her knee. "Can you tell me what's really going on?"

But Natasha had turned to look towards the front seats. "What's the hold up?"

"Rush hour traffic," said the driver.

David craned his neck so he could see through the gap that led to the front seats of the ambulance. Except for Natasha, who was several inches shorter than the men, everyone looked the same in their hazmat suits. He knew only that the man who'd spoken was the American.

"So find another route," Natasha said.

"We have to get all the way up to the Heath," he said.

"What about using the siren?" David said.

Natasha stood to peer into the driver's cab and then sighed, looking down at David. "Too many cars in too small a space." She sat back beside him and made a motion as if to put her chin in her hands but was stymied by her helmet.

"You might as well talk to me while we're waiting," David said. "Who am I going to tell?"

"You never know," Natasha said, but then she leaned forward, her hands dangling next to his IV drip. "Ever since last November, we've been on alert to any change in our readings. Since I was promoted to head of Cardiff station, we've been working on your case full time."

"Up until today, everyone must have been pretty bored," David said.

Natasha shrugged. "It's typical for us to work a case for many months without a lead. Anyway, when Callum called, we already knew you were here, though admittedly, finding you in the middle of the Bristol Channel was a bit of a shocker." Natasha leaned even closer. "Within two minutes, Director Cooke knew as much as I knew. Our response was out of my hands, especially after the disaster of last winter."

"It wasn't Callum's fault that my parents escaped him," David said. "Didn't someone else botch their capture at that hotel?"

"That someone else is now Director Cooke's second-in-command in London," Natasha said. "A man named Smythe. He convinced Director Cooke and her superiors that if she'd left your parents in his hands, he could have salvaged the situation. Since Callum wasn't there to defend himself—"

"It looks like he screwed up," David said.

"That was true until today," Natasha said. "Director Cooke spoke to me after her conference with Callum and admitted, not even grudgingly, that bringing you back here, convincing you that he was on your side the whole time when he was really still working for us, was an impressive piece of tradecraft."

"That's what Callum told her?" David was feeling much better, not necessarily because the drugs had kicked in but because things were happening now and he was out of that interrogation room. As far as he was concerned, the ambulance could take as long as it wanted to get to the hospital. For the moment, he was a tiny bit free.

"I was meeting with you at the time, so I wasn't present myself," Natasha said, "but she seemed pretty pleased with him. Smythe, on the other hand, wasn't looking too chuffed."

Which could hardly be more excellent if David had thought of it himself. That Callum was such a convincing actor had to be the reason Callum and Cassie had been allowed to wander freely throughout the MI-5 building—or freely enough that Driscoll couldn't find them. Not for one second did David believe that Callum had been working for him only because he hoped one day to return to MI-5 with David in tow. That might have been his thought initially, and quite honestly, it was a good one. But David knew Callum better than Natasha did, and he was pleased to learn that his friend was such an impressive liar.

"We've learned—"

But David never learned what Natasha was going to tell him, because the driver of the ambulance chose that moment to jerk the vehicle out of place, the ambulance careening forward, half on the sidewalk, half on the road. Given the way the streets were parked up on both sides, that couldn't last long. Natasha had to grasp a handle above her head, and the third technician who'd been sorting through the contents of the ambulance on David's right let out a yelp.

The ambulance crashed back down to the level road and then swung around a corner to the right. The driver finally turned on the sirens, and he wove the ambulance in and out of traffic, heedless, as far as David could tell, of anyone's safety, even their own. David had never driven a car in the modern world, but when he was young, his mom would often take a circuitous route rather than wait in a traffic jam. She'd insist that even if they arrived at the same time as they would have otherwise, some movement was better than no movement, especially with a sleeping kid in the car. The ambulance driver must have decided having a medieval king with scarlet fever qualified too.

Natasha gasped as the ambulance swerved again, but then it steadied. Natasha didn't say anything else to David. Perhaps she'd thought better of her confidences.

David rested his head back on the pillow and closed his eyes. It seemed Callum had a plan too. David was looking forward to seeing what it was.

14

September, 2017

Callum

As they listened to the warning bell, sirens sounded from outside too. Cassie crossed into the office opposite and looked out the window to the street below. Callum followed and looked with her. Two ambulances and four police cars pulled down the ramp into the underground car park.

"Do you think all that's for David?" Cassie said.

Callum found himself shaking his head in disbelief. "I want to say that it couldn't be, but given the Office's preoccupation with him and his family, I fear it is. We need to get to him now."

Cassie pressed her lips together. "Could they have tortured him to the degree that he needs emergency medical care?"

"Christ, I wouldn't have thought so. Let's go." Callum hit the door to the stairs with his shoulder and led Cassie down them at a run. Along the way, Callum pulled out the paper Jones had given him and opened it, hiding it in the palm of his hand.

"What does it say?" Cassie said. She'd taken Jones' warning about cameras to heart and looked down as she spoke; the cameras were programmed for visuals but not sound.

"Jones has promised to wipe our movements since we left the cafeteria," Callum said. "And he's arranged for a vehicle."

"I thought he didn't want to help us," she said.

"Jones has always been an odd bird," Callum said. "But thank God for him."

At this hour of the day, Callum hoped they wouldn't run into anyone coming up the stairwell. He had to trust that Jones was continuing to track them and would scrub their presence if he could. Other than worrying about the danger involved, if he had to share this adventure with anyone, he was glad it was with Cassie. She never panicked; she rarely became angry; and she knew him so well that she could guess what he was thinking almost before he thought it himself.

They came out of the stairwell at the same instant that the second ambulance pulled into the underground car park. A dozen men in black jackets faced the entrance but none turned around to see them. Callum caught Cassie's hand and pulled her down the long line of parked vehicles to an older model SUV second from the end, which had been backed into its parking space.

"I can't see what's happening from here!" Cassie said.

"You don't need to." Callum traced with one finger the narrow dent in the left fender; this was the very vehicle he and Natasha had ridden in when they'd driven to Chepstow Castle ten months earlier. He moved at a crouch to the driver's side door.

"What are you doing?" Cassie said.

"I still have my ID, which I can show to the guard at the exit. In this vehicle, I can get us out of the car park." Security was designed to prevent unauthorized personnel from getting into the car park, not out of it. Only a person who'd already passed through security, either in the lobby or at the car park's entrance, had access to the cars. Once this was over, this station needed to address that weak point in its defenses.

"Isn't the car locked?" Cassie said.

Callum took out his mobile phone. In the past, it had been an extension of himself. He never turned it off and never went anywhere without it. Now, however, he felt like he was carrying a parasite in his pocket.

Powering it off earlier hadn't sent alarm bells ringing throughout the building. With Jones on their side, he hoped that turning it on for a minute so he could access the program to unlock the vehicles wouldn't either. Jones's note had been cryptic, probably for his own plausible deniability, but Callum had taken it to mean that he would be able to unlock this particular SUV through the program in Callum's mobile, which Jones could update remotely. Callum waved the screen in front of the sensor pad on the door. The lock clicked. Jones had even had the foresight to deactivate the 'beep' that usually accompanied the unlocking of a car door.

Powering off the mobile phone and pocketing it again, Callum pulled open the driver's door of the SUV, pressed the button to unlock the rest of the doors, and then moved back to the boot where Cassie waited. He opened the door, which swung wide instead of up, and urged Cassie inside ahead of him. She pulled it closed once he'd climbed in, and they crouched there for a second, getting their bearings.

While they'd been occupied, the police cars had pulled into the underground car park behind the ambulances. Callum clambered over the rear seat and up to the front of the vehicle so he could look through the front windows. The reflection of swirling lights coming from the top of the ramp that led into the car park from the road indicated that at least one other police car had stopped there to direct traffic. He pressed the buttons in the side door to open the front windows so he could hear what was happening.

The police cars diverged from one another, driving through the lanes of parked vehicles and eventually turning around to face back the way they'd come, towards the ramp and the street. Callum looked towards the door fifty feet away that they'd come through. The stairwell doorway was to the right of a larger opening through which the lift could be found. Callum heard a distant *ping*, and a rush of men in Hazmat suits came through the opening, pushing a stretcher. A tall man with sandy hair lay upon it, with an oxygen mask pushed up off his mouth and nose so it sat on his forehead like a Cyclopsian third eye. He was tall enough to fill the bed from end to end.

"*David.*" Cassie breathed his name. She'd poked her head between the two front seats and put her hand on his shoulder.

"Get back." He gestured with one hand, and both he and Cassie moved into the rear seat of the SUV. The darkened windows in the rear and back would hide them if any agents bothered to look this way, though they were otherwise occupied at the moment.

Cassie hunched down to peer between the front passenger seat and its door, moving her head this way and that so the retracted seatbelt didn't block her vision. "They've IV'ed him. I can't see his face, but he's talking to the people around him. Could they have tortured him?" She glanced at Callum. He'd started searching through the bags in the boot, looking for gear that would make them look more like the agents outside the vehicle.

"The hazmat suits tell a different story." Callum handed Cassie a Kevlar vest, along with a black jacket and a baseball cap. "Put these on."

"So, he *is* sick." Cassie took the vest and inspected it. It consisted of a chest and back pad held together with Velcro. "What do you think? Scarlet fever?"

"Could be anything," Callum said. "He never complained to me about feeling ill, but then he wouldn't have, would he?"

"He must be really sick to have said something to them," Cassie said.

"They'd respond the same way regardless. If it's medieval, it's going to scare them." And then Callum thought again. "Unless ... unless he's not really sick! Or not that sick."

"What do you mean?" Cassie said.

Callum beamed at her. "It could be our David has a plan."

Cassie smiled. "He always does."

Callum grunted his agreement, preoccupied by his Kevlar armor. Cassie hunched down among the second row passenger seats and slipped on her Kevlar vest too. For a moment, the vehicle was quiet except for the *snick* of Velcro sealing and the snap of the vinyl windbreakers as they shook them out and put them on. "This vest is way more flexible and far less bulky than I imagined," Cassie said, patting at her chest. "It's almost like I'm only wearing an extra sweater."

"Technology never stops. We've come a long way since chain mail." If he'd been wearing armor, Cassie would have had to haul it over his head to get it off of him. Sometimes when Callum was particularly tired, he needed two assistants to accomplish the task. As expensive as it was, and as difficult to fit exactly right, it was good that he'd left his armor on the ship. Since he was kneeling in the rear compartment, and Cassie had remained in the back seat, it would have made undressing him even more awkward.

He got himself together, a twin to Cassie, both looking like police extras, and then he plopped into the driver's seat with Cassie next to him. "You're not driving because you're the man, you know," she said as she buckled her seat belt. "It's just that I can't see me having much success driving on the wrong side of the road after five years without driving at all."

Callum laughed. "I love you." He pressed the start button on the vehicle, glancing out of the corner of his eye at his wife as he did so.

She looked very pleased with herself. "You'd better."

In the moments they'd spent putting on the gear, the agents and people in the hazmat suits had dispersed. They'd deposited David in one of the ambulances—the second and closer of the two—and now the police cars lined up to escort the ambulances out of the car park, along with yet another black van full of Security Service personnel.

"Let them get ahead of us," Cassie said.

Callum nodded, the thought having occurred to him too. "We need to keep the right distance behind them so they don't think anything of our presence but the guard assumes we're with them."

If Natasha, or whoever was organizing David's interrogation, was thinking straight, she should have told the security station the total number of vehicles accompanying the ambulances. Callum was counting on her not to think straight, given how urgently she seemed to be treating whatever was wrong with David. For all that he had been lying on a stretcher, the glimpse Callum had seen of David indicated that he was both coherent and calm.

Cassie and Callum waited in their parking space until the first police car and the lead ambulance had gone through the checkpoint at the exit. Then they pulled into the narrow lane between the cars. Callum maneuvered into line behind the last police car, keeping about twenty yards behind it. The security guard stood in the doorway of his box, waving the vehicles through one by one. Callum merely held up his badge as he drove past him and through the raised security barrier, which slowly lowered behind him.

15

September, 2017

Cassie

Cassie was acutely aware that not only was she homeless but she didn't have a badge, money, or any form of ID whatsoever. As they swerved through the lanes of traffic, Callum gunning the engine to keep up with the police vehicles and David's ambulance, she catalogued the number of car chases she'd seen in movies and on television. In almost every instance, the hero and heroine had found themselves beyond desperate, with a stream of police cars behind them. In this case, however, it was they who were doing the chasing of what she had come to think of as 'the bad guys'. She was sorry that they'd been Callum's friends—or at the very least, his colleagues—but she didn't see how anyone could think well of them now.

Betrayed was the word that came to mind. The powers that be had turned them loose in the building itself, but Jones's fears had sparked new ones in Cassie. The hours they'd spent in the Office had shown to Cassie how tightly controlled this world had become in the five years she'd been absent from it. She really hadn't wanted to know the number of cameras in Britain. The only good news about that, as Meg and Llywelyn could attest, was that there seemed to be fewer overall in Wales. Meg had made an offhand comment the other day that modern Wales was like the Appalachia of Britain: treated badly by the larger system, with fewer resources and wealth because England had strip-mined it of everything worthwhile long ago. And sheep outnumbered people in Wales ten to one.

"Do you think Jones was playing us?" Cassie said.

"No," Callum said. "I'm sure Driscoll was, even without Lady Jane's warning. If it turns out he was telling the truth, I'll apologize for mistrusting him and his motives. Meanwhile, I'm just glad to be out of that building."

"Not that we've come very far," Cassie said as Callum cursed and pounded the wheel. The last ambulance and police car were almost a full block ahead of them, stuck with them in rush hour traffic. When they'd come out of the MI-5 building, in short order they found themselves in a long line of cars stretching in both directions. The sirens on the police cars were going, but they weren't making any headway. Both sides of the streets were lined with parked cars, and unless they drove up onto the sidewalk, they weren't going anywhere. "A horse could make it to the hospital faster than we will."

Callum looked over at her. "Missing home, are we?"

"Oddly, yes," she said. "More than that, I don't like seeing David helpless."

"That's what he has us for," Callum said, "to watch his back."

"I have to confess that what Jones talked about—the monitoring and trying to build a time travel device—scares me," Cassie said.

"Me too," Callum said with another glance at her. He hardly had to focus on his driving since they were moving at a snail's pace. They'd made it four blocks in the last five minutes. "What worries you in particular?"

"What would happen if the government actually made the machine a reality? We have to protect that world from them." And then Cassie added softly, "Our world."

Out of the corner of her eye, Cassie saw Callum swallow hard. She hadn't heard him say that he was ready to return to the Middle Ages, but that didn't mean he couldn't clearly see the consequences of exposing those people to more visitors from the twenty-first century.

"From that very first day at Windsor Castle, I understood that general access to the medieval world would destroy it," Callum said, "not because the people wanted to on principle but because money would trump common sense. They'd sell the rights to the highest bidder, who wouldn't have anything but his own interests at heart. Driscoll said as much to me while you were talking to your grandfather."

"Honestly, I think it's a good thing we haven't discovered any other habitable planets in the universe. We'd just muck them up too."

"That's a little random, but I don't disagree." Callum returned his attention to the front, and then Cassie gasped as the ambulance carrying David swung out of its lane and turned down a side alley.

Callum hit the gas and pulled the SUV out of line too, following one police car, which screamed down the alley ahead of them. Cassie put one hand on the dashboard and the other on the handle above her head to steady herself. The traffic had kept the SUV three cars back of the pack of police cars and ambulances, but that fact now allowed Callum to react in a way that the other vehicles couldn't. Concentrating fully on his driving, Callum swung the wheel right and then left, avoiding a cluster of trash cans the police car had gone right through.

Cassie moved her hand to the door handle and gripped it tightly. "I hope David's okay."

"Me too." The SUV screeched around a corner.

"Maybe he's all right but the driver just got frustrated with the traffic," she said.

"Right. That's why the driver's taking him away from the hospital," Callum said. "Something's wrong, and I'm not sure it's with David."

"He did look a little ill," Cassie said, "and he wasn't struggling. In the garage, he looked like he was okay with what they were doing."

"I agree," Callum said.

"Regardless, the policemen in the car ahead of us will call this in to their headquarters and let them know what's going on, right?" Cassie said.

"Yes. If the men in the police car aren't *in* on whatever's going on," Callum said.

When they reached the end of another alley, the ambulance and police car cut across four lanes of traffic. Callum gunned the engine to follow, but Cassie gestured for him to slow down. "Let them get a bit ahead. I know we don't want to lose them, but if what you suspect is correct, we might want them to think they've lost us."

Callum nodded, waited a beat, and then shot across the street during an infinitesimal break in the traffic while Cassie covered her eyes and tried not to shriek. He turned into the alley the ambulance had taken just as the police car disappeared around a right turn a hundred yards ahead. Now Callum floored it and followed, not wanting to lose them at the next corner. "I know where I am at least. My flat wasn't far from here."

"We turned north back there," Cassie said. "Are we getting near the hospital?"

"No," Callum said. "Not one that I know of, anyway. Cardiff has only one hospital equipped to deal with a hazmat-level quarantine. On the other hand, in my absence, the Security Service could have taken over one of the smaller clinics. To send David to a place like that would all but eliminate the risk of spreading whatever has made him sick. But I don't know of any clinics out here either."

With the last few turns, keeping up with the police car through a small miracle, they'd left the traffic behind them. All three vehicles drove northeast at a good clip, away from the city center.

"We could get closer to them if we could change cars," Cassie said.

"Even if we could take the time to steal something less notice-able, it's hard to tail a suspect with only one vehicle." Callum shot Cassie a grin. "I'm doing my best."

Cassie stared at her husband for a second. "You're enjoying this!"

"A little bit." Then Callum pulled sharply to the left-hand curb as four hundred feet ahead of him the ambulance turned into the parking lot behind a ten-story yellow-brick apartment building. Above the first floor, each apartment had a balcony that overlooked the cars.

"Not much of a view," Cassie said.

"I'll get us closer," Callum said, misunderstanding her. Cassie had meant that the apartments didn't have a view, not that she and Callum couldn't see the parking lot. It was a silly joke to make at a time like this.

The police car entered the lot behind the ambulance, and then Callum pulled back onto the road. He drove forward until he found a space to park on the other side of the street from the driveway, al-most directly across from the entrance to the lot. This vantage point gave them a narrow line of vision between the building and a tall hedge that surrounded the whole complex to see what was happening in the parking lot.

The street was tree-lined on both sides, giving them a bit more cover, and mostly residential, with a dentist's office on one cor-ner and a convenience store kitty-corner to it. Otherwise, the neigh-borhood consisted of small houses, duplexes, and other apartment buildings further down the street.

Cassie and Callum remained in the SUV, scrunched down in their seats. They watched as two men, having discarded their hazmat suits, unloaded David from the ambulance, which they'd parked crossways across three parking spaces. It was the emptiest parking lot Cassie had seen in her brief tour of Cardiff. Parking lots in Wales, even from the short time she'd been here, had revealed themselves to be half the size of American ones but still needing to hold the same number of cars, which admittedly were also half the size of American ones. Not this parking lot, however.

David still had the IV in his arm, and the drip bag swung above his head, hanging from a hook attached to the stretcher. He looked to be asleep.

"Tell me this is one of your safe houses," Cassie said.

Callum's mouth twitched. "We do have them. You haven't been watching too many movies—"

"I haven't been watching any movies—"

"—but this wasn't one of ours when I was the head of Cardiff station." Callum stared hard as Natasha took off a hazmat suit outside the ambulance and, dressed as before in what Cassie might call a 'power suit' approached the passenger side of the police car.

Callum made a groaning sound deep in his throat. "Oh no."

"Does this have to be bad?" Cassie said. "Maybe Lady Jane established this safe house in your absence, specifically in case David or one of his family members came back? This could be playing out exactly as she means it to."

"You're too nice."

Cassie scoffed. "I wouldn't ever have said so."

Callum didn't respond to her comment, though she thought she detected a slight twitch of a smile before he went back to chewing on his lower lip and watching Natasha. His former friend spoke to one of the men involved, a tall, gray-haired man in round glasses. Natasha nodded twice and stabbed a finger at him before climbing into the passenger side of the police car. The police car then started up and backed out of its space. It exited the parking lot, took a left, and headed back the way it had come.

"I'll tell you why this bothers me so much," Callum said. "The initial response—the stretcher, the hazmat suits, the ambulances—speaks to me of an abundance of caution. *Someone* was very concerned about David and called in the cavalry. But the sudden departure of the ambulance without its escort indicates fear or extreme recklessness. The former would mean that Lady Jane has grown concerned that someone is trying to get at David. In this case, the initial response—over-response, in fact—would have been for show."

"That would explain Natasha's presence here," Cassie said.

"It would; I'd love for that to be the case and that all this was planned out from the beginning," Callum said. "But when they took David from the ambulance, he was asleep. And that looks like a real IV in his arm."

"So if he wasn't well, they might take him to a smaller clinic, like you said before, instead of a hospital," Cassie said, "but not to a semi-rundown apartment building."

"Exactly," Callum said.

"So this *is* an abduction," Cassie said, "and Natasha is involved."

"Yes," Callum said. "Easier to grab him here than once he's in London."

And really, what more was there to say than that? "You said I was too nice, but this confirms all my fears," Cassie said.

"Which fears are those, in particular?" Callum said.

"That *they*—" Cassie gestured to the men in the parking lot, one of whom had opened a side door into the building and was helping the second man wheel David's stretcher inside, "—are the bad guys. We need to get in there."

"I know we do," Callum said, "but I don't want to rush in without a plan. Watch first, act later."

Leaving the gray-haired man inside the building with the stretcher, the two remaining medics closed the door to the apartment building, walked to the ambulance, and got in. The ambulance started up and drove out of the parking lot, turning right instead of left like the police car had. The occupants of neither vehicle appeared to have noticed Cassie and Callum.

Callum pulled out his phone and stared at the blank screen.

"What are you doing?" Cassie said.

"Trying to decide what I should do next: use my mobile to ring Lady Jane and report what is happening or toss it into a rubbish bin." He turned the phone over in his hands, and Cassie saw that it had a seamless construction. It wasn't possible to remove the battery. "Stupidly, I am only realizing now that it might have a tracking device in it that functions even when it's off."

"You've been away for a while," Cassie said.

Callum grimaced. "That's no excuse. I should have known better than to keep it on me."

"We needed the phone to access the SUV," Cassie said.

"Which has its own GPS system." Callum gestured to the dashboard. "We're probably not fooling anyone."

Cassie's stomach had been in knots from the start over being separated from David. Bad enough to be stuck in a foreign country with a bunch of spies. Far worse not to know what was happening right under their noses or whom they could trust. She was glad to be with Callum, but she was hating everything else about today. It wasn't at all what she'd imagined returning to the twenty-first century would be like. She hadn't even gotten a hot shower yet, and the coffee in the cafeteria had been lukewarm and bitter.

"It may be that everything that has happened so far has been a charade for our benefit, a test even," Callum said.

"I wouldn't go that far," Cassie said. "David wouldn't be playing along with them to test your loyalty."

Callum held up the phone. "What do you think? If I turn it on, I can use it to help find David."

"How could your phone possibly help with that?" Cassie said.

"I'm a secret agent man." Callum gave her a wicked grin. "It has a program to scan for heat signatures."

"Wow." She pursed her lips. "You can turn off the GPS, can't you?"

"Technically, but if the mobile is on, Jones could turn on the GPS remotely. If anyone is looking for me, he needs about a minute for my signature to come online and another minute to trace my location," Callum said. "A lot depends on how far Jones is willing to go to help us and how much pressure he's under to find us."

"Would he know about a new safe house?" Cassie said.

"I don't know," Callum said. "I don't dare ring him to find out until we at least know more about what's happening here. So far, we haven't done anything wrong or illegal. We were concerned about David's safety and tailed his ambulance. I need a bit more information before I can make that call."

"I say turn on the phone, then," Cassie said. "It's worth the risk of them coming after us. At the very worst, they'll catch us and haul us back to MI-5. But all that means is that we'll end up right back where we started. No harm, no foul."

Callum reached for Cassie's hand, squeezed it, and then opened his car door. Cassie got out too. The parking lot stayed as it had been, empty but for two cars. The day had been warm before they were shut up in the MI-5 building, but with evening coming on and clouds arriving that looked like rain, the air temperature had cooled considerably. If she hadn't been wearing the Kevlar vest and the windbreaker, she would have been cold. She wished for her cloak, left in the bathroom back at MI-5, and then dismissed the thought. It had sentimental value, but it was a *thing*. Callum would commission her another one.

With the phone in Callum's hand, though still not turned on, they crossed the street and entered the parking lot. Callum signaled for Cassie to stay back while he approached the remaining two vehicles. He didn't pull his gun from the holster at the small of his back, but he did sidle down the side of the nearest vehicle—a minivan—

towards the driver's door as she'd seen police and agents in television shows do a million times. He kept his eyes fixed on the side mirror.

When he reached the driver's side door, he peered through the window and then opened the door, which was unlocked, and poked his head inside. Cassie thought he might climb into the van, but then he pulled back and looked towards Cassie, shaking his head. *Nobody.* She shrugged and pointed to the side door of the apartment building through which the men had wheeled David in his stretcher.

Callum closed the van door gently, hardly making more noise than a click, and crossed to the building. He put a hand on the apartment complex door, at which point Cassie realized that it was a solid sheet of metal, without windows or adornment, not even a handle. That meant, though she hadn't noticed it at the time, that the door had been opened from the inside for the ambulance men. Yet another person was involved.

Callum came back to where she waited at the near corner of the building. "Let's try the front."

Unsurprisingly, like the side door, the main door to the apartment building was locked. Cassie shaded her eyes with her hand to block the glare of the setting sun and pressed close to the glass. Peering through the window, she saw an actual human being sitting behind a counter on the opposite side of the foyer. She knocked on the window to get his attention while Callum flattened his badge against the glass. When the man looked up from his computer, Callum crooked a finger at him. "Open up."

The man's eyes narrowed, but he stood and came around the counter. He glanced at Callum's badge and then twisted the lock to open the door. "What is it?" He had a very stiff, upper crust British accent, which made Cassie wonder what he was doing managing an apartment complex instead of drinking tea and eating strawberries and cream at Wimbledon. He was dressed well to match his voice, in a button-down shirt, slacks, and a tie. He wore flip-flops instead of loafers, however, and the incongruity of it had Cassie biting her lip and looking down at her feet to hide her amusement.

"I have some questions about someone who has leased one of the flats in your building," Callum said. "What's your name?"

"Anders," the man said. "Which flat do you mean?"

Callum pushed passed Anders and crossed the foyer to the counter without answering. Anders and Cassie hustled after him. Anders seemed anxious to reach the counter first, and Cassie understood why when she saw the images on Anders's computer screen just before he slammed the lid down on his laptop.

Callum cleared his throat. "I don't have a name, only that he may have entered through a side door a few minutes ago, pushing a stretcher."

"A stretcher?" Anders said. "I didn't notice anything."

Neither Cassie nor Callum mentioned that if Anders spent more time paying attention to what was going on around him and less time surfing the web for pictures of naked women—or watching pornographic videos—he might have noticed something like that.

"I'd like to see your security tapes," Callum said.

'Tapes' hadn't been used in a lot more years than the ten months Callum had been in the Middle Ages, but Anders knew what he meant. He didn't ask for a search warrant either, if one was even required in the UK, just gestured towards a door behind him. Perhaps he was worried about Callum reporting his visual stimuli. Callum's glance at Cassie showed his self-satisfaction with their progress so far; he put his hand at the small of Cassie's back, and they followed Anders into the little room behind the counter.

The apartment's security system was minimal but efficient. Two cameras watched the parking lot, with a wide angle of vision. More cameras monitored both the front and side doors and all the hallways on all ten floors. Anders fiddled with the video, moving forward and back until the image of the ambulance driving into the parking lot appeared. Even though he'd seen it live when it happened, Callum cursed again at the appearance of Natasha. After that, they had full coverage of a man opening the door, the ambulance men unloading David in his stretcher, and two men wheeling him through the side door, into the corridor, and down it to the last apartment on the end, number 118.

"When did you let this flat?" Callum said.

"A month ago; a bloke paid in full for a year."

"Is he one of the men you see here?" Callum said.

Anders's leaned forward, squinting. The resolution on the screen wasn't great. "I can't tell."

"Might he appear elsewhere? How about when he rented the flat?" Callum said.

"We delete the video after a fortnight. In fact, I don't remember seeing him since then." He gestured to the screen. "I could try to find him for you."

"Thank you," Callum said.

"Should be a doddle." Anders's forehead wrinkled up, and he suddenly looked wary. "Do you want to wait?"

"I wasn't planning on it. Let me know if you find him." Callum gestured the corridor. "We'll be down there."

Anders indicated their armor and windbreakers. "Are you here to arrest him?"

"We'll see," Callum said.

"We'll do our best to keep it peaceful," Cassie said without any real knowledge of what they were going to do but because she thought that's what an agent might say.

Callum shot her a grin as he turned away; they left Anders in the security room and headed down the corridor towards apartment 118. Cassie looked back to see the manager's head just peeking around the corner. As she noticed him, he pulled his head back, but she knew that with his cameras, he would be watching them. "Are you just going to knock on their door?"

"I'm thinking about it," Callum said.

"You could call Lady Jane," Cassie said. "She could be freaking out at this point since we're missing."

"Or she isn't because she knows I'm doing as she asked. My job." Callum tugged on Cassie's arm, pulling her into a maintenance closet located halfway along the corridor. He left the door slightly ajar so they could keep an eye on number 118.

"Given time, I could think of things to do with you in here that are more fun than this," Callum said with another smile.

Cassie smiled, too. She'd never made out in a maintenance closet at school, not being adventurous that way at the time. Then she looked away, and her smile faded. Callum appeared to be in his element. It was a little daunting to think that the Middle Ages had less life and death peril than one day at MI-5, and if she wasn't mistaken, Callum had missed it.

"Remember, we have two minutes," she said.

Callum pressed a button on the side of his phone and turned it on. Almost immediately after the main screen came up, before Callum had a chance to do anything else with it, the phone lit up with an incoming call. They stared at the name of the caller for a few seconds before Callum took in a deep breath and pressed 'talk'. "Hello, Driscoll."

16

September, 2017

Cassie

"Where are you?" Smythe's voice burst from the phone. Both Cassie and Callum jumped, and Cassie's elbow hit a stack of sponges on one of the shelves in the closet. Fortunately, they made no noise as they fell. Callum turned down the sound, though he didn't put the phone to his ear and instead started flipping through its many screens and programs. Cassie put her head near Callum's shoulder so she could hear the conversation better.

"Out." As Callum spoke, he found where the GPS application was on his phone and turned it off.

"What? Did you say *out?*" It was still Smythe speaking, for some reason using Driscoll's phone.

With a grimace, Callum turned down the volume another notch. A thud, followed by rustling and fumbling sounds, came from the other end of the line, as if Smythe had dropped the phone, and then a woman's voice came on. "This is Jane Cooke. All of us can hear you, Callum. David has been abducted."

"I know," Callum said.

"Where are you, exactly?" Smythe said.

"Why don't you know?" Callum said.

Cassie mouthed "Jones?" at Callum, who nodded and said, "Is Jones there?"

"I'm here, Callum," came the familiar voice. "You took the one vehicle in the car park without a working GPS, and I see you've turned off the GPS on your mobile."

"It would be quicker if you just told us where you were," Smythe said.

"I'm less concerned that you don't know where I am than that you don't know where David is," Callum said. "You were supposed to look after him."

"We were looking after him, as you so succinctly put it," said Lady Jane, "until his ambulance took another route. Is Natasha with you too?"

Callum frowned even though the people on the other end couldn't see his expression. "No, though we've seen her. The ambulance David was riding in doesn't have a GPS either?"

That prompted a buzz of conversation on the other end of the line, none of which Cassie could clearly distinguish. It rose and fell, and then Lady Jane came back on. "Callum—"

"I'm doing my job." Callum cut her off. "I'll ring you back as soon as we have David." He closed the connection and looked at Cassie. "That was less than two minutes."

"Do you think Jones really doesn't know where we are?" she said.

"If he does, he hasn't told anyone else," Callum said.

"I've had a thought." Cassie unzipped her jacket, took it off, and removed her Kevlar vest. An apron had been hanging on a hook on the wall, and she slung it around her neck.Callum stopped fiddling with his phone, watching her without asking what she was doing, and when she turned around, he tied the apron at the back for her.

She turned back to look at him. "I'll knock on the door to the apartment, and then you do your thing."

"My thing?" Callum said, but he stepped into the corridor without asking her to elaborate. Cassie followed, hauling a mop bucket on wheels behind her.

Callum pulled out his gun and held it loosely in his right hand, pointed straight down at the floor, while still holding his phone in his left. They approached apartment 118, Cassie walking down the center of the hall, wheeling the bucket behind her, and Callum sidling along one wall.

"How many men do we think are in there?" she said.

"You can see for yourself." Callum showed her the screen on his phone. The room contained three men in shades of green, red, and black. One man was clearly sitting down and from the way his body was shaped, Cassie guessed he was sitting on a couch or a squishy chair. A second man lay flat. On the screen, it looked as if he was suspended in mid-air. A third man stood beside him. The phone recorded no other heat signatures in the apartment.

Cassie tried to calculate how long the phone had been on. Their actual conversation with Smythe and Lady Jane had stayed within the required two minute time frame, but that didn't mean Smythe wouldn't have had Jones punch up the specifications of Callum's phone and turn on the GPS remotely as soon as they hung up.

"How about you get the two men who are not David to open the door, and I go through it?" Callum said.

"That was the sum of my plan." Cassie eyed him. "You realize that Lady Jane does trust you, or she wouldn't have left you with your gun."

"That's a nice thought. Perhaps it was on her orders that nobody patted me down. I'm not sure what's going on except that if we wait until the Security Service arrives in force, David's chances of getting out of this alive decrease significantly."

"You really think agents would come in here guns blazing?" Cassie said.

"I don't know what to think," Callum said.

Not for the first time, he showed Cassie his underlying self-confidence. He could admit how much he didn't know and yet push through this problem anyway. He wasn't hampered by fear or indecision. He thought he knew what they had to do, and by God, they were going to do it.

"We've come a long way since rescuing Samuel and James Stewart at that fort in Scotland," Cassie said.

Callum gave a snort of laughter. "We did all right then. We can do this now, and this time we don't have a horde of angry Highlanders after us." He looked down at his gun. "That was the last time I held this gun with the intent to use it if I had to."

"Let's hope you don't have to."

"Very little of what has happened so far makes sense to me, Natasha's defection—if that's what it is—being at the top of the list."

Cassie unwound her hair from the bun at the back of her head and let the long braid fall over her left shoulder. Then she pulled out the mop, dry as it was, and began sweeping it around the floor in front of the apartment door. Callum pressed himself flat against the wall to the left of the door, on the opposite side from the handle.

After a quick intake of breath for courage, Cassie bumped the handle of the mop into the door and then a few seconds later did it again, this time making it scrape along the wood a little longer. Footfalls came from the apartment, but the door didn't open. Cassie passed the mop along the floor, scraping the door a third time and then a fourth.

The door opened abruptly, and Cassie straightened. She had made sure she was more to the right than the left of the door, so whoever opened it would look towards her and not to Callum. When the man opened the door, his mouth was agape, as if he was ready to curse her out—or whomever he found scraping at his door—but at the sight of Cassie, his teeth snapped together.

Until Callum, she'd never thought of herself as beautiful—certainly not enough to stop a man in his tracks—but the man who faced her was so struck by her appearance that he didn't speak. She gave him a shy smile.

"Who is it?" Someone spoke from behind the first man, who turned his head to talk to his partner. "It's just the maid—"

Callum shoved his left shoulder into the door, knocking it from the man's hand. The next second, he snapped his right elbow into the man's throat. He staggered backwards, his hands coming up to his neck and his face a rictus of agony. The man's calves banged into the couch behind him and, because he was still unbalanced, he fell sideways and cracked his head against the side wall of the room.

Callum didn't wait to see any of that. He continued through the door, which flew inward and slammed against the wall to the left. Callum's gun was steady in his hand and pointed at the second man, who had the sense to put up his hands.

"Step away from the stretcher," Callum said.

Cassie's eyes flicked from Callum to the fallen man, who moaned and curled into a fetal position. She moved into the doorway, the handle of her mop at the ready. If he tried to get up, she would whack him.

"You don't want to do this, son," the man by David's stretcher said in an American accent.

"I really think I do," Callum said. "Cassie, help David."

Cassie abandoned her vigil, leaving the mop and bucket just inside the doorway. She sidled behind and around Callum, so she wouldn't get in the way of his line of sight, and went to where David lay.

"He's alive," the man said.

"He'd better be." Cassie leaned over David, patting his cheek and speaking softly to him about how he was going to be fine. After a few seconds, David took in a deep breath and then coughed. He tried to turn onto his side, gasping a bit at the effort, and she shushed him, though that cough was the nicest sound she'd ever heard. "It's okay. It's me."

David hadn't really opened his eyes until that moment, and now they widened in recognition. "Hey," he said.

"Hey yourself. We've come to get you out of here."

"That'd be nice." David's words came out slurred.

Cassie looked more closely into his eyes: his pupils were very dilated. The IV drip was almost completely full, so whatever it was, it hadn't taken much to put him out. Cassie had never turned off one before, but there was a little dial on the tube that led to David's arm and she turned it.

"What did you give him?" Callum said.

The man's chin jutted out, and he didn't answer.

"Tell me," Callum said.

"Or what? You'll shoot me?" the man said. "Then you'll get no answers."

"Don't push me," Callum said.

"He can shoot you in the leg," Cassie said. "Your mouth would still work."

"Get him out of here, Cassie," Callum said.

She got behind the stretcher and pushed David towards the door, out it, and down the corridor, aiming for the exit door through which the men had brought David an hour earlier. As she reached it, Anders met her.

"Thank you," she said.

He helped her lift the stretcher over the threshold and into the parking lot. A chill wind greeted her, reminding Cassie that she'd left the windbreaker in the maintenance closet. More days like this and she'd have clothing scattered all over Cardiff.

"Where are you going with him?" Anders said.

Cassie pointed to the SUV, still parked on the street. She couldn't remember if Callum had left the doors unlocked, but it didn't matter because by the time she and Anders got David across the street, Callum was hurrying out of the apartment building, still with his gun in his hand. He unlocked the SUV from across the street. Apparently, he had a button for that on his mobile too.

Cassie opened the rear door and crawled inside in order to put down all the seats but the front ones. While she worked, Anders and Callum dropped the height of the stretcher to a few inches above the ground so it would fit inside the vehicle. Then Cassie slid out to allow the men to lift David into the back.

When David was securely inside, Callum got in the driver's side. He started the engine, and Cassie turned to Anders. "Thank you, again."

"Always happy to help the Security Service," he said, but as he turned to leave, he hesitated. "You know, though. I'm pretty sure the bloke who rented the flat was one of you."

"Why would you think that?" Cassie said.

Anders looked a little sheepish. "He took a stack of pound notes out of his wallet to pay the rent but then dropped his keys. When he bent to pick them up, I took a closer look at his wallet and saw that he had an ID like his underneath." Anders pointed to Callum, who had turned around to look at them from the driver's seat.

"What was that?" Callum put a hand to his ear.

Cassie flapped a hand at her husband. "Just a sec."

Cassie didn't ask Anders if he'd taken a few more bills from the man's wallet too and instead said, "But you didn't see who he worked for?"

"Sorry," Anders said. "I didn't have time."

Cassie nodded at the apartment manager. "Thanks for the information—and the help."

"No problem. I never liked that bloke anyway."

Cassie climbed in after the stretcher, and Anders shut the rear door. After another wave, he crossed the street and returned to the apartment building. Thinking about the mess he had to clean up, she stuck her head out the window. "You might call the police, just to cover yourself."

Anders shot her a grin and waved a hand in acknowledgement.

Cassie crouched by David's head. "Do you hurt anywhere?"

David was struggling to wake; he rolled his head from side to side but didn't seem to have the wherewithal to answer properly.

Callum looked at them through the rearview mirror. "You two okay back there?"

"I guess," Cassie said.

While they'd been inside, the daylight had faded, and though it wasn't yet fully dark, evening had arrived, along with a few scattered drops of rain. Callum allowed several cars to pass him before pulling into the street heading east. The rain began to pick up, and he turned on the windshield wipers and the headlights.

"I'm really glad you came." David's eyes were open, and he struggled to push up onto his elbows. Cassie shushed him and forced him to lie back down.

"Did you find out what they gave him?" Cassie said to Callum. His hands were clenched around the steering wheel, and he was driving faster than the weather and the streets might normally allow.

"A cocktail of pain killers and something to get him to talk," Callum said. "He wouldn't tell me anything else without more effort on my part, and I was in a hurry to get back to you."

"What did you do to him?" Cassie said.

"I didn't kill him if that's what you're asking." Callum gave her a quick glance over his shoulder to let her know he was joking and that he didn't believe she would think that.

Cassie just shook her head at him.

"If you must know, I duct taped them both with a roll they'd kept handy for use on David and phoned the police." Callum held up his cell phone. "But not before I took their photos. If they're in the system, facial recognition software should get us an ID."

"Anders thought one of them was MI-5," she said, "though that wouldn't account for him being an American."

"They did look ex-military," Callum said.

"What'd I tell you?" David threw an arm across his eyes, and Cassie wondered if the bit of light coming through the windows hurt them. "If you think someone's out to get you, you're paranoid only if it turns out not to be true."

Cassie smiled. For the first time since they arrived in the twenty-first century, his mind and hers were working along the same lines. "I'm pretty sure, in this case, paranoia is our only hope."

17

September, 1289

Lili

From the entrance to the castle on the northeastern end of Windsor town, it was a matter of three hundred yards to the gatehouse where the King's Road ended at the city gate and an equal distance to the town end of the bridge across the Thames River. Messengers, young boys and girls mostly, scurried back and forth from gate to bridge to castle and all around the city in a near constant stream, keeping Math updated on the status of the defense and what was coming against them. Lili had heard men say that watching the lower lands outside the moat fill up with enemy soldiers as darkness descended upon the castle and town was more terrifying than fighting an actual battle, and she had to agree.

Lili remembered her first fight at the battle of Painscastle; it was the same day she'd admitted to herself that she was head over heels in love with Dafydd. She'd stood with the other archers to shoot, and shoot, and shoot again. Tonight she hadn't even nocked an arrow, and she was already tired. Math had sent her away twice to see to Arthur, but she had refused his entreaties not to return. As Math had confessed, he needed her—maybe not more than Arthur did, but Arthur could do without her for a time tonight more easily than Math.

"Keep your heads down." The command came from below. "We don't want that bastard to know how many we are."

Lili smiled to hear Bevyn's gravelly voice. He had come with Math to Windsor to confer with Dafydd, though Lili thought the real reason was to check up on her husband and make sure he was still the same boy he'd taken under his wing nearly seven years ago. Bevyn had been disappointed to find Dafydd gone—and in particular, gone to Ireland—without him. Bevyn had made do with a few days' consultation with Math and Ieuan about the state of England's defenses, staying longer than he perhaps needed to. He had been planning on departing for his home on Anglesey tomorrow. Nobody was sorry tonight that he was among them.

Now he stomped up the steps to the top of the wall and crouched beside Lili before taking a moment to peer between two of the battlement's merlons at the darkness below them. It was so quiet Lili could hear the lap of the Thames against the wharf.

"How are you, lass?"

"I'm well," Lili said.

"Is Dafydd going to have my head for letting you fight?"

"I thought it was Math's head he was going to have," Lili said.

"Mine's a little lower to the ground." Bevyn chuckled, the sound coming low and melodious. "I'd fall on my sword for you if need be."

Lili patted his arm. "I love you too."

Oddly, Roger Bacon had been instrumental in developing the plan they were following: to remove the torches from the walls all around the town and let no man poke his head above the top of the battlement. The idea was to lure Valence's men closer than they might have come otherwise and to convince them not so much that Windsor was undefended but that it was poorly defended. If Valence couldn't calculate their numbers, he would have a harder time deciding where to strike.

"Lights or no lights, someone will have told Valence by now that Dafydd isn't here," she said.

"Valence came here to challenge your husband. That I believe absolutely. Dafydd's absence will increase Valence's confidence, and his well-established prejudices will tell him that Dafydd's rule is incompetent and that he has succeeded up until now out of pure luck," Bevyn said. "Lord Math intends to do nothing to dissuade Valence of his opinion, right up until he is proved otherwise."

"I hear something!" The message was passed down the wall-walk from one man to the next. The archer on the other side of her, a man named Hywel, wiped the sweat from his brow. Lili could just make out his expression in the faint glow of the torch that lit the street below them. He looked at her, and they both nodded, finding courage in their camaraderie.

Lili listened hard, brushing the baby hairs that had come loose from her braid out of her eyes and peeking over the wall with Bevyn. They stood on the north rampart, overlooking the bridge across the Thames River. To the south, on the opposite side of the town, a hundred camp fires lit up the farmland. Valence was making a big show of numbers on the south and east side of Windsor, but where Lili and Bevyn looked remained dark.

Half of the archers were posted here, Lili among them. Their job was to defend the bridge. They all hoped that the first assault would be on the other gatehouse. The host of men posted there had every intention of throwing Valence's army back. But everyone knew by now that Valence was tricky. At times like this, silence was louder than marching feet. It wasn't to be trusted.

"There!" Lili pointed and then quickly dropped her hand and her body below the level of the crenel.

"My eyes aren't what they once were," Bevyn said. "What do you see?"

"Shadows move along the road." Lili wished for the binoculars, but Math had them at the main gate. She squinted into the darkness, pulling at the corners of her eyes to expand her vision. "I can't make them out well and strangely, I can't hear them."

"Valence wouldn't be the first commander to muffle the feet of his horses and men." Bevyn cat-walked to the town side of the wall-walk and waved a hand at an approaching messenger, a girl not yet grown into womanhood. "Tell Lord Math that he was right. Valence comes at us from the north as well as the south. We can't yet say as to his numbers." The girl nodded to indicate she understood and departed at a run.

Bevyn patted Lili's shoulder. "I have men to see to. Wait for my signal." He disappeared into the darkness under the wall-walk, heading towards the gatehouse that guarded the bridge.

The idea that Valence had left the London road dark to lure them to send out their women and children—possibly Lili herself—in a lightly defended force was one that Lili had immediately accepted, but she was still a little stunned that it had been proved true. If she had fled as Roger Bacon suggested, Valence would have captured her, and the war would have been over before it started. Dafydd, or Math in Dafydd's name, would have agreed to anything, promised anything, to get Lili and Arthur back.

Would Dafydd really have given up the kingship? That she couldn't say, and in truth, it wasn't his to relinquish. The people had chosen him to rule them, which appeared to be something Valence had yet to comprehend. Some of these Normans had spent so long dominating the Saxons they'd conquered that they'd forgotten how to rule by anything other than force, if they'd ever known it.

Lili huddled behind a merlon near the other archers, every so often peering around it to see what was happening beyond the walls. Directly below her lay a cleared space in front of the gatehouse and then the wooden bridge across the Thames River. Over fifty feet in length, it was easily wide enough for a cart to cross, though not for two to pass side-by-side.

"Waiting is hard," she said to nobody in particular.

"It's always like this before a fight." Nicholas de Carew appeared at her left shoulder in the place Bevyn had vacated. Lili glanced up at him, taking in his patrician profile outlined against the glimmerings of stars in the night sky, and then she shifted her eyes to the front again, straining to make out the shapes of Valence's men. The shadows bobbed and weaved in places, coalescing into individual men here and there as they came on. She still couldn't hear their marching feet or make out their exact numbers.

"You've participated in many battles," she said, not as a question.

"I've fought some beside your husband." Carew paused as if he was thinking to add to his statement and then turned to look at her fully. "Tell me, my queen, have I offended the king?"

Lili's eyes widened. "No ... no ... why would you think that?"

"I used to be much in his confidence, but these days he turns more to Clare or this new Earl of Shrewsbury, Lord Callum."

This wasn't the first time one of the Norman lords had come to her rather than Dafydd for an explanation of his actions. For some reason, they found her more approachable. She wouldn't have thought this was the best time for it, but that Carew would speak to her about his concerns in this moment was an indication of how troubled he was. So she did her best. "My lord Carew, if you fear that you have lost my husband's favor, I assure you that you are in all ways incorrect."

"I pray that you are right. Please tell me, in what way have I misunderstood?"

"Has he not put the whole of southwest Wales into your keeping?" she said. "With that and your new lands in Cornwall and Somerset, your estates have doubled in size compared to what they were before you threw in your lot with us. He has given you this authority and power because he *does* trust you."

Carew nodded. "And yet, he no longer calls me to court. I care for his estates and mine, I pay my taxes, and yet I had heard nothing from him, barring the announcement of the birth of his son, for the past three months until this week. And then when I do come to London, he isn't here to greet me."

Lili bit her lip, searching for the words that would convince Carew how completely he'd misunderstood the situation. "Dafydd has a saying. Perhaps you've heard it before, and it certainly applies to you in this case: *keep your friends close and your enemies closer.*"

Carew's face was shadowed. He stood totally still, making his emotions difficult to read, but she forged ahead anyway. "If Bohun sails with my husband to Ireland, it isn't because Dafydd trusts him or his counsel more than yours. It's because he *doesn't*. Dafydd can leave a large portion of his lands in your very capable hands and never worry that you will betray him or undercut his rule. He has left you alone because you do very well on your own." She canted her head. "I can tell you that just the other day he said to me that he misses your companionship, but he wasn't calling you to court because he didn't want you to think he didn't trust you to manage his and your affairs without his direction."

Carew took in a breath and let it out. "You comfort me. I have lived so long among those whose mouths speak nothing but falsehoods that I sometimes become confused by a king who tells me the truth. You have eased my mind and yet—" He paused and looked at her carefully. "I am concerned as to *why* he asked me to come to Windsor on the heels of his own departure."

"Why would you be concerned about that?" she said.

"I came here in a temper, angry because I believed him to be mocking me by requesting my attendance on you instead of him. I couldn't understand why he wouldn't speak to me in person."

"He would never mock you," Lili said. "Never. Don't you know him well enough by now not to think it?"

"Your courtesy has shamed me." Carew gazed out over the battlement, and Lili realized that he was fully exposed to the enemy across the river. She didn't feel she could tug on Carew's cloak to get him to drop down, and perhaps by now it didn't matter. The oncoming soldiers would expect at least one sentry on the wall. They didn't have to know how many additional men awaited them.

"I will beg his forgiveness next I see him. I should have known that for the king to ask for my presence at Windsor while he was absent meant no more or less than it appeared on the surface and was an indication of trust—"

"Of extreme trust," Lili interjected.

"He requested that I watch over you." Carew shook his head. "With Lord Math and Lord Ieuan at Windsor, why would he choose me? Why place you in my keeping?"

"They had many duties already, so he relieved them of the most important one by giving it to you."

Carew nodded but didn't speak, and it seemed to Lili that even an old soldier like Carew could find himself undone by a gesture from her husband.

And then she added, "It isn't so much *me* that he charged you with, is it, Lord Carew? He charged you with the protection of our son."

She didn't know why Dafydd hadn't made sure he was here when Carew arrived, but then, why would he bother? He knew that he could rely on Carew, and that was the end of the matter. It was too bad he hadn't explained all that to Carew, however.

She put a hand on his arm. "Have you ever had any reason to mistrust Dafydd's instincts?"

Carew cleared his throat. "Never."

"Then don't question them now," Lili said. "You are here because he wanted you here, and for my part, there is no knight among all of Dafydd's men whom it suits me more to have by my side tonight."

Carew bowed. "No matter what Valence brings against us, I will be your shield."

"I am grateful," Lili said.

As Lili spoke those words, the sound of marching feet finally came to her. She braced herself, eyes searching for Valence's banner, but then a shout from across the Thames split the silence. "We're friends! Let us through!"

Lili peered into the darkness beyond the river. Bevyn shouted, "Who goes there?"

"Rhodri ap Gruffydd! Uncle to the King! Hurry! Valence's men are right behind us!"

"It has to be a trap," Lili said.

Bevyn signaled that the torches on the bridge be lit. Once done, they revealed upwards of fifty men. They'd arrived at the far end of the bridge and at their head was a small man who'd removed his helmet, exposing his pure white hair. Bevyn stepped to the front of the men who guarded the city gate, a broad door with iron fittings and hinges. He looked up at Lili, who leaned through the crenel to speak to him. "I know of this Rhodri," she said, "though I've never met him."

"I have," Bevyn said. "I don't trust him."

"You trust no one," Lili said.

"I will speak to him." Bevyn lifted his chin. "Let Lord Rhodri through!"

The soldiers on the bridge gave way. Some of Bevyn's men formed a circle around him, hemming him in, and he met Bevyn at the near end of the bridge, right underneath Lili and Carew.

"I am Rhodri ap Gruffydd. I have brought fifty men to aid Windsor." He trained his eyes on the battlement, observing the people watching him through the crenels. "I believe I can be of service in this matter."

Lili had never met him, but this uncle Rhodri was one of the four brothers born to Dafydd's grandfather, Gruffydd. Owain, the eldest of Gruffydd's sons, had died in 1282 before Dafydd had come to Wales. Llywelyn, the second son, was Dafydd's father, and Dafydd, the youngest and most wayward of the brothers, had died a few years ago after allying himself with King Edward against Llywelyn. Rhodri, the third son, had never involved himself in the struggles for Welsh independence. He'd been a very small boy when his mother had taken him to England in the 1240s when Gruffydd had been imprisoned in the Tower of London. Rhodri had never returned to Wales.

In 1272, Llywelyn had paid Rhodri a large sum of money to relinquish his inheritance in Wales, an amount which by all accounts Rhodri had gladly taken. Dafydd had always meant to meet this uncle and had even invited him to his coronation last December. Rhodri hadn't come, and Dafydd had, in a way, respected him for it. When Rhodri said that he didn't want to involve himself in politics, he'd meant it, even if it meant not taking advantage of his blood relationship to the new king of England and, effectively, forgoing the new king's favor.

That he would come out of the woodwork now, however, and bring fighting men with him, defied all expectation.

Bevyn bowed. "You understand our reluctance to admit you to Windsor."

"*Y Ddraig Goch ddyry gychwyn.*"

Lili laughed in surprise at Rhodri's words, spoken loudly in fluent Welsh: *The Red Dragon will show the way*. The phrase had been cropping up here and there over the past few years in reference to Dafydd himself. Lili wouldn't have expected Rhodri to even know Welsh, much less declare his loyalty so starkly.

"If you will admit me, I will leave my men to fight alongside yours. I will be your hostage."

Bevyn glanced up at Carew, who nodded his agreement, though with narrowed eyes as he observed the former Welsh prince.

"I should greet him," Lili said.

By the time she reached the bottom step, Rhodri's men had joined Bevyn's, more than doubling the number defending the gate, and Bevyn had brought Rhodri inside Windsor. Rhodri bowed as Bevyn gestured to Lili. "Our queen, my lord."

"You fight, my lady?" Rhodri indicated her bow.

"We all must do our part," Lili said.

Rhodri bowed again. "I will stand with you on the battlement."

Lili led him up to the wall-walk, accepting Carew's offered hand that steadied her at the top. He glowered past her to Rhodri. "Why have you come?"

Rhodri waved a hand in a dismissive gesture. "I was raised by my mother to hate my brother, Llywelyn, but hate isn't in my blood for anyone but that bastard, William de Valence."

Carew blinked.

"How is that?" Lili said. Rhodri's frankness was disarming.

"My brother, Dafydd, and the late King Edward were brothers in all but name. When Edward's father brought Valence to England, over time he displaced Dafydd in Edward's affections. I could have abided that fine, since their circle of trust never included me. But Valence went out of his way to persecute me at every turn." Rhodri leaned closer, tapping the spectacles that rested on his nose. "I am no fighter. Never have been. I was a great disappointment to my family."

Lili could see how that might have been. She'd never met Senana, Llywelyn's mother, but by all accounts she had been fiery and opinionated. She'd ruled her family like a general, all but Llywelyn, who'd made his own way and refused to come to heel.

Carew was still looking daggers at Rhodri. "When you didn't come to the king's coronation—"

"That was my failure," Rhodri said. "The hate in me for Llywelyn is long gone, but the distrust remains. He bought me off, you know."

Lili and Carew both nodded.

"It was in my mind that if I put myself in the king's hands, I would find myself clapped in irons in the Tower of London."

"What changed your mind?" Lili said.

"We're not in London, are we?" Rhodri actually laughed. "But that's not it. The king has ruled with a fair hand since he took the throne, far more than any king in my experience in any land, past or present. I am neither a fool nor blind. It was time we mended this family. He tried, and I scorned his offer of peace. This is mine." He gestured beyond the battlement to his men.

"How far behind you were Valence's men?" Carew said.

"Not far. A half mile, no more." Rhodri rubbed his hands together in overt glee at his expectation of Valence's ultimate defeat.

And then men's voices roared into the darkness on the other side of the Thames River. Valence had finally come.

18

David

Seeing Cassie at the door and then Callum come through it with a gun was possibly the best moment of David's life. That was saying something, since he'd led a mostly charmed existence, and he'd had plenty of great moments. Among them were the day Lili agreed to marry him, the day his son was born, the morning his mother returned to the Middle Ages, and the day his father had told him that he was his father. At those times, however, David hadn't felt his life to be in danger. Today, from the scarlet fever, to his up-close-and-personal acquaintance with a stretcher, to his apparent abduction by a kindly eyed American in a run-down apartment on the outskirts of Cardiff, David thought he'd give the day's events a slight edge.

David had tried to let Cassie know that he appreciated her rescue of him, but it seemed that his entire body had been covered with lead weights. With the little strength he possessed, he reached over with his right hand and tugged on the lead to the IV.

"Hey!" Cassie grabbed his wrist before he could pull the needle out of his vein. "It's okay. I turned it off."

"Oh." David closed his eyes, exhausted by that small effort but glad to know that whatever poison they'd been giving him wasn't continuing to drip into his system. Before the ambulance had come and he'd been taken out of MI-5, he'd been feeling sick but functional. Since they'd strapped him to the stretcher and all hell had broken loose, he'd been unable to rise or he would have unhooked himself sooner.

"You're going to be okay," Cassie said.

"You're sure of that?" David said.

She gave him a quick smile. "Now I am."

David closed his eyes, listening to the rumble of the engine and the sudden onslaught of rain on the roof of the car. Both were incredibly comforting, making him feel safe. He also liked that night had fallen. Hiding was easier in the dark. "Where are we going?" he said.

"While we have a mystery to solve and treachery within MI-5, my first priority is your safety, my lord. I'd love to take you to Chepstow, but I'm worried about getting that far without my colleagues intercepting us. An all-points bulletin must be out by now on this SUV, even if Jones will try to protect us as long as he can," Callum said. "Do you know if any castles around here have a moat?"

David coughed a laugh, feeling more upbeat by the minute, just to be in motion and with his friends. "Our world shifting occurs when my life is in danger. I'm not sure that jumping tamely into a moat is going to cut it."

"I knew it couldn't be that easy." Callum turned his head so his voice would project to Cassie and David from the front seat. "Did your abductors tell you anything about themselves?"

"No. My sense is that they weren't MI-5, even though they were working with MI-5 agents," David said.

"Whoever they are, they have infiltrated the Security Service to the extent that they not only could evade detection leaving the Office but entering it too," Callum said. "Before we rescued you, Director Cooke claimed not to know where you were. Every ambulance has a tracking device built into it. Even if the men who abducted you turned it off, it can be turned on again remotely. The Security Service couldn't."

"Maybe David's abductors disabled it," Cassie said.

"Then the engine isn't supposed to start," Callum said.

"Maybe it wasn't a real ambulance," Cassie said.

Callum was silent for a moment. "I should have thought of that."

David felt he should have thought of that too, if his brain hadn't been currently made of mush. "What happened to Natasha? Are you saying that she's one of them?"

Callum sighed. "I don't know. We have too many unanswered questions, my lord, not the least of which is why everybody seems to be lying to me, even those people I thought were my friends."

"Welcome to my world," David said.

"Yes … well … I'm not saying that your life hasn't been in danger before from all those conniving barons back at home, but what happened today is outside of my experience," Callum said.

"Before you came to the Middle Ages, you were in charge of the Office," Cassie said. "Now you're on the outside looking in, and it looks different."

David thought Callum might take that as an insult, but instead he laughed. "Are you implying that I'm naïve, *cariad?*"

Cassie looked startled. "No-no-I didn't mean that; what I meant to say is that navigating all the politics and the lies and the shenanigans was second nature to you when you worked for MI-5. You saw the political maneuvering in Scotland a few months ago for what it was too. But this … this is different, and maybe what is so confusing is that we are dealing with another organization in addition to MI-5."

"Natasha is an agent," Callum said, "and I don't understand her at all."

"What if that's because she's working for this other organization, one with no rules, one which would abduct David and give him drugs to question him—" Cassie broke off, swallowing hard. "You didn't hear Anders—" She poked David in the shoulder, "—that's the guy who was helping us back at the apartment. He told me that the man who rented the apartment had a badge."

"What kind of badge?" Callum said.

"He didn't get a good look," Cassie said, "but Anders thought he was 'one of you,' meaning MI-5."

"He could have intended Anders to see his badge and think exactly what he did think. That way, he wouldn't ask questions or tell the apartment owner," Callum said.

"I suppose," Cassie said.

"I suggest it because, to my eyes, this is too haphazard to be government sanctioned," Callum said.

"But what if Anders is right at least a little?" Cassie said. "What if the guy was working for an American spy agency? There are enough of them these days that it could be any of a dozen. And Jones did say that the Americans wanted in."

"In?" David felt like he was walking into the middle of a conversation he'd never had but was expected to keep up with anyway.

While Callum drove steadily north, ducking around corners and pulling over to the side of the road every few hundred yards to make sure they weren't being followed, Cassie gave David a quick summary of what she and Callum had been doing and what they'd discovered since they were separated. When she finished, he related what had happened on his end, which felt like very little indeed compared to what they'd been doing.

"Let me get this straight," Cassie said. "You really do have scarlet fever, but you made it seem like you were sicker than you were to get them to take you to a hospital. They gave you a huge shot of antibiotics—"

"—it was a big one. Hurt like nobody's business." David knew he was interrupting, but he couldn't seem to control either his brain or his mouth, which kept firing off at random.

"I'm really glad they did that," Callum said, "even if it hurt."

"How would you know how to treat scarlet fever?" David said. "It isn't common in the modern world any more."

"All agents know about contagious diseases," Callum said. "Besides, if I didn't know from my work, we were given a lecture on them when I was in Afghanistan, where scarlet fever and many other infections like it are still common. The cure is one shot. You should be on the mend."

"I hope so," David said. "I feel like crap."

"You have strep throat, too. I had it once, and I remember it." Cassie, very kindly, didn't smack either of them for interrupting her, but now that they'd covered his illness, she picked up the thread of what she'd been saying. "To continue, on the way to the hospital, your ambulance is hijacked by rogue agents in MI-5 or a third party. Either way, the culprits had maybe half an hour to implement this plan."

"Half an hour, tops," David said.

"Thank God for that," Callum said. "It's why we were able to rescue you so easily."

"That was easy?" Cassie said.

David liked listening to his friends' banter. When Callum had first arrived in the Middle Ages, David had seen him as stiff and sober, which wasn't his true personality at all. In retrospect, it would have been hard for Callum to have been anything but awkward and uncomfortable, given that he'd been thrown into the deep end of the proverbial pool, what with the various murders, weddings, and coronations going on at the time and the fact that he didn't speak any language that anyone but a handful of people understood. Callum had also been suffering from PTSD, which had initially been made worse by suddenly finding himself in 1288 Britain.

"Suppose the man—the American—really is CIA or NSA or even Homeland Security," Callum said. "Suppose he convinced Natasha to work with him. Just because we arrived in the twenty-first century today doesn't mean he couldn't have been planning how to get his hands on David, or whoever came here next, for months."

"Point taken." David rubbed both eyes with the heels of his hands. Callum's obvious concern was causing his own heart to beat faster. "Isn't that what you said MI-5 had done, Callum? That they've been working on how to deal with one of us ever since Mom and Dad returned home with you?"

"Yes," Callum said.

"I like the Americans for your abduction, though," Cassie said.

"You've watched too many movies," David said. "Governments, especially the American one, are rarely shown in a positive light."

"True. But that doesn't mean the CIA isn't involved," Cassie said.

"Why would Natasha betray her country to the CIA?" Callum said. "What could they possibly offer her?"

"A lot of money," Cassie said.

"It would have to be walking-away money," David said. "Not impossible, I suppose."

"We're talking about time travel," Cassie said, "so already you know that we're in the realm of the impossible. And Jones did say that the Americans weren't happy with MI-5 for not sharing."

"MI-5 is starting to seem like the lesser of two evils," David said.

"Evil is right," Cassie said, though only to David and not loud enough for Callum to hear over the engine noise and the pattering of the rain.

David touched her arm. Given that all of her suspicions had so far proved right, it was hard to fault her cynicism. Then he spoke louder so as not to keep Callum out of their conversation. "Don't forget that we still have the small matter of my illness to deal with and perhaps some kind of antidote to whatever that American gave me." David checked the IV drip to make sure it hadn't spontaneously turned itself on again. "Whatever they gave me is making me feel even sicker than when I just had scarlet fever. If I didn't before, I think now that I really do need a hospital. And probably one with good security. Maybe some big bodyguards you can trust, Callum."

Cassie leaned across David and tried to read the writing on the IV drip bag. "It says *Rohypnol* and then in parentheses, *flunitrazepam*, whatever that is."

"To use the American term, you've been roofied," Callum said.

"Great." David rested his head back against the pillow. "And to think all I got out of it was a headache. Though ..." He shifted uncomfortably. "Does it change anything that I can't feel my feet very well?"

"What was that?" Callum swerved the SUV, almost running it into a parked car on the side of the road before correcting the steering.

"He said he can't feel his feet," Cassie said. "He doesn't look good either; he's a little green around the gills."

"Roofies shouldn't be doing this," Callum said. "What else did they give you, David?"

"I don't remember." David rubbed his forehead. He was feeling hot again. "I think back in the ambulance someone mentioned *Roxanol*."

"Bloody hell." Callum executed a U-turn, causing Cassie to lose her balance and fall on top of David's chest. He put up a hand to contain her, but he was weak and could do little more than push at her arm. She reached for the handle above the window to right herself. Callum flipped on the vehicle's siren and screamed down the road.

Little bits of scenery flew by the windows above David's head: trees and the tops of houses and apartment buildings, lit by streetlights and distorted by the raindrops on the window. He couldn't see much out the rear window besides the headlights of other cars receding into the distance. He didn't know in which direction Callum had been driving, and thus he didn't know where they were going now.

Cassie cupped her hands around her mouth and called up to Callum: "What's going on?" The sirens even drowned out the sound of the rain.

"*Roxanol* is an opiate," Callum said.

"And that's bad?" Cassie said.

David twitched his legs, grateful that he wasn't paralyzed from the waist down, and concentrated really hard on wiggling his toes.

"It's reacting with the *flunitrazepam*." Callum swerved through traffic, which was thinner than before. "Together, they can suppress respiration."

"So he stops breathing?" Cassie said.

David looked up at the ceiling. As soon as Cassie spoke, he found he was having trouble filling his lungs. He wanted to say something, but nothing came out.

Cassie gripped his hand. "Don't try to talk. Just keep breathing."

Several tense minutes passed before a red 'emergency unit' sign appeared in the back window, indicating a hospital entrance. Callum braked with a jerk, scrambled out of his seat, and darted around to the rear of the SUV, by which time Cassie had the door open. Medical personnel flocked to them, and a minute later David was being wheeled into the hospital. He was really getting tired of this stretcher. It felt like his back had been glued to it.

"You saved my life," David said to Callum as he jogged beside the stretcher down a long corridor.

"I'm just glad we got to you in time," Callum said. "All that planning involved in your abduction and instead they almost killed you."

19

September, 1289

Lili

Valence had been just as tricky as they should have expected, which was to say, he'd outdone himself this time. Over the last few months, he'd made a habit of concocting more and more elaborate plans and ruses; the most dangerous ones—the ones that they knew about—had ended by tripping him up badly and tangling him in his own net. Lili prayed that the same would be true this time, but right now, with five hundred men racing towards her, she didn't feel very hopeful.

"Dear God. Here they come." Carew held his sword at his side, ready to defend the town. He wasn't needed yet, not on the wall-walk. Soon enough, if the defenders were routed, Valence's men would be able to bring their ladders to bear on the walls, and then he would have more than enough to occupy him. Lili had an arrow resting in her bow, ready for the moment Bevyn told her to release it.

Valence's men surged onto the bridge across the Thames. The town's defenders had begun by standing at the far end, but faced with the rush and heavy press of Valence's men, the foremost defenders fell back, pushing at those behind them to make room for their retreat. As the leaders of the enemy force gained ground, those in the rear of Valence's army cheered and pushed forward with more force.

Meanwhile, the defenders screeched at one another and gave way, at first step-by-step and then all at once. The defense of the bridge collapsed completely, and the men came racing back to the Windsor side of the bridge in a panic. Bevyn's cries of, "Steady! Steady!" fell on deaf ears.

Now that the assault had come, there was no point in keeping the lights doused; men with torches ran back and forth below Lili in front of the gate, shouting at each other. Lili couldn't make out most of their words, and it seemed that half the men in their army had lost their senses.

Hardly ten heartbeats later, the last of the defenders reached the near end of the bridge. At that point, they calmed, most appearing to return to their right minds. With a few barked orders, the company regrouped and formed their lines again. Behind them, the city gate, which had opened to admit a few men as they retreated, closed and remained closed.

Bevyn exhorted his men, calling to them to *be* men, to uphold their honor and their duty. Honor, as he well knew, would do none of them any good if they were dead, but his words seemed to achieve their goal. Before Valence's men were halfway across the bridge, the defenders had created a solid wall of shields in front of the city gate, leaving forty feet of open space between them and the bridge for Valence's men to fill.

"That's more like it," Rhodri said, under his breath. "I've never seen my men run like that."

"They are outnumbered," Lili said, though she wasn't sure why she was defending them. She'd been surprised by their panic too.

Valence's men slowed as they approached the end of the bridge, those in the lead showing concern at the sudden discipline in their opponents and their near total silence. The press of men behind the leaders was too great, however—and victory too near—for them to stop. Gathering themselves again, they poured off the bridge in a rush, swords and axes raised high and faces contorted as they screamed their war cries to the skies.

Bevyn's men held their ground. They didn't race to meet the oncoming soldiers, even though (as Lili thought about it) that might have been a better plan. A few men posted at the end of the bridge could have held it for a while, since Valence's men couldn't outflank them in so small a space. By that measure, Bevyn's force outnumbered Valence's three to one. But that hadn't been Bevyn's choice, and Lili shrugged her criticisms away. She raised her bow and aimed her first arrow at the foremost of Valence's men, determined to take down the leader if she could. She took in a breath and held it. For a moment, battle—or at least the idea of it—held the two sides suspended, and then—

Kaboom!

Between one breath and the next, the bridge across the Thames River disintegrated, along with the two hundred men who'd been on it. Although Lili wasn't close enough to the blast to be knocked flat, it shocked her enough that she might have fallen off the wall-walk if Carew hadn't grabbed her around the waist and spun her back to safety. No wonder Bevyn had looked so confident, even triumphant, when she'd last looked into his face. She was annoyed that he hadn't warned her about what he and Math had planned. She eyed Carew, who looked self-satisfied himself. "You knew? Why didn't anyone tell me!"

Rhodri was standing on the wall-walk with his mouth open.

Carew glanced at him and then at Lili. "I thought Math had told you."

She would take up her grievance with Math later, though it may well have been that each of the three men—Math, Carew, and Bevyn—had assumed that one of the others had revealed the plan to her. Lili shook her head to stop her ears from ringing and gazed at the carnage before her. Those of Valence's men who'd crossed the bridge now found themselves caught between the city gate and the Thames, outnumbered, their hearing ruined by the blast, and pieces of the wooden bridge (and, horrifyingly, their companions too) falling from the sky.

Bevyn's men had known what was going to happen, even if Lili hadn't, and in retrospect, their acting had been worthy of Easter mummers. They'd convinced Lili of their fear and equally of their change of heart, and though they must have been shocked by the force of the blast, their foreknowledge allowed them to recover more quickly than their enemy could. With a command from Bevyn, Windsor's defenders attacked with a roar to match the confident one Valence's men had cried when they'd seen the city before them and thought it lightly defended.

Lili's vantage point allowed her to look right down on the men as they fought. She'd seen men and boys spar with wooden swords in courtyards of castles from here to Dolwyddelan, she'd fought at Painscastle, and she'd been in skirmishes since, but she'd never seen hand-to-hand like this. It was a slaughter. Bevyn called up to her from below, but she was so focused on what she was seeing that she didn't hear him until Carew touched her shoulder. "Lili, it's time."

Bevyn waved at her. "Put the men to work, Lili."

Shaking her head to clear it, she raised her bow to draw the attention of the dozen archers along the wall-walk. "Pick your targets carefully! They're packed in close down there, and we don't want to hit our own men!"

The archers nodded. They had heard Bevyn too and were already getting ready. Taking Lili's warning to heart, within a few moments they had begun loosing their arrows at soldiers coming out of the water on the other side of the Thames, as well as at the remainder of Valence's army, still some two hundred at least, milling about on the far bank. Lili herself was picking her targets carefully on this side of the Thames, trying to relieve the pressure on the men defending the gate, which still needed defending.

In order to achieve the maximum effect of the explosion, Bevyn had allowed fifty enemy soldiers to reach their side of the bridge before he blew it. Their swords and axes hadn't dulled just because they were alone. If anything, they fought with greater ferocity.

Lili focused on one large man with a thick beard and black hair. He seemed to have unusual strength and had cut down three of Bevyn's men before they had time to raise their own axes. At the moment, he was fighting a man who'd lost his helmet. Lili stared at the soldier, recognizing the blond head and fine features of Henry Percy. The boy *had* traded his pen for a sword, though Lili was stunned to find him fighting here and now, a novice among more experienced men.

Before she could bring her bow to bear, the enemy fighter drove his axe at Henry with such force that he lost his sword. As Henry scrambled back, Lili loosed an arrow that missed the attacker's head by inches, the arrow flying past him and landing in the mud of the riverbank.

"No!" Lili hadn't realized she had shouted until Carew's voice came softly in her ear.

"Focus, Lili. You have time."

She loosed a second arrow that took the man in the center of his mass. He fell, but as he did so, she caught sight of Percy on the ground nearby. She couldn't tell in the torchlight if the blood on his tunic was his own or another's. She leaned far over the edge of the battlement, her eyes searching, but then Carew hauled her back. "Keep shooting. Lord Rhodri and I will see to the boy."

"What? Yes, of course." Rhodri followed Carew down the steps.

Lili nodded, knowing—and maybe for the first time believing—that her place was not in the press of men below. She forced the death before her out of her mind, along with her fear for Bevyn and Percy and Carew—and all the men whose wives and daughters would miss them if they didn't return tonight—and returned her attention to picking off the last of Valence's fighters. It had been only a quarter of an hour since the bridge had exploded, and the battle had become a rout. The few remaining of Valence's company battling before the gate decided all at once that retreat was wiser than fighting and chose a quick dive in the Thames over death. Some of them could even swim.

Another quarter of an hour and Lili was out of arrows. She'd turned away to search for the cart that held the extras when she was stopped in her tracks by Anna, who looked up at her from the bottom step, a grave expression on her face.

"What is it? Does Henry Percy live?"

"Carew and Rhodri got him out in time," Anna said. "He lost blood, but we've sewn up his arm. He should be fine, particularly if the penicillin paste that I made to smear on wounds works. That's not it."

"Then—" Lili almost stumbled down the steps in her haste, her heart leaping into her throat at the thought that something was wrong with Arthur.

Anna caught Lili's arms, holding on firmly. "Papa sent a pigeon from Cardiff. There was a storm in the Irish Sea. Humphrey de Bohun's ship was driven back to Wales, but he fears that David's ship went down."

Lili's hands clenched around her bow. "It's not true. It can't be."

Anna moved in closer, holding onto Lili as if she would run away screaming if she didn't. "Papa wouldn't have sent the message if he didn't think it could be true. We all know that anything can happen at night in a storm. David could arrive in Ireland in two days, safe. We'll need to hear from Clare before we really worry."

Dafydd didn't have any pigeons that had been trained to fly across the sea. It meant that if Dafydd did arrive in Ireland, Lili wouldn't know it until he sent word on the next ship or finished his business with Valence there (not that there would be any business to finish given the fact that Valence had come to Windsor) and returned himself.

"You must come with me to the castle," Anna said.

Lili gestured towards the wall. "I was just—"

"You are the Queen of England and the mother of the heir to the throne," Anna said. "It's just clean-up work now. Bevyn can manage here without you."

Lili opened her mouth to argue with Anna, but the fierceness in her sister-in-law's eyes had her reconsidering. Anna's earlier confession had tugged at Lili's heartstrings. Anna hadn't grown up in this world, but she'd suffered losses along with everyone else since she'd arrived. In private, Lili had wondered to Dafydd how his family could have chosen to stay in the Middle Ages when they had a choice not to. Him she understood. Not only was Llywelyn his father, but even a blind man could see that the role of prince, and then king, was one he'd been born to play. Anna, however, for all that she and Math loved each other, had given up a life in the modern world where she would be educated and free.

Lili longed to see that world. Dafydd had almost taken her in the midst of Arthur's birth. The labor had been a long one, nearly two days with hardly any progress. Dafydd was within moments of scooping her up and jumping with her from the highest tower in the castle when she'd succeeded in birthing their son. Arthur had been turned wrong, face-up. Bronwen said that in the modern world, a physician might have cut her open to take the baby. In this world, if not for a last minute position change that gave her renewed strength, she might have died in childbirth.

Anna hadn't been able to attend the birth, but she'd heard about it; the careful way she'd looked at Lili when she'd arrived at Windsor, and the lengthy embrace, should have warned Lili about how Anna was feeling now.

But Lili didn't believe for a moment that Dafydd was dead. She put her arm around Anna. "He's okay, Anna. I know he is. If you look into your heart, you'll know it too."

"That's not very scientific," Anna said, though she managed a small smile.

"See," Lili said. "I'm right, aren't I?"

Anna took in a deep breath and let it out. Then she nodded. "I can believe it if you can."

"It isn't that I'm cavalier about death—my own or anyone else's," Lili said, "but I do understand it in a way that's hard for you. My mother died, you know."

"I know," Anna said. "I didn't tell you about David because I don't think you can fight. This isn't about that."

"I believe you," Lili said. "But you need to know that I'm not leaving because I'm the Queen of England. I'm leaving because I love you, and even if your feelings aren't rational or logical or helpful, you still feel them, and I don't need to add to your pain."

"Besides, we've won this particular battle," Anna said.

Lili wrinkled her nose at her sister-in-law; she was right. Then Lili glanced ahead to see Carew walking towards them. He had blood on his tunic, but his long stride and posture told her that the blood belonged to someone else, probably to Henry Percy.

"Thank you for rescuing Henry," Lili said as he halted in front of them.

He bowed at the waist. "The boy fought bravely, for all that he has little experience in battle. He was trained well; he just wasn't ready to face a giant."

"He was very contrite once he was able to speak," Anna said, turning with Carew and Lili back towards the entrance to the castle, which rose above them, as yet untouched by war.

"He has even less experience than I," Lili said, unable to resist pointing out that fact.

"Which means that he shouldn't have been where he was," Carew said. "I will speak to Bevyn and Math as to how it came about that he was fighting there."

Anna stopped and put a hand on Lili's arm. "I want you to know—"

But whatever Anna was going to say was lost in a sudden uproar from the battlement. "Look out!"

Fifty flaming arrows arched above their heads coming from the south side of the town, and the trio dove for safety to the base of a nearby wall. The arrows fell among the shops and huts of the village. The barrage was followed by a second and then a third.

"I thought they didn't have archers!" Anna said.

"Valence must have held them back until he saw how his first assault went," Carew said.

As it hadn't gone well, Valence might be putting all the more weight into this attack. A fourth flight came, adding to the chaos in the streets. "The infirmary!" Lili gasped to see a spout of flame rise up from the low building beside the Abbey.

"Come on." Anna set off at a run, smartly keeping to the shelter of buildings not yet damaged instead of heading directly towards the church. Lili followed, with Carew protesting, even as he kept his arm around her shoulders. He forced her to run at a low crouch, as if that would prevent an arrow from hitting her.

"Let others see to the sick!" Carew shouted ahead to Anna. "I must get you to safety."

Yet another flight of arrows soared over the wall and came to land on the rooftops around them. Villagers hurried back and forth, bringing buckets that they'd filled in preparation for exactly this eventuality. Fortunately, with the river so close, they had plenty of water.

The roof of the stone Abbey was made of slate, so it hadn't yet been harmed. The infirmary hadn't been so lucky. In the few minutes it had taken for Anna and Lili to cross half the distance from the gatehouse, fire consumed the roof. With a blaze and a crash, it collapsed in on itself. Anna screamed; Lili raced to her and wrapped her arms around her, stopping her from getting any closer.

"All those people." Anna bent her head, tears coursing down her cheeks.

Carew wrapped his arms around both of them. "I'm taking you to the castle." He tugged hard, and both women had all but consented to go with him when Anna spied one of the nuns, her veil missing and her normally undyed robe blackened with soot. Her name was Joan, and she was the herbalist at the Abbey. Although she was well into middle age, she'd been one of the first to embrace Anna's new methods.

"Lady Anna!" Joan picked up her skirts and ran towards them.

"They're all dead—" Anna choked on her words.

"No! No, my lady! All is well!" Joan said. "We had already moved them into the church for their safety. Because the infirmary was separate, we didn't worry about saving it. That's why it burned so fast."

Anna listened with her hand to her heart. Then she threw her arms around the nun. "Thank you!"

Joan stepped back, renewing the distance between them. Anna's hug had been typical for the Americans but was much more exuberant than most English were used to.

"We'll keep them safe. Don't you worry." Joan looked past Anna to Lili. "Why aren't you on the wall, my queen? Surely you would be of better use up there than down here?"

"Isn't that what I've been saying?" Lili said.

"Excuse us." Carew tugged on Lili's arm. "We are all needed elsewhere."

20

Callum

"**I** need you in here, Callum." Lady Jane tipped her head towards an empty hospital room. It had been nearly twenty-four hours since Callum and Cassie had brought David in, and Callum was beginning to think he might lose his mind with the waiting and doing nothing but watching David sleep. Thus Lady Jane's summons, as perfunctory as her manner was, came as a relief.

Callum had been hoping for a chance to speak with her. He put a gentle hand on Cassie's shoulder to indicate that he was going and followed Lady Jane into the room she'd chosen. It was three doors down from the one in which David slept. They hadn't needed to intubate him, but he hadn't spoken since they'd brought him in. From what Callum could gather from the attending physicians, they were concerned he might not ever wake again.

That wasn't to be tolerated. For now, however, Callum could do nothing for David. Lady Jane, on the other hand, had some explaining to do, and it looked like he was finally going to get some answers.

Once inside the room, she turned on the fan in the private loo and indicated that he should follow her inside. It was more than a little awkward to be crammed into the small space between the sink and the tiny shower, but he braced his shoulder against the wall and composed himself to listen.

Lady Jane closed the door. "We can't be overheard in here."

Callum folded his arms across his chest and waited for her to explain what she wanted. Lady Jane would tell him what she wanted him to know in her own time.

"I have arranged for documents, detailing what I know and what I suspect, to be sent to individuals in the highest levels of government *and* the press should something happen to me," she said without preamble, raising the stakes as high as they could be raised, short of nuclear war.

Callum dropped his arms to his sides. "You believe yourself to be in danger?"

"In the past month, there have been three attempts on my life that I know of. Each was intended to look like an accident. I might not be so lucky with the next one. I feel them closing in on me. My movements are being monitored, along with my email and whom I speak to. They'll be after you next. I'm putting your life in danger even now if someone notices that we are both absent at the same time."

"Murdering a director of the Security Service is no small act," Callum said. "How can you be sure—"

Lady Jane was already shaking her head before he could finish his sentence. "Ever since you left us, the influence of special interests on the Security Service, Whitehall, and Parliament has increased with every week that passed. At first, I thought it was no more than business as usual, but as the months went by, it became clear that the corruption goes to the highest levels. Perhaps all the way to the top, though I have been unable to confirm that."

"You're speaking of the Prime Minister?" Callum said.

"To Downing Street," Lady Jane said. "Beyond that, I cannot say."

"And you've chosen to speak to me because … ?"

Lady Jane gave him a sharp look. "You are the only one whose record is beyond reproach. You've spent the last ten months in the Middle Ages and thus are uncorrupted. Not to mention *incorruptible*. Everyone knows you would never sell yourself, not to another government, not to corporate interests, no matter how much money was offered."

Callum couldn't argue with that.

"You've proved yourself once again by rescuing David and returning here with him," Lady Jane said, "though I wish you'd phoned me so we could have arranged for a more anonymous admittance."

"I didn't know if I could trust you," Callum said. "I deliberately made our arrival as public as possible."

"That's honest, I suppose," Lady Jane said. "Do you trust me now?"

"I believe you," Callum said, "but all I know for certain is that I need to get David away from here as quickly as possible."

"There's a safe house—"

"I don't mean to a safe house," Callum said.

Lady Jane pursed her lips. "You intend to return with him to the Middle Ages."

"I'm sorry, but his well-being is my first priority, and what you've just told me only confirms my worst fears and increases my urgency. He can never be safe here."

"If I guarantee his safety—"

"You've just said that you fear for your own life. How can you guarantee his safety when you can't ensure your own?" Callum didn't mean to sound harsh, but the moment called for truth. He was seeing with a clarity that he'd been missing the whole time they'd been here.

Lady Jane didn't continue the argument. "I have to tell you that things are coming to a head. I've laid a trap that may well cost me my life."

"Director—"

"No. Hear me out. I've been laboring alone for months, and it's a relief to tell someone. Natasha was only one of several agents whom I fear have betrayed us."

"Driscoll among them?" Callum said.

"I assume it, though I have no direct evidence of his betrayal beyond impression and instinct. My sense is that Natasha and Driscoll don't—or rather, didn't—know of the other's involvement. In regard to Natasha, she did what she set out to do, which was to deliver David. She's done a bunk, and I don't expect to see her again."

"To whom did she deliver David? Can you tell me who's behind all this?"

"They're called the Dunland Group: defense contractors with their own private security force," Lady Jane said.

Callum sucked on his teeth. "They made a fortune in Iraq, working for us as well as the Americans."

"If I didn't already know they were behind these events, I know it now," Lady Jane said. "The facial recognition just came back on the two men you subdued. They are known employees of the Dunland Group."

"That's why you're telling me this now." Callum nodded. "Those faces are all but public now, and with that fact, the Dunland Group will know that you know of their involvement—and that others do too, people who can do something about them."

"The Dunland Group will swing into full damage control. I imagine that the men you encountered will be disavowed as a rogue operation," Lady Jane said. "All the politicians they've bought will pray nobody noticed them pocketing their pound notes and clamor for an investigation."

"Everyone implicated will be wondering what else you know and whom you've told," Callum said.

Lady Jane bit her lip. It was the first time Callum had ever seen her uncertain. "It's not just you I've put in danger. It's Cassie too."

Callum licked his lips. He'd needed to know what Lady Jane knew and was glad of the information, but the repercussions of the Dunland Group's actions—and this conversation—stretched out in all directions. "We need to move David."

Lady Jane shook her head. "He cannot be moved, not yet, not until he wakes."

"If he wakes," Callum said.

"As long as he remains unconscious, he buys us time," Lady Jane said. "After that, I will be forced to bring him to London, at which point he will be out of my hands."

"That cannot happen," Callum said. "You need to release what information you have *now*."

"No," Lady Jane said. "I don't have solid evidence yet. It's enough to cause a scandal, yes, but not enough to bring the culprits down. I need a few more days, that's all, to bring my plans to fruition."

"You're going to get yourself killed, and us too," Callum said. "I don't know that I cared as much before about that as I do now."

"I'm working on alternatives," Lady Jane said. "You need to stay by David's side until then."

"What alternatives?"

"That's my headache," Lady Jane said. "I will do my job."

"And damn the consequences?" Callum barked a laugh. "David and Cassie are my first priority, not the Security Service, but I swear to you that I will do *my* job as long as it is possible to do it."

"I would expect no less."

21

September, 2017

David

David woke to quiet darkness. He was in a hospital, but whether on the same day he'd been rescued or a different day, he couldn't have begun to guess. He didn't see a clock anywhere in the room to tell him the time. For all he knew, he could have slept for a week. Living in the Middle Ages had given him a better natural time-sense than he'd had as a kid, but the transition to the twenty-first century—and probably his illness and the drugs—had thrown it out of whack ever since he got here. If he had to guess, he would have said that the time was early evening. It was dark outside but not past midnight.

The curtains in his room had been left open, and for a while David studied the spray of rain on the window and the little rivers the water made down the glass. The drops sparkled in the light coming from outside: streetlights, or maybe spotlights shining from outside the hospital. For the first time since before he left medieval Cardiff,

David felt like his mind was clear. He could breathe easily too, and his throat hurt no worse than if he had a mild cold. The shot the medic had given him had hurt like hell, but it seemed to have done the trick.

Cassie reclined in a chair beside the bed, between him and the outside window. Near the end of his bed, the door to the corridor was open. He had a private room, or at least one that could be made private. A full bank of windows starting at waist height and going all the way to the ceiling lined the interior wall of the room, separating him from the corridor. Blinds covered the top half of the windows, but he could see through the gap between the bottom of the blind and the window frame to a cluster of people standing in the hallway.

Unfortunately, he couldn't hear what they were saying, though from the apparent twitchiness of those involved, the conversation was heated. Callum was tall enough that the blind cut off his head from David's sight, but David would have known him anywhere by the sword in his hand. He must have retrieved it from wherever he'd stashed it. He certainly hadn't been wearing it earlier when he'd come through the apartment door. Some of David's tension eased. By holding the sword, Callum was declaring his loyalty and what he stood for.

Everyone, including Callum, wore business suits, trench coats, and ties, even the one woman. If her stabbing finger was any indication, it was she who was in charge. David guessed that she was Director Cooke. Her build was all wrong for Natasha, who was the only other woman David knew of who was involved in his case, not that MI-5 might not have dozens of female agents. He just hadn't seen any others.

David turned his head to look over at Cassie, who opened her eyes. He wouldn't have put it past her to have a sixth sense about people watching her.

"Hey," he said.

"Hey yourself." Cassie shifted in her seat. "God, this chair is uncomfortable."

"How can you say that after living in the Middle Ages for five years?"

"Nobody pretends that you can sleep in a medieval chair," Cassie said, "though that rocker you had made for Lili is pretty nice."

"How long have I been asleep?" David said.

"A long time," Cassie said. "We brought you in around nine in the evening yesterday, and it's almost that time again, though a day later."

David pressed the 'up' button on the bed to raise himself to a sitting position and pulled up his knees too.

"Can you feel your feet?" Cassie said.

David wiggled his toes. "Yes." He looked at her warily. "Is there some reason I shouldn't be able to?"

"They were numb," Cassie said. "How much do you remember?"

"Apparently, not a lot." David thought back. "I do remember the interrogation room and seeing you two come through the apartment door. But nothing after that."

"I guess that's not surprising, given the drugs they gave you," Cassie said. "Fortunately, the man who abducted you had just gotten started when we rescued you or you would be in a lot worse shape than you are."

David swallowed hard, unnerved to hear how close it had been. "Thank you, if I neglected to say it before."

"You are most welcome," Cassie said. "Clearly, you're feeling better."

"The medic wasn't kidding when he said the antibiotic shot would work. My throat is only a tiny bit sore and my head is clear." David flexed his shoulders and arms, pleased to discover that at the moment *nothing hurt*. Triumph shot through him at the knowledge that this wasn't over yet. Not by a long shot. "And I'm hungry."

"I'm sure that can be remedied soon enough," Cassie said, "though hospital food is nothing to write home about."

"Tell me what I missed," David said.

Cassie grumbled. "I did this already," but then she obliged with a long soliloquy on everything that had happened while they'd been apart.

David felt like he'd slept through three-quarters of a movie and missed all the best parts. He gestured towards the door. "What's the argument about in the hallway?"

"They don't know you're awake yet, of course, but they've been talking nonstop since we brought you here about what to do with you. Callum is being treated like the hero he is, so we're good there, but skeptics in the Home Office are having a field day with how screwed up today—" She glanced at a small digital clock on a side table which David hadn't noticed until now. It said 8:30, "—or rather, yesterday, got."

"Is one of them Smythe?" David said.

"No," Cassie said. "While you were asleep, Smythe left for London on Lady Jane's orders. He was to brief representatives from the Home Office on the situation in person."

"Lady Jane?" David said.

"Callum's name for Director Cooke," Cassie said.

"Why *in person?*" David said.

"Probably for his own self-aggrandizement, but Lady Jane isn't trusting any open form of communication, even a secure cell phone, with your whereabouts," Cassie said. "That woman has ice water for blood."

David peered up under the blinds. "They really ought to include me in this conversation."

"You're not very good at letting other people take charge of things, are you?" Cassie said with a laugh.

"It hasn't been my experience that doing so generally turns out well," David said. "I am the King of England, after all."

"Oh sure," Cassie said, "but I bet you were this way before. In fact, I've talked to Anna, so I know you were."

Even though David hadn't seen his sister for months—hadn't even met her new baby—Cassie and Callum had traveled to Shrewsbury and then into Wales to meet the rest of their new family. That was after they got married and had returned from Orkney, which hadn't turned out to be much of a honeymoon. While David and his companions had thwarted several of Valence's schemes over the last year, he didn't know how many he'd failed to thwart. The rogue baron couldn't be allowed to roam free any longer.

What David wasn't so sure about was what he was going to do with Valence once he captured him. All of his counselors insisted that the man had to die. They thought Valence's fellow conspirators, whom David still had locked up in the Tower of London, should be executed too. David wasn't yet medieval enough to feel right about ordering the death of a man in cold blood. He was probably king enough to do it if he had to, but he didn't know what it would take to live with himself afterwards.

All of this was presuming, in Valence's case, that they could take him alive. Or that they could take him at all. If Valence knew what was good for him, he would have left Ireland once he realized David was on his way and sailed for America. Never mind that its existence was a discredited Welsh myth or a Viking rumor. He should know that nothing was going to stop David now. Not even being displaced in time.

That dilemma was for another day, however, and another place. David had to get better, though he realized as he swallowed again how much better he already was, and then get himself back to the Middle Ages. *How* he was going to get back was the only problem that interested him currently. He pursed his lips as he observed the group in the corridor again. He had to get past all of them to make it happen.

Fortunately, he had allies in Cassie and Callum, and maybe he would garner a bit more sympathy now from Lady Jane and the others than he'd been given before. He was a valuable commodity. They didn't want to let him go, but he'd been badly mistreated on their watch. Maybe that fact was something David could use to his advantage. It was a mercenary idea and not entirely like him, but he had a kingdom to run and a wife and child he desperately needed to see again.

The cluster of people talking in the hallway broke up, and Callum came through the door to the room, pushing it wider with his shoulder. He saw David sitting up and smiled. Cassie sat up straighter and said, "You are ridiculously handsome when you smile."

Ignoring his wife, except for the fact that his smile broadened further, Callum put his heels together and bowed. "Sire."

David waved a hand. "Shut up and tell me what's happening."

Callum took a deep breath. "A great deal, none of it good. You've given some people a bad headache. The threat is not just from outside the Security Service but within it too."

"Which makes it even worse," David said. "Natasha wasn't the only one?"

"No," Callum said.

"And she hasn't come in?" David said.

"Neither she nor the ambulance men nor the police officer who drove her away. Who knows how many more conspirators we have to contend with." Callum straightened David's blanket until the edges were perfectly aligned. "We've spent the last twenty-four hours looking for all of them."

"I'm sorry about Natasha, Callum," Cassie said.

"Do we know yet who the men in the apartment were?" David said.

"Both men are ex-military black-ops, working now for the private security firm, the Dunland Group. It has ties to defense contractors in the US, UK, and Europe."

"So not CIA," Cassie said.

"If they were secretly working for the CIA or any other agency, the Americans aren't claiming them," Callum said.

Cassie slouched further in the uncomfortable chair so she could put her feet up on David's bed and cross them at the ankles. "Would the Americans claim them if they were theirs?"

"It is customary to acknowledge your own agent when talking to foreign agencies who are your allies." Callum leaned against the wall between the two windows, folding his arms across his chest and crossing his ankles in a mimicry of Cassie. "Admittedly, the Americans are at least as likely as the French to lie to us."

David fiddled with his remote control to alter his position. He shifted so he could see his friends better and contemplated getting out of bed. He wondered how badly that would freak out his guardians. "What would a defense contractor want with me?"

"The same thing everyone wants, David," Cassie said. "What makes you tick."

Lady Jane pushed through the door, looking not at David but at Callum. "We need to move him. Now."

Callum straightened against the wall. "What's happened?"

Lady Jane came a few steps further into the room and stopped at the end of David's bed. "I apologize on behalf of the Security Service and the British government for what befell you when you were in our care. We didn't do our job."

"Thank you," David said.

"We will do everything in our power to ensure your safety going forward." She waved a hand. "Get him dressed."

It was unmistakably an order and not directed at him, but David swung his legs out of bed anyway. He couldn't get out of here soon enough. Cassie crossed to the closet and opened the door. David was pleased to see his duffel propped upright against the back wall inside.

"What have you not yet said?" Callum said.

Lady Jane closed the door to the room. "The Home Office is sending a helicopter to collect David and bring him to London."

"Already?" David said.

Lady Jane looked at her watch. "It will arrive within the hour."

"Do you trust her?" David asked Callum. The time for pretense appeared to be over.

"I guess I do," Callum said.

"Then I'd better take this out." David gingerly removed the IV needle from his arm.

"Did that hurt?" Cassie dropped the duffel bag to the floor at David's feet.

"I expected it to, but it didn't." David crouched by the bag and pulled out its contents, setting them aside one-by-one until he found his breeches. He tapped the packet of papers that had been at the bottom of the duffel. "Thank you for bringing it all." He stood to shove a foot into one leg of his breeches.

"You wouldn't have printed out that lot if you didn't need it," Callum said.

David might have been embarrassed to have two women in the room while he dressed, but it seemed silly to worry about modesty under the circumstances. Lady Jane faced away, going to the door with Callum to peer into the corridor. David glanced at the windows in the inner wall and saw nobody there.

"Did you order everyone to leave?" David tugged his shirt on over his head.

"I made sure they'd be occupied for the next few minutes," Lady Jane said. "Time enough to find our way to my vehicle downstairs."

David stopped, his hands to the ties of his shirt. "Isn't that a huge risk for you?"

"Even if it is, I'm past caring," Lady Jane said. "The time has come for risk-taking."

Callum pointed at David with his chin. "Put on that vest."

"What?" David said. "Where?"

Callum snapped his fingers, indicating the Kevlar vest poking out of the duffel. "That vest. Put it on."

David looked at it dubiously, but Cassie picked it up.

"What about you two?" David said.

"We're not anybody's target," Callum said, leaving the door. "We don't know what situation we might be getting into. You have no armor so you need to wear the vest. For all our sakes. It has ceramic plates in key locations that will even stop an arrow."

"How nice for me," David said, but took the vest from Cassie and held it to his chest. Then he looked up. "I couldn't agree with Director Cooke more, by the way, that the time has come for risk-taking. Why don't we go up to the roof right now and jump off?"

"Do you think you're ready for that?" Cassie said.

David looked at his friends with a completely calm expression. "I have my clothes. Five minutes and we're gone."

"You're really willing to risk your life, jumping off a ten-story building, on the off-chance you'll be transported to the Middle Ages?" Lady Jane said.

"What choice do I have? Last time, I got home by causing a car wreck. This world-shifting thing only works when my life is in danger." David gestured to his bed. "Almost dying of a bad drug interaction is apparently not good enough."

"We would have to jump with you," Cassie said.

"I understand your difficulty." David rubbed at his jaw and saw blood trickling down his arm. Callum noticed it too and handed David a tissue from a box on the side table. David pressed it to the cut. He was probably lucky the vein hadn't opened more. "I do. I just don't see an alternative. *I need to get home!*"

"He's right," Cassie said. "Instead of going with Director Cooke to her car, we could slip up to the roof."

"We could take the car and try the balcony at Chepstow, like I suggested before," Callum said.

"Even if we could reach it without getting caught, I'm afraid that's not going to be enough," David said. "Believe me, I'm glad it worked—both times—when my mom and dad jumped. If it hadn't, they would have lived through it. I just don't feel like that's going to be good enough for me."

"What's the downside of trying?" Cassie said.

"We get wet," Callum said, "and end up in the Wye River."

David sat on the edge of the bed and clasped his hands in front of his mouth, looking at them both over his fingers. He didn't say anything. They could argue with him until they were blue in the face, but it wasn't going to change his mind.

"I'm willing to risk my life for you, but ..." Callum glanced at Cassie.

David switched to medieval Welsh. "You don't want to risk Cassie's. I understand."

"I don't know what you just said, but I don't care either." Cassie had arranged the chest and back pieces of the Kevlar vest on David's torso and was systematically velcroing the shoulder pieces, adjusting the sizing so it fit snugly over David's shirt. She stopped in the act of cinching the chest piece tighter and looked into David's face. "Do you believe jumping off the roof will take you home?"

"Yes." David spoke with utter resolve.

"Then I do too," she said.

Lady Jane had been watching them with her arms folded across her chest.

"Thank you for your help," David said to her, "but I have every intention of getting out of your hair as soon as possible."

Lady Jane's lips pinched together, and she glared at David. "I am loath to lock you up—"

"—because that's worked so well so far," Cassie said.

"—but you are forcing my hand." Lady Jane transferred her hostile glare to Cassie.

Cassie shrugged, not at all cowed. "David seems to get what he wants most of the time. I suggest you let him do what he needs to do, and perhaps in the end you might get something out of it. Knowledge, if nothing else."

David had been pleased to let Cassie talk back to Lady Jane, but then Lady Jane snapped back at her. "Do you want to see your grandfather again or don't you?"

"Hey now." Callum took a step towards Lady Jane, but in that instant the window between David's bed and the corridor exploded in a shower of glass.

"Get down!" They all shouted at once, and a second later, David found himself on the floor between Cassie and Callum, who had dived at him at the same time. Cassie had gotten there first, shoving him flat onto his bed, and then Callum had scooped them off the bed to land in a heap on the other side. Cassie lay flat on the floor beside David, with Callum stretched across them both.

David turned his head to look under the bed and found himself looking at Lady Jane. Her eyes were open but sightless. She was dead.

22

September, 2017

Callum

It had taken Callum a half second—which in retrospect could have been too long if the killer had been aiming for David instead of Lady Jane—to realize that when the window exploded, it was because the bullet had come through the plate glass window on the street side of the room and hit the window in the corridor after passing through the room and its victim. Lady Jane's skull had slowed it and spun the bullet enough to shatter the glass instead of punching through it like it had the outside window. Callum expected that when someone examined the hole in the outer window later, he would find that the bullet had created a perfect circle the width of the bullet itself.

"Agent down! Agent down!"

Men shouted to one another, repeating Callum's words, and then someone much closer to the doorway said, "Callum?"

"Stay down, Driscoll! The shooter has a clear line of sight into this room. He may still be out there," Callum said.

"Who's down?"

Callum watched the doorway as Driscoll, appropriately attired in Kevlar, peered around the frame, his head only eighteen inches above the floor. Driscoll's eyes widened at the sight of Lady Jane's body, and then he focused on the three of them huddled behind the bed a few feet away.

"Christ." Driscoll brought his mobile phone to his lips. "Man down, man down."

"We're moving!" Callum hooked his arms under David's to get him going, while Driscoll reached for Cassie. They left the room at a low crouch, their noses only a few inches from the floor. A phalanx of men in black Kevlar gave way as they exited the room, and Cassie, Callum, and David hustled away down the hall. The hospital was set up so one bank of rooms took up one half of ICU, and a second bank took up the other, with the nurse's station, administrative offices, and lavatories in the middle. Callum went down the right-hand corridor and opened the second door on the left, which said 'Family Members Only'.

They entered a small sitting room. "You'll need to secure not only the hospital but anyone who knows about this project, even peripherally. Take the time you need. We're good here," Callum said, even if it wasn't true.

"I'm on it." Driscoll disappeared.

Don't trust Driscoll. Don't trust anyone.

The litany resounded in Callum's ears as he pushed away any thought of Lady Jane but what she'd said to him. He kept seeing the blood pooling underneath her body. Even in the small time they'd remained in the room, it had started a slow trek to the door. Up until that moment, it would never have occurred to him that the hospital floor was uneven.

"Are you all right?" Callum crouched in front of Cassie, who had found a seat on a small sofa next to David. Shouts came from the corridor, but he ignored them for now. Lady Jane was dead, so his priority was the living. "I wrenched your arm pretty hard."

"I'm okay," Cassie said. "A sore elbow is better than being dead."

David was staring at nothing, so Callum said, "Look at me, David."

David obeyed, swinging his eyes up to meet Callum's. David hesitated for a second, and then he nodded. "I'm fine, too. Really. My hip is sore where we landed—neither of you are exactly lightweights, you know—and my arm is bleeding again, but other than that, I'm fine."

"Was the bullet meant for David or Lady Jane?" Cassie said.

"Lady Jane," Callum said with certainty. "She told me earlier tonight that she feared for her life. And she told me why."

"Do you know who—?" Cassie cut herself off at Callum's sharp nod. Sirens wailed and footsteps pounded in the corridor as an assault unit approached the doorway. Driscoll poked his head into the room, put up a thumb, and then pulled out again. *Cleanup and control commenced* would be what he wrote in his official report, but

Callum didn't think those words quite did justice to what needed to happen next. Agents would scour not only the hospital but all the buildings within line of sight of that room, looking for evidence of the shooter.

Callum wasn't an investigator, so he would have to leave that to others. He didn't plan to be around to find out what they learned, however. If the shooter knew what was good for him, he would be long gone by now, anyway.

"Is it Smythe?" David said. "He's Lady Jane's second, right? With both her and Natasha gone, he'll take over Thames House *and* Cardiff station."

"I can't accuse anyone or talk about it here," Callum said. "It's enough to know that there are traitors in the Security Service and the government, more than just Natasha. And that a helicopter may be arriving at any moment to take you from Cardiff."

"When Anna and I first came to Wales, we drove into it in my aunt's minivan," David said. "How did we get from there to here? How did our lives become fodder for international intrigue?"

"It happened the moment your Uncle Ted spilled the beans to Lady Jane's husband," Cassie said, taking his question literally.

David rolled his eyes at her but then said to Callum, "I'm sorry Director Cooke is dead."

Callum was peering through the narrow slit of a window in the door and just nodded his head in response.

"Are those guards still there?" Cassie said.

"They are."

"We should go." David rose to his feet. "Director Cooke had a car for us, but we should go to the roof, like I said before."

Callum found himself agreeing with more certainty than before. He swung the duffel over one shoulder, opened the door, and gestured the others through it. "Head to the left; we'll take the stairs."

David left the room and trotted down the corridor towards a door on the end that showed a graphic of a set of stairs and said 'way out'. Cassie followed, but Callum stopped in front of one of the guards.

"I'm moving David for his safety," he said. "Smythe's orders."

The guard saluted, and Callum walked quickly away, catching Cassie's elbow when he reached her and hurrying her along. They started up the stairs, all three of them taking the steps two at a time. They circled around and around, and Callum lost count of the number of steps.

"I'm scared, Callum." Cassie's eyes were on her feet as her legs moved rhythmically beside his.

"I am too," Callum said. "I'm afraid of losing you."

"It's going to work," David said from a few steps ahead.

"He's done it four times," Callum said.

"That knowledge is keeping me climbing these stairs," Cassie said.

Callum found Cassie's hand, and they weaved their fingers together in a tight clasp.

"I wouldn't be leading you up here otherwise," David said.

Then a door banged below them and feet pounded on the stairs. Callum looked down through the stairwell. Driscoll was coming up the stairs behind them, his gun in his hand.

23

September, 2017

Cassie

Driscoll was still several floors below them, but he was coming on fast. Cassie's breath caught in her throat at the sight of the gun. "Oh God." As if Lady Jane's death wasn't bad enough. She felt like throwing up.

"Stop!" Driscoll shouted up at them.

David didn't even break stride. "Not gonna do that."

Cassie glanced up at him. When David had talked about jumping, Cassie hadn't heard the slightest hitch in his voice that might indicate fear or uncertainty. At a few inches over six feet and two hundred pounds, dressed in his freshly laundered clothing (MI-5 was good for something, it seemed), he'd transformed himself into the medieval man he'd grown to be. The last two days had put some uncharacteristic lines around his eyes and mouth, from exhaustion, Cassie guessed, but that only made him look more forbidding.

"Just get to the top." Callum pulled out his own gun. "I can hold him off if he starts shooting."

"Why doesn't Driscoll have anyone with him?" she said.

"He doesn't have anyone he can trust any more than we do," Callum said.

Because they'd paused to look down, David was now a half a staircase ahead. "Come on, guys. Keep up!" he said.

Cassie and Callum ran, moving side-by-side in a steady motion. They caught up with David, and Callum passed off the duffel to him. David slung it over his shoulder. The papers in the bag might mean the difference between life and death—a lot of lives and a lot of deaths—if they could take them home, but Callum shouldn't be carrying the bag as well as the gun if Driscoll started shooting. They passed the seventh floor and then the eighth. The pounding below them grew closer.

"Don't look," Callum said.

Cassie didn't. She didn't dare hesitate even for a second.

The stairs ended at the ninth floor. David hit the safety bar on the door and went through it. Cassie and Callum followed. She didn't know where David was going, but he seemed to because within a few seconds he found a second stairwell to the right of a pair of elevators.

No stairs led down from here at all, and steps went up only one floor, to what Cassie prayed was going to be the roof. She was terrified—absolutely terrified—of jumping off. They were completely insane to consider it. She didn't want to do it; she didn't want Callum to do it, but neither could she see letting David go alone. The possibility of failure had her throat squeezing closed, but the utterly insane idea that it really might work kept her following both men up the steps, around a corner, and out onto the roof.

Bank after bank of solar panels took up most of the roof space, along with a massive air conditioning unit, some other industrial-looking boxes that might have been for power and gas, and an extensive antenna array like on the MI-5 building. Other than the equipment, the roof was empty and lit up as if it were day, with torchlights and strobe lights crisscrossing the night sky. Cassie started across it after David, heading for the edge. She braced herself with every step for what she had committed herself to doing:

Jumping off.

They were insane. And yet, she was going through with it anyway.

"Don't make me shoot you, Callum!" The shout echoed across the rooftop.

Cassie stopped and turned to see Callum facing away from her, standing between her and Driscoll, who blocked the doorway of the stairwell.

"Let us go, Driscoll!" Callum said. "This has nothing to do with you."

Driscoll brought up his gun.

"Get down!" David caught Cassie in his arms, and they rolled together behind one of the metal boxes.

Two shots rang out, followed by two more and a shriek, cut off sharply.

"Callum!" Cassie screamed his name and, after extricating herself from David, scrambled to her feet. Callum ran towards her, and Cassie almost collapsed with relief.

"Go! Go! Go!" He caught her arm and spun her around, urging her towards the edge of the roof. "Driscoll's dead. We have to get out of here now."

Before they'd gone three steps, however, the *whuf-whuf-whuf* of a helicopter sounded overhead.

"That's for me." David backed away from the helicopter's searchlight, which panned across the roof towards them as the helicopter descended.

Callum moved towards David but then staggered—and it was only then that Cassie saw the blood dripping from his fingers.

"No!" Cassie threw her arms around his waist, holding him tightly as she sagged with him to their knees. Another scream rose in her chest.

At last, another agent appeared in the open doorway that led to the stairwell. He pulled up at the sight of Driscoll's body at his feet. David pointed at him. "You! Agent Callum's been shot! Go for help!"

The man hesitated.

"Now!" The word split the air.

The man went, his hand to his ear as he spoke into his phone.

Cassie's eyes blurred with tears as she and David together lay Callum down on the hard concrete of the roof. She kissed Callum's forehead while David ripped open his shirt. At the sight of the bullet wound and the blood, David bent his head, but it was in relief, not despair. "It missed his heart, Cassie. The bullet hit him high in his shoulder. I think it even went all the way through and came out the other side."

"Oh, thank God." Cassie doubled up the edge of Callum's suit jacket and pressed it to the wound, her tears dripping onto the back of her hands, mixing with Callum's blood on her fingers.

"If we get him help soon, he'll be okay." Then David nudged her, forcing her to meet his eyes. "But not if he comes with me."

Callum bent his right arm at the elbow, holding up his hand for David to clasp. He wheezed in pain. "Go. Go before anyone else comes to stop you."

David squeezed Callum's hand. "One of us will come back for you. If not me, it'll be Anna or my mom. I swear it."

Cassie meant to tell him not to be ridiculous, that he didn't have to, but all she got out was, "He's weakening."

"Where's the medical team? Isn't this a hospital!" David glanced towards the elevator doors, which at that second opened. A team of medics with a stretcher surged towards them.

Then the backwash of the helicopter blades swept over them again. "We've got your back, whether or not we ever see you again," Cassie said.

"I know you do." David released Callum's hand, grabbed the duffel, and ran to the edge of the building. Without stopping, thinking, hesitating, or looking back, he launched himself upwards and over the edge, arms and legs pin-wheeling in the air.

And then he fell below the level of the roof and was gone.

24

September, 1289

David

David rolled onto his back and stared up at the star-strewn sky. *I made it.*

He almost didn't care where he'd landed, just so long as he wasn't a flattened pea on a side street in Cardiff. He'd known that ten stories was over a hundred feet high, but though he'd launched himself from the roof with a clear vision of what would follow, the sight of the street below him had been heart-stopping. He'd fallen, his faith failing him at the last minute, but even without faith, the familiar-yet-foreign black abyss had opened beneath him, and he'd been sucked into it.

An eternity—that is, three seconds—later, he'd landed with a thump on the turf of a field amidst a herd of sheep. The animals had scattered at first but had started to creep back towards him, cropping the grass and no longer concerned about his presence. "Good thing I'm not a wolf," he said to them and then got to his feet. The ground was wet but not overly so, and his cloak had soaked up most of the dampness.

"Okay." He brushed off the seat of his breeches and took inventory. The place in his arm where he'd tugged out the needle hurt a little, his throat was sore only at the tail end of swallowing, and he was utterly starving. The fish and chips in the interrogation room had been good but he'd eaten them over a day ago. All he'd had since then was what they'd fed him through the IV: salted sugar water and drugs.

All in all, for someone who until half an hour ago had been unconscious in a hospital bed in the twenty-first century, he was doing pretty well.

He couldn't see much of his surroundings due to the darkness of the evening, but the stars gave him some light, and gradually his eyes adjusted. Only two days in the twenty-first century and he had already forgotten what it was like to walk in an unlit landscape.

His surroundings, as far as he could see, were relatively flat, consisting of fields and pastures. In the distance, a dark line gave the suggestion of trees and indicated that he was near a river—not that every spot in Britain was within hailing distance of a river, so that didn't tell him much. He slung the duffel over one shoulder, thankful it was made of a muddy brown canvas that didn't look overly modern, and started walking towards the river. He assumed that if he followed it, he would eventually reach a village. Once there, the inhabitants could tell him where he was.

David was very conscious of how alone he was. The whole time he'd been in the twenty-first century, he'd told himself that nothing was going to stop him from bringing Cassie and Callum home with him if they wanted to come. To find himself here without them had thrown him off-kilter. They'd all felt urgently that David needed to leave in that moment or he would never have been able to leave. He also knew that he couldn't have brought Callum with him, not with a bullet hole in his shoulder. David had to trust that decision, and that Callum really would be okay. Modern medicine being what it was, David didn't have too much trouble convincing himself of that.

It was a bit harder to convince himself that his promise to retrieve them was one he could keep. But as David had found over the years, certain problems had to be put aside to deal with ones that were more immediate. Callum needed time to recover from his wound. A few weeks, a few months. It mattered to all of them that they remained behind, but Cassie and Callum were together, and they were alive; David could commit them to the care of others, or God, until he could figure out how to get them back.

After half a mile of walking, David approached the river, which was good-sized—at least fifty feet across. The moon had risen, and the shadows of trees interspersed with the pinpoints of starlight rippled on the surface of the water. Without too much stumbling around, David found a trail and followed it south on the east side of the river, which flowed north-south at this location. He pulled his cloak tighter against the chill of the evening, and it was only then that he remembered he was still wearing Kevlar. He suspected that it had been Callum's, but there was no point now in cursing Callum's generosity in giving it to him. What was done was done.

David couldn't wear the vest out in the open, however, so he took a moment to rearrange the order of his clothing, putting his shirt and cloak back on over the vest. Television had made him think that Kevlar was a half inch thick. Callum's Kevlar, however, was thinner than that, three layers of woven fabric that felt like nylon, with hard plates inserted in key places. Though black, not silver, it bore a greater resemblance to Frodo's mithril coat than the Kevlar from TV.

He could have put it in the duffel and not worn it, but something told him he might be better off wearing it, just until he could put on his own armor again. And then he groaned as he remembered that he'd left that armor back on the cog in modern Cardiff. The historians would be having a field day with it, he was sure, but he would miss it. It had fit him perfectly.

It was just as well that he'd remembered about the Kevlar, because within another quarter-mile, he reached a bridge across the river he'd been following. Torches lit both ends, and a phalanx of farmers-turned-soldiers guarded it. At the sight of them and their village, David knew precisely where he was. He would have laughed but for the grave expression on the faces of the men who confronted him.

"Who goes there!"

David halted fifteen paces from the end of the bridge. He didn't answer right away, deliberating as to what, exactly, he was going to say. That the gray-haired guard who asked belonged to the village of Maidenhead, established just ten years ago when a bridge was built here across the Thames, changed everything. Maidenhead was five miles north of Windsor. David had no men-at-arms or knights with him, but he was the King of England. He'd been to Maidenhead. The men here might recognize him.

Arms spread wide, David entered the ring of light thrown out by the torches and approached the group of men. "I am your king, David."

For a moment, David wasn't sure if he'd used the right form of English because the men stared at him, pikes and axes at the ready. And then the man who'd spoken first dropped his pike head to the ground with a *thunk*. "Sire!" He whipped off his hat and sank to one knee, hastily followed by the other six men with him. "I am John Wade, headman of this village."

David almost laughed at what a difference half an hour could make. It wasn't that he wanted or needed the obeisance, but after being tossed around for two days by people who didn't respect him at all, it was nice to finally be treated like a human being. "Rise, gentlemen," he said. "Why do you guard this bridge so assiduously?"

The men rose to their feet, shuffling a bit, and then John answered, "Lord Ieuan sent us word that Valence's men might try to use our bridge to cross the Thames, now that the bridge down in Windsor is gone. But we haven't seen or heard anyone so far other than you."

David just managed not to gape at the man. He'd been gone less than a week, but clearly bad things had been happening in his absence. Struggling to keep the dismay off his face and not openly curse, he made a very painful, and yet sure, guess. "Valence has Windsor surrounded?"

"Yes, my lord," John said. "You didn't know?"

"Where is Lord Ieuan now?" David said, not answering the man's question.

"He hoped to surround Valence's forces himself by today but only if he had the men," John said. "We have not seen or heard from him since this morning."

"Sire, where are *your* men?" A younger man than the first stepped forward. "Tom Longman, my lord." He ducked his head as he introduced himself. Given that he was taller than David, his surname suited him. "Word was that you'd gone to Ireland."

"I never made it," David said flatly. "And I am alone, as you can see."

All of the villagers swallowed hard. "Sire, if there's anything we can do—" John said.

David held up a hand to stop him from speaking. He needed to think. He already missed Callum's guidance and hadn't realized until this moment how much he'd come to depend on it. He could almost hear his friend's voice in his ear, telling him to determine the facts first and then objectively examine his available options. Finding creative solutions to huge problems was something Callum had been particularly good at. "Windsor is surrounded, you say?"

The men nodded vigorously.

"How many men does Valence have?"

"Some say two thousand, my lord," Tom said.

David eyed him. "You can count?"

"Yes, my lord."

"And Lord Ieuan? How many does he have?"

"Fewer," Tom said. "I don't know how many. And they say that only a hundred defend Windsor."

"Windsor town is burning. You can smell it from here." John gestured towards the south, and now that David was paying attention, he could smell the smoke. His stomach knotted, and suddenly he wasn't hungry any more.

"The queen is there—" Tom cut himself off and looked down at his feet.

"Thank you, Tom," David said. "I assumed it."

"Valence hasn't taken the town or the castle yet," John said, trying to comfort him. "They've held out a night and a day so far."

"It's only been a night and a day since the assault began? That's all?"

John and Tom nodded together.

That was far better than David had feared. It seemed he and Valence had made the same decision—each to confront the other—but had just missed each other going in opposite directions. He wondered if Valence knew yet that he wasn't at Windsor or that he'd gone to Ireland and might even now be laying siege to Valence's own castle. It was a lesser prize, certainly, and if Valence could take Windsor, he would gladly make that exchange.

"So we have a little time, perhaps," David said. "You're telling me that the defenders destroyed Windsor's bridge across the Thames?"

Another nod. "Your sister's husband, Lord Math, defends," John said.

"And the moat is full of water?"

"It worked perfectly, my lord." Tom grinned. "My brother and I helped build the sluice gates."

During this discussion, they'd remained standing on the eastern side of the bridge, but now John remembered himself. "Please come into Maidenhead, sire. There you can refresh yourself."

"Thank you." David walked with the men onto the bridge. "I do need food. But even more, I need men."

"We have few," Tom said. "All the rest who could fight went with Lord Ieuan. None of us are soldiers, but still we do his bidding."

"England has always relied upon its people to fight for her in times of need," David said, sounding pompous even to himself. "Does anyone in the village possess a horse?"

A man who stayed in the back of the group lifted a hand. He was nearly as large as Tom and twice as wide. "I do, my lord. Lord Ieuan instructed me to send him word at once if Valence came for this bridge."

"You, if I may make a guess, are the village blacksmith," David said.

"Yes, my lord. Rob Lincoln is my name. Many a horse needs a new shoe by the time he reaches Maidenhead from London."

"All right. You three come with me." David pointed to John, Tom, and Rob. "The rest should stay and guard the bridge as before. We'll send you a few more men to help."

They entered Maidenhead, which like Windsor consisted of houses and shops clustered on both sides of the main road. The normally busy wharf was quiet now that night had fallen. A village green sat to the south of the London road, and John led David to his house just off of it. No wall surrounded the town, which meant that if Valence's men chose to approach from this side of the Thames River, the villagers could do nothing to stop them. At the same time, there would be no reason for Valence to come here unless, as John had said, he wanted to use the bridge.

They entered John's house. Even at this late hour, the family was up, and the smell of baking came from the back of the house. "Emma!" John raised his voice, and a teenage girl came into the room through the door opposite the main one.

"Yes, Father?"

"We have a noble guest," John said, without naming David. "We must eat and then go."

The girl smiled and curtseyed, her eyes on Tom instead of David or her father. "Yes, Father."

John gestured to a table with six chairs around it that took up the center of the room. A fireplace was set into the right hand wall, with a low fire burning in it. The chimney appeared to work better than most since smoke wasn't choking the room. David sat, and even though he indicated that the others should sit too, none of them took a chair at the table. Sitting in the presence of the king just wasn't done.

David had wanted to be recognized, but three minutes into life in the Middle Ages, he'd already had it with the formality of his position. "Sit!"

Eyes bulging, John sat, and then Tom did too. Rob bowed. "My lord, I dare not. I know who made those chairs, and I will break one if I sit in it."

SARAH WOODBURY

David laughed, and waved a hand in acceptance at Rob, who leaned against the frame of the door with his arms folded across his chest. "Two things: I need to know the current location of Ieuan and his men," David said, "and I need to know what is happening in Windsor. Who in Maidenhead, other than you three, knows how to ride?"

The three men in the room looked at one another. "No one," John said. "Tom and Rob do, of course, as you say, but all the other men with that knowledge have gone, and there weren't many to begin with. Some of the farmer boys might ..." John's voice trailed off.

"I know how to ride." The girl, Emma, had returned to the room, this time with a tray containing bread and beer.

Carbohydrates for dinner were better than no dinner at all. David resigned himself to leaving the table unsatisfied, but then he sighed in relief at the sight of the tureen of soup with steam rising from it in the hands of a second girl who'd entered the room after the first.

"You can't." Tom's eyes were fixed on Emma.

"Is she speaking the truth?" David said.

"A little daredevil, isn't she?" John said. "But—"

"If I go, none of the enemy will think anything of it," Emma said. "I'm a girl. I'm the one who *should* go."

David took a long drink of beer, which had never been his favorite (he preferred mead), and then a sip of soup. He closed his eyes, glad to have something in his stomach again. Then he got back to work. "If she can find Ieuan, I need her."

"It isn't safe," Tom said.

"And it's safe staying here if Valence's men come?" Emma said. "What will his men do to me if he catches us sitting here doing nothing?"

Tom ground his teeth.

John appeared caught between Tom and his daughter, and appealed to David. "Sire—"

The pitcher that held the beer Emma had been pouring into Tom's cup crashed to the floor. She whipped around, her color high and beer frothing at her feet. "Sire!" She gaped at David and then gave a deep curtsey.

"Rise, Emma," David said.

She came forward, ending up on her knees beside his chair, making David deeply uncomfortable. "Please. I can find Lord Ieuan. Let me go."

John nodded. "She's capable, Tom."

"Then give me leave to go with her," Tom said.

"We have only one horse," Rob said.

"I'll take old farmer Blidworth's. She's a nag but sturdy. We'll cover more ground with two and find Lord Ieuan all the sooner."

John looked at David, who shrugged. He honestly didn't care how he got news of Ieuan, and the news of his arrival *to* Ieuan, only that the communication occurred—and the sooner the better. "Meanwhile, we'll gather a second army here," David said.

"How's that, sire?" John said. "We have no more men."

"We need bodies, not men," David said. "Valence cannot maintain a siege if attacked from both the castle and from behind. He will know that and raise the white flag. We just need to put on a show. Every person who can walk, of whatever age, should gather on the green as soon as possible."

Emma's eyes lit as she rose to her feet. "I'll tell Mum to get ready!"

John was aghast. "You already took Emma. You mean to use the rest of the women too? To arm them?"

David beamed at him. "That's an excellent idea." He clapped a hand on John's shoulder. "I'm so glad you thought of it!"

The five miles—less—between Maidenhead and Windsor would take two hours of walking on a flat, well-used road. The night was cool but dry, and the villagers got on board with David's plan almost before David asked for their help. A few protested, like John, that the women shouldn't be involved. David could understand their reluctance, but he was impatient with it too. He'd stood by helplessly while Lili had given birth to Arthur, and he'd lived with Anna most of his life. He had Meg for a mom. Women were a lot tougher than these men gave them credit for.

Several of the more able-bodied older men set off immediately to gather as many other people as they could from outlying towns, such as South Ellington and Cookham. David stood on the Maidenhead green, watching the villagers come in, making sure each had a weapon of some kind, even if only a broom, and the makings of a torch. He aimed to depart as close to midnight as he could, which meant they should reach the outskirts of Windsor by three in the morning. David didn't know if Valence would be continuing the assault throughout the night to press what he saw as his advantage before Windsor's reinforcements arrived. He had to know that they would come; it was only a matter of time.

"Ho there! What news of Windsor?"

David spun towards the voice. He would have recognized it anywhere, even with it having settled into a lower register over the last few months. "William!" David raised a hand and hastened towards the bridge across the Thames. He shouldered his way through the men guarding it, who gave way the best they could in the tight space. He reached the end to find Maidenhead's villagers holding the Norman youth off with the same pikes and axes they'd pointed at David a few hours earlier.

"Put up," David said, pressing on a pike himself to get the villager to lower it. "He's a friend."

William de Bohun dismounted and dropped to one knee in front of David. "Sire."

"Rarely have I been so glad to see anyone in my life." David grasped William's upper arms and lifted him to his feet. "How many men have you brought me?"

"Some five hundred. It was all I could gather on short notice." He leaned in. "Between you and me, most of them barely know the hilt from the point of a sword."

David shook William's shoulder. "It is no matter. I need men more than fighters. You should see what we're doing here." He led William from the bridge towards the center of the village, which torches lit up like it was day.

William stopped on the edge of the grass. "What is this?"

David spread his arms wide, laughing. "My army!"

"But—"

"Windsor is under attack and has been since yesterday evening," David said.

"I saw from a distance," William said. "I have no idea how Valence managed to progress so far so quickly. When I went for help two days ago, he was entrenched at Winchester."

"I know nothing about that," David said. "Nor do I know where Ieuan and his men are, but we must relieve the defenders, by any means necessary, before Valence breaks through Windsor's defenses."

"But the women—" William was struggling with the sight of mothers and daughters in their husbands' and sons' spare breeches and coats.

"I have no intention of having them fight, if that is what worries you," David said. "I have no intention of leading anyone into battle today. Whether or not women are capable of fighting is something we can argue about another day. Right now, I need bodies, as many as I can find."

William blinked but then nodded. "You mean to deceive Valence into thinking you have more men than you have."

"That is exactly what I intend." If his trip to the twenty-first century had taught David anything, it was to take advantage of the power he had been handed to change the world. There, he'd been treated like a valuable but semi-inanimate object, to be passed around for whatever information anyone could get out of him. Otherwise, his thoughts, opinions, and contributions had been ignored. He was a twenty-year-old kid, to be humored, at best. At worst, it had been implied, even if not said, that he was to leave the thinking to the grown-ups.

Well, screw that.

Now a shout came from the other side of the village. William de Bohun leapt in front of David, his sword out.

"Sire!" It was Tom.

"It's okay, William." David nudged the boy's arm. "He's a friend too." At the green, David caught the bridle of Tom's horse as he dismounted. "Where's Emma?"

"Safe with Lord Ieuan," Tom said. "He agreed that I should return on the better horse without her."

David didn't ask how long it had taken Tom to persuade Emma that he should return alone. David had believed her when she'd said that she was the superior rider. It wasn't David's problem, however. Tom and Emma were going to have to work that out between them.

"How far away is Lord Ieuan, and how many men does he have?" David said.

"He marches with over a thousand strong," Tom said. "Lord Ieuan asked me to tell you that he would be grateful if we met him at St. Leonard's Hill as soon as possible."

Ieuan had named a spot that in the modern world was adjacent to the Windsor Legoland (David knew this through Callum). Rather than mention it, David raised a hand, calling his new captains to him.

"This will put us to the west of Valence's main force, is that right?" David said to Tom.

"Lord Ieuan says so," Tom said.

William made a fist and slammed it into his palm. "We will crush him, once and for all."

David narrowed his eyes at the young man. "Do other barons of your acquaintance share your animosity towards Valence?"

"The day you banished Valence was a day of celebration among my father's peers," William said. "Didn't you realize? I know of nobody who doesn't want to see him hang."

25

September, 1289

Lili

When Anna thrust a piece of bread wrapped around slices of cheese and meat at her, Lili just stared at it, too tired even to know what was in her hand.

"What is this?"

"It's called a sandwich. You need to eat it," Anna said.

Lili looked at the food dubiously. She'd seen Dafydd eat something like this—wolf it down in four or five bites, in fact—on many occasions, but to her, each of the different components, the buttered bread, the cheese, and the meat, should be eaten separately.

"Is Arthur awake yet?" she said between bites.

Anna shook her head. "Perhaps this will turn into a long stretch. It's nearly dawn, and he's been asleep since midnight."

"That's when he usually nurses the most." If she spent more than two hours away from Arthur, Lili felt the tether that connected her to him stretching tighter and tugging on her. Since the attack began, Anna, Bronwen, or one of the maidservants had come to get her whenever Arthur needed to eat. It had kept her connected to him, but the strain of being apart from him so much had long since grown wearing. She wanted nothing more than to lie in bed and snuggle him against her chest.

One of the other archers appeared behind Anna. "My queen," he said.

Lili gestured that he should speak, preparing herself for the latest bad news he was bringing. "What is it?"

"Our stock of arrows is all but depleted."

Anna gasped in dismay, but Lili nodded and dismissed the archer. She'd been expecting to hear that since the sun had gone down. They were all thankful that Windsor had been prepared for an assault to the degree that it had been, but they hadn't been prepared enough, not for what Valence was throwing at them.

"We've been in a lull since midnight," Anna said. "The bowyer and fletcher are working overtime. All is not lost."

"I know," Lili said. "I haven't given up hope."

"Math wanted me to tell you that the men need to be prepared to shoot at the siege engines—or rather, the men working them—when they come against us," Anna said.

"How soon?" Lili gazed over the wall towards the enemy lines. The fields of barley and wheat, or grass for sheep, had been trampled by Valence's army. Fallen men, some wounded, some dead, lay every few feet. Windsor's arrows had held out long enough to kill many, and any attempt to rescue the wounded had been met with more arrows. It was cruel, inhuman even, but Math had insisted that it was necessary. He wanted to sow discontent among Valence's men and push him towards raising the white flag when they faced more resistance than he was prepared for.

"Not long. Dawn, he thinks," Anna said. "You need to be aware that Valence will focus first on the towers that defend the sluice gates." The sluice gates were what diverted the water from the Thames around Windsor. If Valence could close the northwestern gate and open the northeastern one, he could stop the flow of water and clear the moat.

"As he should," Lili said.

When the captain of the archers had been hit—not killed, but badly injured—somehow it had fallen to Lili to organize the men on her section of the wall. With the destruction of the bridge, Valence's men had abandoned any attempt to attack the north side of the castle and village, so the defenders had turned their focus elsewhere too. Lili had moved to a section above the postern gate of the castle. This position overlooked the northeastern sluice gate, which made it a doubly weak point in their defenses. She was inside the castle, however, and that made Carew happier.

The two women looked at each other, and then Anna put her arm around Lili's waist.

"I know I'm not the first to wonder who those men on the other side are," Lili said. "But ... do they fight for Valence because they love him and believe? Or are they following their lord because they must, because they can't imagine any other life?"

"There's some of all of that, I'm sure," Anna said. "And then there are those who are paid. Many may believe that it makes no difference who is king. That's for noblemen to worry about while common folk struggle to put food on the table."

"How did I come to be in an English castle, married to the King of England, fighting for a country which up until a year ago was my sworn enemy?" Lili said.

"I don't know the answer to that any more than you do." Anna shook her head. "It seems a strange path for all of us to have taken."

"I want this over and Dafydd home safe," Lili said.

"When he returns, ask him to take you home to Wales for a time," Anna said. "He'll do it gladly."

"I haven't wanted to burden him—"

Anna took Lili's face in her hands. "You are his wife. He won't know what you need if you don't ask for it."

Lili put her head into the hollow of Anna's shoulder. They stood still a moment, their heads bowed. Then Anna took a breath and stepped back. "I have a sliver of hope that our penicillin paste might be working. We have treated every injured man with it, and so far none of the wounds have suppurated."

"That is good news!" Lili said.

"That is the best news!" Nicholas de Carew mounted the stairs. "And there's more."

"What more?" Lili said.

"I have to show you," he said.

Lili was reluctant to leave her post, but after a quick word with the five archers who shared her particular stretch of wall, she walked with Carew and Anna around the battlement until they reached the stairway that led to the lower bailey of the castle. Arthur and the other children slept in the castle's northwest tower, and though part of her longed to go to him, even if he was asleep, she allowed herself to be tugged along, out the gate, and into the town of Windsor.

"Where are we going?" Lili said. "I thought you wanted me to stay in the castle."

"Some things are worth making an exception for." Carew smiled. "Have you heard the king say that it is always darkest before the dawn?"

"You're awfully cheerful for someone who's found himself in the middle of a war we're currently losing." Lili gestured to the sky, which had gone from pitch black to murky while they'd been walking. "Dawn is coming. Anna said that Valence will attack with the rising of the sun."

"We aren't going to lose," Carew said.

"How do you know that—?" Lili cut herself off at the sight of dozens of men—archers, scholars-turned-soldiers, and villagers—crowding onto the southwestern wall-walk above her. They'd reached the exact opposite corner of the town from where she'd been standing earlier.

"Make way for the queen," Carew said, and everyone did.

Lili climbed the stairs up to the wall-walk and rested her hands on the stones of the crenel, staring southwest through the gap. Valence's men were there, of course, though fewer than their original two thousand strong. But beyond them, covering the entirety of the hill behind the enemy encampment, torches shone.

Hundreds of them.

As Lili watched, a campfire blazed up, and then a few more, until the whole of the land to the south and west of Windsor was covered with light. "How—?" Lili couldn't speak more.

A smile split Carew's face from ear to ear. "They appeared less than half an hour ago, all at once, as if every soldier had lit his torch at the same time, which perhaps they did."

"How many have come?" Anna pressed between Lili and Carew, drinking in the sight of the oncoming army as eagerly as Lili was.

"From the number of torches, I would have said more than a thousand," Carew said, "but they keep lighting more—"

"A thousand, did you say?" Anna said. "That's more like five thousand."

Roger Bacon wended his way through the crowd. "It's Valence's decision now whether or not to attack. The fact that our force has taken the high ground puts him at a further disadvantage."

"We're sure they're here to fight for us?" Lili said.

Carew pointed. "Look there, at the very top of the hill where there are no trees."

Lili squinted. The torches shone all around the hill, and many seemed to be directed at its peak. "Is it ... is it a flag?"

"I would say so," Bacon said, squinting too.

"It's a flag with a dragon on it. How many armies that fight for Valence would carry such a thing, do you think?" Carew said.

"That's David's personal banner." Anna's brow furrowed. "Normally, it isn't flown unless David is physically present on the field."

"Ieuan must be flying it." Pride in her brother rose in Lili's chest. He deserved every bit of trust that Dafydd had placed in him.

"Has to be," Carew said. "Though I have no idea how Lord Ieuan found so many men so quickly."

A clamor came from below. "There's a boat coming down the river!"

Archers all along the wall-walk shouted and leveled their bows at the intruders. They had been expecting some renewal of Valence's assault on this side of the town, and with such a force hemming them in, now would be the time for an attack. The window of opportunity for taking Windsor was closing.

"Don't shoot! Don't shoot! We're friends!"

The color drained from Lili's face. That was Dafydd's voice. She knew it like she knew her own face in her looking-glass. But it couldn't be him; it had to be a trick and a very cruel one to deceive her in this way.

Anna ran along the wall-walk, screaming at the archers, her skirts pulled up to her knees to free her legs. "Stop! Stop! It's the King!"

Several archers were so focused on the river, they didn't hear her. Breathless that Anna could be right, Lili sprinted after her.

Bevyn, who still maintained charge of the northern gatehouse tower, bellowed at the men: "It's just one boat! Put up, you fools!"

By the time Lili made it down the stairs that led to the gate, Bevyn had it ajar. She and a dozen others darted through the opening, making for the narrow wharf, located to the east of where the bridge had been and almost directly under the castle walls.

The wharf was long but not wide, jutting out into the river only the length of a man but with many indentations, much like the crenellations on a battlement, where boats could tie up. Fortunately, a few men had the foresight to bring torches, and as they raced towards the oncoming boat, Lili could see that it had two men in it. One reached for a rope tied to an iron ring attached to the dock, and as he grasped it, he looked towards the crowd coming from the town.

Lili pulled up short, drinking the sight of Dafydd in. Even after a year of marriage and the birth of their child, he never lost the power to stop her in her tracks. He caught sight of her and lifted a hand; then Bevyn reached down to help him scramble onto the dock. "What are you doing here, my lord?" Bevyn said in Welsh, always the one to get straight the point.

"It seems I was needed." As he spoke, Dafydd turned in time to catch Lili, who barreled into him, wrapping her arms around his waist and pressing her face into his chest. He hugged her, bending his neck to rest his cheek on the top of her head.

Then her brow furrowed. She pulled back and pressed a hand to his chest, feeling the smooth yet hard armor covering his torso underneath his shirt. It had felt strange to her cheek. "What are you wearing?"

He grasped both of her hands. "It's not of here, *cariad*."

Not of here. That was a code she understood, for Dafydd had used it often, as a way to talk about places and things in that far-off world of his. She swallowed hard. Given that *he* was here, against all expectation, Lili was willing to wait for an explanation. She nodded, letting him know she understood. Then she looked towards the boat and back to Dafydd. "Where are Cass—?"

Dafydd's grip tightened on her arms. "I had to leave them. I swear I didn't want to, but I had no choice."

A chill grew in Lili, starting deep in her bones. "You mean—?" Lili hadn't known Cassie long, but she missed her already and didn't want to think about what she might be doing now, stuck in a foreign land, even if it had once been her land. Cassie wasn't going to be happy there.

"I believe they're safe. The three of us went together, but only I could return. Callum was wounded, and I couldn't bring him home—" Dafydd caught Lili up in a fierce hug, kissed her, and only then turned towards his companion in the boat.

Most of the crowd that had followed Bevyn from the gate had sunk to one knee at the sight of their king, but when Dafydd reached down a hand to haul his companion out of the boat, several scrambled forward to help.

Lili looked at the newcomer curiously. Like Dafydd, he was fair-haired and tall, though less muscular. He wore no armor or cloak, just a simple shirt and breeches, damp now from the river. Like Dafydd, his eyes were bright.

"This is Tom, from Maidenhead. One of many villagers who have come to our aid tonight." Dafydd looked over Lili's head to the men behind her. More continued to spill from the gate. "We should get back inside. This isn't over yet."

"By God, it won't be long now." Bevyn's mustache quivered. He was more pleased than Lili had ever seen him. "Not with the army you've brought."

"I did very little." Dafydd strode towards the gate, getting the people to their feet and herding them ahead of him with wide sweeps of his arm.

Lili hurried to catch Dafydd's hand, and Bevyn hustled along behind her. When Lili had plunged through the crowd to greet Dafydd, Carew and Anna had held back, but they met them at the gate. Dafydd embraced his sister and then reached out to shake Carew's hand. "Thank you for being here."

"I am honored that you requested my presence," Carew said.

"I never considered asking another," Dafydd said, proving true what Lili had told Carew. She wondered if Carew would ever tell Dafydd that he'd felt mistrusted. Probably not. From the way the two men were nodding at each other, Carew's concerns were long gone.

Dafydd looked down at Lili. "How is Arthur? Not ill at all?"

"He remains well. Sleeping now," she said.

"Good."

Lili peered up at her husband, suddenly suspicious. "Is there some reason to worry?"

"That is another matter to discuss with you—Anna, Bronwen, and you—later," Dafydd said. "For now, I bring word from Ieuan to Math, as I hear he defends Windsor."

Carew bowed and gestured towards the street that led to the southeastern gatehouse and Math's headquarters. "This way, my lord."

When they entered the house that served as Math's command post, they found Math leaning back in a chair with his feet propped up on the table in front of him. His eyes were closed and remained closed, even amidst the clamor in the room. A group of men were gathered around the table, among them a bandaged Henry Percy, Dafydd's Uncle Rhodri, and Sir George, the castellan of Windsor. The men were arguing and gesticulating at one another, a fact to which Math appeared oblivious. At the arrival of the newcomers, Sir George recognized Lili. "My queen! Lord Ieuan has come!"

"So I have seen," she said.

Then at the sight of Dafydd entering the room right behind her, Sir George's jaw dropped. "B-b-but—"

Dafydd merely held up his hand in greeting.

Anna went to Math and rested her arm on his shoulder. Without opening his eyes, he put an arm around her waist.

Anna leaned down to him. "I brought you someone you'll want to see."

"Who is it?" Math didn't open his eyes.

The other men had given way for Dafydd, as they always did. "Sleeping on the job, are you?" he said in Welsh. "That's hardly what I pay you for, is it?"

Math's eyes popped open, but he must really have been tired because it took him a moment to recognize Dafydd standing before the table. Then his feet hit the floor with a thud, and he was upright and coming around the table to embrace his brother-in-law. "Good God! How is it that you are here?"

"That's the first question everyone has asked me in these last hours and the one I can't answer," Dafydd said. "Brother, you really don't want to know."

Math stepped back, his eyes focused on Dafydd's face. Lili knew Dafydd didn't want to say more and hoped Math would know exactly what he meant.

"But I want to know," Carew said.

Dafydd turned to look at the Norman-Welsh lord and then glanced at the onlookers and Lili. She raised her eyebrows and shrugged. She didn't have any idea what would be the right thing to say. Dafydd's eyes flashed—with intelligence and a bit of that reckless streak he usually didn't let show—and then he said, "I meant to go to Ireland but went to Avalon instead."

The men in the room gasped. While on the wharf, Lili had worked out what had happened, of course, but Anna seemed not to have understood until now how Dafydd had reached Windsor. Her face drained of color. "What?"

"I know, I know." Dafydd reached for his sister's hand and clasped it.

"Where are your men? Where are Callum and Cassie?" Anna said.

"Once the storm hit, I lost track of my men," Dafydd said. "I arrived here tonight as you see, alone and without a guard."

Anna had her hand to her mouth, staring at her brother and more shocked than Lili might have expected, given the frequency with which time traveling happened to her family. Maybe because Lili had never been to that other world, she was more accepting of it.

Usually, she managed to forget about Dafydd's origins in the daily business of living. Dafydd was her husband, the father of her son, and the King of England. That was all that mattered most of the time.

But that was the crucial word, wasn't it? *Time.*

"Callum was wounded. He and Cassie stayed behind," Dafydd said. "I'll be going back for them as soon as I can."

Carew absorbed Dafydd's news with a pinched look on his face. "How did that happen?"

"I cannot tell you how," Dafydd said, "only that it did. In this, I know little more than you."

"Tell me something." Carew clenched his hands into fists and strained forward. "Tell me *why.*"

"It seems I wasn't meant to go to Ireland because I was needed here," Dafydd said.

Those simple words had Carew settling back on his heels. His expression cleared. "That certainly is true."

Dafydd stepped towards Carew. "Sometimes, against all expectation, good things do happen. I—"

Someone knocked at the door, and Dafydd swallowed down whatever he'd been about to say.

"Enter!" Math said.

The door opened, revealing a messenger standing on the doorstep, sweaty and unkempt. He stuttered a bit, looking from Dafydd to Math, perhaps thinking about whose presence he was in for the first time instead of the news he brought.

Nobody held his appearance against him. "What is it?" Math said.

"My lord!" The man stepped through the doorway. "Lord Valence has raised the white flag!"

Other men murmured *thanks be to God!* And *the Lord has delivered us*, but Math pursed his lips and said, "Thank you. Wait outside for my response."

The man bowed and departed to the street. Everyone else in the room fell silent, looking between Math and Dafydd. "It's what I wanted—hoped for—but I didn't expect him to fold his tents this quickly," Dafydd said.

"It feels too easy," Anna said.

"What do you intend, my lord?" Carew wasn't looking at Math but at Dafydd. While Math was still the commander of Windsor's forces and thus had spoken to the messenger, everyone in the room knew that the ultimate decision lay with the king.

"I intend to talk to him, of course," Dafydd said, "but to take some additional precautions, some of which some of you aren't going to like."

Carew stood with his hands on his hips, still looking defiant. "We need to capture him. He cannot be allowed to wiggle away this time to incite new mischief elsewhere."

"Agreed," Dafydd said.

"What are your orders?" Math said.

"We will show our good will by allowing him to gather his wounded on the field in front of the town, even sending down our men to assist the efforts of his soldiers. We will provide medicines and healing herbs as needed." Dafydd glanced at Anna, who nodded.

"I imagine in the chaos, certain ... things ... might be left behind, hidden in the grass."

Roger Bacon's eyes went wide and flicked from Carew to Dafydd to Math. "Surely, you will abide by the rules of safe conduct, my lords?"

Dafydd eyed him. "You forget yourself."

Roger Bacon swallowed hard and took a step back. Dafydd didn't often show this side of himself. His face had turned to granite, and his blue eyes had gone cold. Lili shivered. She wouldn't want to be wearing Valence's boots this morning.

"I don't care how you capture him." Anna was one of the few people in the room who didn't concern herself with Dafydd's temper or status. "But I do care what you do with him afterwards. The sooner you think about what that is going to be, the better."

"I have thought about it. I've spent far too much time thinking about it." Dafydd ran his fingers through his hair and began to pace, too restless to stand still. Anna had told Lili that he'd always been like that, ever since he was nine months old and decided walking and talking went together.

"I know what you should do," Anna said, "but it won't be easy."

"What that is worthwhile ever is?" Dafydd lifted his chin. "Tell me." If some of the men in the room thought it was odd for the King of England to be taking advice from his sister, none of them said so, even when Anna's next words were meant for them as much as for Dafydd.

"Are we a rabble seeking revenge or civilized men seeking justice?"

Some of the men shifted uncomfortably, but Dafydd gave Anna a small smile and said, "The latter, of course, but I'm not sure what that means to you."

"Do what you have to do to take Valence in, but once he's in custody, you have to do this the right way. He should be tried by a judge and jury of his peers, not beheaded or hanged from the battlement at Windsor, even if it would provide a good lesson to others."

Lili was surprised at her sister-in-law's adamancy, but she wasn't the only one nodding, either. All three traditions—Welsh, Saxon, and Norman—had developed a court system by which fines were leveled and men punished or set free. In fact, in this instance, the Normans had expanded upon the justice system of the Saxons, codifying trial-by-jury in *Magna Carta* and other documents, for all men. No nobleman wanted an all-powerful king, even one as popular and as even-handed as Dafydd, and for more than a hundred years had pressed for the ability to rein in their ruler.

Dafydd studied his sister for a long moment and then nodded. "We will do as you say. There never really was another choice. Not for me. Thank you for making me see it."

26

September, 1289

David

The sun was fully up by the time Valence rode from his command tent with his entourage and David rode out of the castle with his ten men. He'd left everyone else—Ieuan, Math, Carew, Edmund, William, this new Uncle Rhodri, and a dozen others—behind. It wasn't to slight them. David could have brought any number of men instead of these few. But he meant to send an unmistakable message to Valence. *He*, David Arthur Llywelyn Pendragon, King of England, ruled here. And neither Valence nor anyone else would be wise to forget it.

David could feel his wife's eyes on him as he came to a halt two hundred yards from the town gate and an equal distance from Valence's camp. Lili had her bow in hand and stood with most of the archers who could still stand on the wall-walk above the southeastern gate. Valence had pitched his tents out of arrow range, but the designated meeting point was within it from both sides. David eyed Valence's lines, and particularly the archers, wondering from which one treachery would come. A well-placed arrow had killed more than one king in England's history.

He'd set the parameters of the meeting very clearly, even to the point of having his men stake out how far Valence's men should ride and where Valence's horse should stand when Valence greeted David. He'd carefully orchestrated every aspect of this meeting, except, of course, for Valence's response. David hoped Valence would take these actions as David's attempt to control the situation (which it absolutely was) and not grasp that it was also an artful mask over his back-up plan should Valence fail to come to heel.

Up until now, Valence had shown a tendency to underestimate David, even as David defeated him. He believed David to be lucky but naïve. David wanted to do nothing to dissuade Valence of this opinion. He couldn't know that David was dispensing with any pretext of inherent goodness today. He was planning—if Valence forced his hand—to show the world that he could be just as merciless as his predecessors.

David hadn't yet looked at Valence himself. It was petty of him, but he didn't trust himself not to give the game away. The less interaction he had with Valence the better. David held up his hand to stop the men with him from continuing and rode the last yards to meet Valence alone. They were actors in an ancient play, each reliving the role of innumerable men who had come before them. Some traditions would have had them both dismount, but neither side trusted the other enough for that.

Finally, David brought his eyes to meet Valence's. The hatred in them shocked him, and bile rose in his throat at how much he shared it. Valence had been responsible for more deaths, more disunity, than any baron he'd ever met, barring King Edward himself. The two men stared at each other for a count of ten, and then Valence said, "What are your terms?" Since Valence had been the one to raise the white flag, it was his job to speak first. He was the supplicant, though David wasn't sure he knew it.

"Total surrender to me," David said. "Lay down your weapons and end this war you started."

"If I do not?"

David gestured to the fields around them where men were lined up as far as the eye could see. "You are outnumbered and surrounded. More men come every hour to join my ranks. How many of your soldiers will you sacrifice to your pride?"

Valence scowled. "What of my captains?"

"I will allow the common soldiers to go free, without their weapons, of course," David said. "I will decide the fate of the noblemen among you on a case-by-case basis. Some may go free; some may share your fate. It is up to them."

"What does that mean?" Valence sounded genuinely puzzled.

"You have attempted to incite my people to rebellion," David said. "You didn't do it alone. Your captains may have sworn fealty to you, but each has a soul and must answer for his actions."

"You will have their heads," Valence said.

"Did I say so?" David said. "Do I look like King Edward to you?"

"If I surrender, what are your plans for me?"

"I have chosen to remain detached from any decision," David said. "We are not rabble but civilized men. You will be judged in a courtroom by your peers."

Valence's face paled, and some of the belligerence seemed to leave him. But then he recovered himself, and his chin jutted out defiantly. "And if I refuse your terms?"

"You sign the death warrants of all of your men."

Silence fell between them. David watched Valence, who was looking beyond him to the battlement of the town. David didn't turn to look too, but he knew what Valence was seeing: the wall-walk was lined with the people of Windsor and David's men.

"This wasn't how it was meant to end." Valence's voice was soft, almost contemplative. It annoyed David. Valence had proved time and again that he responded to little else but overt displays of power. He had no business feeling regret.

"The moment you took up arms against me, it could end no other way."

"So be it."

For a moment David thought he'd won—until Valence gave him a wolfish grin and added, "We will fight to the death rather than surrender our honor to you!"

Valence's last words were shouted to the sky as he turned his horse and raced back towards his own lines. The men who'd accompanied him made an opening in their ranks for him to pass through, pulling out their swords and raising their shields as they did so.

As Valence raced away, a single arrow shot from his lines, straight into David's chest at the breastbone. That the archer must be a Welshman passed through David's head in the second before he was knocked back in the saddle and thrown head over heels off the horse by the force of the shot. He did a complete flip, landing on his feet behind his horse.

The arrow stuck out from David's chest, the tip caught in a link of his armor. The padding beneath his armor may have saved him without the ceramic plate in the Kevlar vest underneath that. But with both, he'd have no more than a bad bruise on his chest. Regardless, the arrow was meant to kill him. This was more like what David had expected from Valence, and something for which he'd prepared.

As his men converged on him, David straightened and thrust his sword into the air. "Now!"

The trampled and distressed wheat all around Valence's soldiers burst upwards, revealing armed men. Horses whinnied and reared, and chaos engulfed the field. Arrows flew from Windsor's battlement. One of Valence's soldiers was hit in the neck. Blood spurted from the wound, and he fell to the ground. Five men had been given the specific task of subduing Valence's horse and capturing the renegade baron. At their sudden appearance out of the grass, Valence's horse spooked. The baron jerked at the reins, while two men grabbed the horse's bridle and three others hauled Valence to the ground.

The arrows continued to fly from both camps, adding to the carnage. David leapt back into the saddle. Standing in the stirrups, he raised his sword high again and bellowed, "Hold! Hold I say!"

David's cry to *hold*, combined with the sight of him plucking the arrow from his chest and throwing it to the ground, stopped all the action.

The men David had tasked with taking Valence wrestled him towards the spot where David waited. Valence had lost his helmet in the struggle, and his normally well-coifed hair was askew. He was a blond man going gray, with a paunch and jowls. With a wolfish grin of his own, Bevyn reversed Valence's sword and handed it to David.

"This is an outrage!" Valence said. All he had left was words, so David didn't begrudge him the opportunity to speak them. "I spoke to you under the white flag. You have no right to take me!"

David dismounted and walked to stand in front of Valence. He knew he was making his retainers uncomfortable by approaching his prisoner, but Valence couldn't harm David now.

"I have every right," David said.

Valence spat on the ground. "You have no honor!"

"On the contrary," David said. "It would be far less honorable to allow you to sacrifice more of your men and mine when you are already defeated."

"No lord will ever parley with you again! You—"

David cut him off with a laugh. "Why? Because I was prepared for you to throw the peace terms back in my face? To betray the white flag yourself? That arrow that hit me was—what?—a mistake? You have no leg to stand on."

Valence wasn't used to being interrupted. "Among noblemen—"

David cut him off with a bark. "I am far less concerned about the sanctity of the white flag than winning this little war you started. The next time I face another baron in battle, he will treat with me for the same reason you did: because he has no other choice. And he will wonder as he does so if I will do to him as I've done to you."

"You—"

"What you don't seem to understand is that the laws of chivalry don't apply to a traitor. You seem to think that you have the right to stand before me and speak your mind as one free man to another. You do not." David lifted his voice so everyone within hailing distance could hear what he had to say. "By capturing you now, I have sent a message to any other baron who resents my kingship. I was chosen by the people to rule them."

Valence tried to sputter a response, but David stepped closer and took Valence's chin in his hand. "Your rules don't apply to me. You, and every other baron who defies me, should look upon this day and *fear*."

27

September, 1289

David

"Keep your eyes closed and open your mouth." David obeyed his wife from his supine position on a blanket with Arthur asleep on his chest.

The family had gathered for a picnic on the lawn by the Thames River: Lili and David, Math and Anna, Bronwen and Ieuan, plus all the children. David missed Cassie and Callum acutely, for they should have been here today. His mother and father were absent too, as they remained in Wales, and he resolved for all of them to journey there before winter came. Maybe they could celebrate Thanksgiving at Aber.

Lili popped something cool and juicy into his mouth, but as the taste hit him, he gagged and half sat up. "What *is* that?"

Lili stared at him, but Anna giggled. "It's a cantaloupe!"

David spit out the offending piece of fruit. "Not a moldy one, I hope!"

"Of course not." Lili took Arthur from David, looking disgruntled. She laid the baby on his back on the blanket. "We saved one for eating. I think it's lovely."

"What David isn't telling you, sister of mine," Anna said, "is that he has always despised most fruits and vegetables. The fact that we can't get the same variety here as we did in the modern world has never bothered him in the slightest."

"I'm with you." Bronwen raised a hand to David, who slapped her palm. "In graduate school, my four food groups were Diet Coke, coffee, onion rings, and doughnuts."

"And pizza," David said.

Bronwen laughed. "Clearly, I've been starving since I got here."

"You two are disgusting." Anna pinned her brother with her gaze. "Enough with the stalling. You need to tell us everything that happened since you left Windsor. Start at the beginning and talk until I don't have any more questions."

David saluted his sister.

"Yeah, David, do tell," Bronwen said. "And what's with the empty duffel? You bring us back another ream of paper and nothing else? Where's my Chapstick? My coffee?"

"I was incarcerated and sick the whole time I was there," David said, "as you already know."

Bronwen rolled onto her stomach and put her chin in her hands. Ieuan and Math had taken Cadell and Catrin to the river to throw rocks into the water, so she was momentarily childless. "Did you ever consider not coming back?"

David scoffed. "Of course not."

"You could have been killed, you know," Bronwen said.

"I was nearly killed about a dozen times, both here and there," David said. "Today is the first day since I returned that I'm not wearing the Kevlar, and you can bet that I will wear it under my armor from now on."

"Do you think we'll ever discover who informed Valence that you were sailing for Ireland?" Lili sat cross-legged, slathering butter on a slice of bread. "Or who sabotaged the rudder of your ship?"

"Only if we're very lucky," David said. "Dad is pursuing all leads from the Cardiff end, but it's hard to think that finding the individual saboteur matters. Like the Welsh archers who fought for him, he was paid by Valence, and Valence is going to pay for his crimes."

"You hope," Bronwen said. "You and your justice system. You should have hanged him from the battlements like everyone wanted."

"That I didn't is Anna's fault." David put out a hand out to his sister. "If Valence is exonerated, it will be a miscarriage of justice, but I rule by the law, which isn't something I should use when I feel like it and not when I don't. Besides, Clare took Valence's castle in Ireland, and all of Valence's supporters have come crawling to me asking for forgiveness. He's finished."

"Valence has pride," Anna said, "I'll give him that."

"His trial is already a circus, and it hasn't even started," Bronwen said.

"I don't know what a circus is," Lili said, "but I think I know what you mean anyway."

David mumbled to himself. "I was arrogant enough to think I could control the situation."

Anna punched his shoulder. "When are you not arrogant?"

"Hey guys!" David called over to Math and Ieuan. "The girls are ganging up on me. Again!"

"It's only what you deserve," Anna said.

"I thought the whole point was that you didn't control what happened next," Bronwen said. "You aren't even going to testify against him, are you?"

"No," David said. "That would be unfair to the jurors. Bad enough that many of Valence's crimes were committed against me and mine."

"You're probably right," Anna said. "This isn't a true democracy. Your barons can't vote you out of office if they don't like what you do, but you can punish them if you don't like what they do."

"You can only change so much so quickly," Lili said.

"I've told myself that for years. I don't know how much longer I can continue to believe it," David said, turning serious.

"You are too hard on yourself," Lili said.

"If I'm not hard on myself, who will be?" He took back his son and lay down, adjusting Arthur's little shirt, which was warm from the sun. A hat shaded the baby's face, and he slept with his little fist just touching his lips. "Not you, I don't think."

"Bevyn always tells you what you don't want to hear," Lili said.

"Less so than in the past." David had never told Lili—or anyone else—how Bevyn had conspired on his behalf, but without his consent, in the run up to David's coronation. He didn't intend to either.

"You've still got me," Anna said.

David laughed. "Thank God for that!"

For a moment, they sat quietly, and then Bronwen said, "I hope Cassie and Callum are okay."

"I have to believe they are," David said. "I could say *I wish things had been different* a million times, but it doesn't help. I've gone over and over again in my mind the events leading up to my departure from that world, but at the time, our choices made sense."

"Bad things happen," Lili said. "They happen all the time. That's what I've been trying to explain to Anna. But as you well know and have said many times yourself, it's how you respond to the bad things that determines what kind of man you are. Or woman," Lili amended.

"You comfort me." David felt himself drifting off to sleep.

And then Lili spoke again, quietly and not for anyone's ears but David's, "My love, you have changed the world. I think Callum, wherever he is, would be proud."

28

September, 2017

Cassie

The black SUV came for them at midnight on the fourth day after Callum had been shot. They'd been told it was coming, of course, and where they were going, but when the Security Service agents came through Callum's hospital room door, Cassie still didn't quite expect to see them. She found it hilarious that she was wearing a dress, given where she'd spent the last five years living; Callum had a new suit, one without a dark red stain across the lapel and a hole in the shoulder.

They showed Callum their badges but didn't tell Cassie their names, and she didn't ask. A near continual stream of nameless and faceless men wearing earpieces and dark suits had come and gone since Callum had been shot and David had left. Cassie had given up trying to make small talk. One of the men wheeled Callum in a wheelchair down to the garage and helped him into the SUV. Cassie knew they didn't want her to come, but Callum had insisted.

"I know you're sick of being baggage," Callum said in the moment they were alone inside the car.

"You're sick of being sick, so I guess that makes us even," Cassie said, which was her attempt not to be sour about this whole thing. She restrained the rest of her thoughts, such as the hope that she could stop being baggage soon.

Callum took Cassie's hand as they drove through the deserted streets of Cardiff, a far cry from that frantic afternoon chasing David's ambulance. It was the end of a long day in a string of long days. If Cassie never saw the inside of a hospital again, it would be too soon.

Callum was *fine*. Or would be once his wound healed. It seemed that David was fine too, given that he'd disappeared before he hit the ground. Cassie hoped that he'd landed gently on the other side.

The SUV rolled up to a side door of the government building. The First Minister of the Welsh government greeted them as they got out. This time Callum declined the wheelchair and walked into the building, holding Cassie's hand in his good one.

They took an elevator to a large office on the third floor; once there, the First Minister held out his hand to indicate that Cassie and Callum should enter without him. "This is where I stop."

This interview was too top secret even for him.

The men inside the room stood as they entered: the Prime Minister of Great Britain, his Minister of Defense, and the head of the CIA. They introduced themselves, each one shaking Cassie's hand

and looking into her eyes, though the Prime Minister almost made to kiss her cheek but held himself back at the last second.

"Please sit." The Prime Minister indicated one of the soft couches arranged in a talking group.

Callum walked to an upright spindle chair instead. "If I sit there, I may never get up again." And then he smiled to indicate that he meant no offense. Cassie sat at the end of one of the couches, next to Callum's chair.

"Before we get any further," the head of the CIA said, "I'd like you to have this." He took a United States passport out of his breast pocket and handed it to Cassie.

She opened it and stared at the picture. She didn't know where they'd gotten it—off a camera somewhere, clearly—and wasn't entirely unhappy with the likeness. She looked up. "Thank you."

"Since you lived in Scotland for five years and are married to Agent Callum, you may apply for a UK passport as well, but we hoped this would be enough to be going on with," the Prime Minister said.

Cassie nodded, oddly moved by the gift.

"You have my personal assurance," the CIA director said, "as well as that of the United States government, that we had no hand in any of the events leading up to David's disappearance."

Cassie nodded again, but with the formalities over, they weren't looking at her any more and had moved on to Callum and the real purpose for this meeting. "You've read the newspapers, of course." It was the Defense Minister's turn to talk. "And I understand you also received a copy of Director Cooke's files."

"I did," Callum said. "Before she was killed, she told me about them and that she'd arranged to have them made public."

As Lady Jane had said to Callum an hour before she died, her documents exposed a host of individuals in the government—from MI-5 to Whitehall, the Home Office, and Parliament, to the cabinet itself—as being in the pocket of the Dunland Group, the organization that had orchestrated the abduction of David. As the information had been disseminated throughout London, the halls of government had run red with blood, figuratively speaking.

With Lady Jane and Driscoll dead, Natasha on the run, and a half dozen other agents also incriminated in the documents, MI-5 in particular had been decimated. Smythe hadn't been named in Lady Jane's files, but he'd kowtowed to those who had. All in all, it was a mess.

On top of that, MI-5 sorely missed Lady Jane's leadership. She'd had her finger in more pies and known more about more things than anyone had given her credit for. Callum had decided that the manner in which he'd been treated from the start by MI-5 had been intended by Lady Jane to drive him towards the path he'd ultimately followed. He hadn't yet asked Jones if he'd waited eight seconds to report to Lady Jane after they'd left or ten. But neither he nor Cassie doubted now that they'd been a part of Lady Jane's carefully laid trap from the moment she learned of their appearance in the Bristol Channel. Cassie was just sorry that her machinations had ultimately ensnared her too.

"Then you know that Thomas Smythe was not implicated directly in the scandal," the Defense Minister said.

"So I understood," Callum said. "Are you telling me that he has been appointed director of the Security Service?"

"No," said the Prime Minister. "That has yet to be decided. At issue today is your future. I spoke with Director Cooke only hours before she was killed. She suggested at that time that I name you head of the Project."

Callum canted his head. "I am unfamiliar with that file."

The CIA Director laughed. "That's because we just invented it." His British companions shot him sour looks, but he ignored them. "Seriously, given the current upheaval, our two governments have resolved to create a joint task force to address and oversee what we are otherwise calling *the time travel initiative*."

"We are asking that you, Agent Callum, accept the posting as Director of the Project, reporting directly to Downing Street," the Prime Minister said, "not the Home Office."

Callum and Cassie had talked about this—not about the Project (with a capital 'P') specifically, since the terminology was new, but about the role that Callum might play in MI-5 in the future. His absence over the last ten months, and his unswerving loyalty, had left him the last man standing at Cardiff station. And Cardiff station had the *time travel initiative* file, to use the CIA man's phrasing.

Callum didn't want the job, but he feared the consequences if he didn't take it. The issue for him was the balance between the unpleasantness of the job, with all the politics and behind-the-scenes maneuvering becoming director entailed, and what might happen if he left the Project in the hands of someone else. Someone he didn't trust. Since Callum didn't trust anyone, it was hard to see how he could refuse it. It could be disastrous if someone with Smythe's sensibilities was running things the next time David—or Anna or Meg—appeared.

"Would I still be a member of the Security Service?" Callum said.

"Only on paper," the Prime Minister said. "But in point of fact, you would be the director of a new agency, with the commensurate compensation, of course."

"I'm concerned about oversight," Callum said. "I would need the freedom to run the agency as I saw fit, without meddling or micro-management."

"Whitehall and the Home Office have been severely implicated in the Dunland scandal," the Prime Minister said. "I cannot, and will not, promise you free rein, but we have read your report and believe we understand your position."

"Just so we're clear: my position is that David's world—the medieval world—is not an opportunity to enrich our government or private interests," Callum said. "No agency under my direction will pursue such a directive."

The three men exchanged glances; they all nodded. "You are the right man for the job," the Prime Minister said.

"Then I accept your offer," Callum said. "I will direct the Project."

While the three politicians congratulated each other, smiles all around, Callum reached over and took Cassie's hand. "Am I making a mistake?"

"We promised we'd have David's back," she said. "This is the way to do it."

Callum sucked on his teeth. "What about you? I'm hoping you're going to be my first hire."

Cassie almost laughed. They'd spent so much time plotting out what would happen with Callum's job, she hadn't given any thought to what she was going to do. As the men called Callum's attention to them once again, it occurred to her that perhaps it wasn't only David who time traveled because he was needed somewhere. Maybe those who were caught up in it with him were needed too.

Maybe *she* was needed too.

Cassie took out her passport and waved it to catch the attention of the Prime Minister. "Are our relations with the Home Office amicable enough to extend to a work permit?"

Callum's eyes crinkled at the corners, and for the first time since Lady Jane's death, he genuinely smiled. Cassie squeezed his hand. They'd been through a lot in the few months they'd been together, but she had a feeling that their adventures were only just beginning.

The End

Acknowledgments

First and foremost, I'd like to thank my lovely readers for encouraging me to continue the *After Cilmeri* Series. I have always been passionate about these books, and it's wonderful to be able to share my stories with readers who love them too.

Thank you to my family who has been nothing but encouraging of my writing, despite the fact that I spend half my life in medieval Wales. Thank you to Deborah and Leonora for their invaluable help with medical issues. All errors are, of course, my own. Thank you also to my beta readers: Gemini, Anna, Jolie, Melissa, Cassandra, Brynne, Carew, Dan, and Venkata. I couldn't do this without you.

About the Author

With two historian parents, Sarah couldn't help but develop an interest in the past. She went on to get more than enough education herself (in anthropology) and began writing fiction when the stories in her head overflowed and demanded she let them out. While her ancestry is Welsh, she only visited Wales for the first time while in college. She has been in love with the country, language, and people ever since. She even convinced her husband to give all four of their children Welsh names.

She makes her home in Oregon.

www.sarahwoodbury.com

Printed in Poland
by Amazon Fulfillment
Poland Sp. z o.o., Wrocław
18 November 2020

87cd9db1-d781-4d45-ac51-8fa1893292b5R02